Hold Me

Isla Rayn

Cover art by stayvblue on Instagram, Cover by getcovers

Proof-read by Marc Edits

Sometimes, one person can make a difference.

Trigger Warnings

All in all, I would describe this as a light and rather sweet and cozy read.

Trigger Warning for: Mentions of substance abuse, alcoholism and childhood abuse.

ONE

ADEN

I go through a couple of folders on my desk; one with the description of the venue and the exact layout, one with the plan of the artists presented in this exhibition and the paintings that were chosen to be on display, and the final one including estimated payments, funds and our expenses. After reading them properly, I close them and hand them back to my assistant. "Good job, Cedric."

The young man lights up at my simple praise. "Really?"

He looks like such a lost golden retriever, I don't have it in my heart to dismiss him, although I am tired enough to fall asleep on the spot. "Yes, you thoroughly researched everything, you listened well to what we planned in the meetings, the venue is prepared to the last detail, and we are set for the opening tomorrow."

"Thank you so much, sir. I... I am so lucky you gave me this chance!"

Frankly, the kid was my last attempt at hiring an assistant. Most of the others had the education and experience, but they just didn't click with me. Or I didn't click with them. They just see the perfectionist in me and don't even want to bother. I hired Cedric, despite coming with zero experience and a Master's degree in Literature instead of art or business, because he showed interest and motivation. He had no idea what type of work I was doing, he only had a very vague knowledge of artists and their work, but if I have learned one thing, it is that this is knowledge that can be acquired with a little time. However, no one can magically become motivated.

My hiring him meant the world to him because it was his first job. As for me, I got an assistant who doesn't drive me up the walls. He just drives me insane *occasionally,* because of his overly bubbly personality, but I can live with that.

"Go home for tonight," I tell him. "It's late. I will see you for the opening tomorrow."

"I am so looking forward to it! It's my first art gallery opening that I helped organize. I am so excited for all the new artists." He beams.

Here. That's exactly why I hired him.

I smile briefly at him. "Let's make it a success tomorrow. For now, go home. We are the last to leave the office. I will lock up behind us."

Cedric grabs his bag before shuffling out of my office and then out of the building, not without wishing me a good night before leaving. I gather my own things and grab the folder with the artists we are going to show tomorrow, and decide to go home too. I want to skim through the plans once more, to get a true feeling of the artists' work. I have spent the last months hand-picking them, but it's my little evening ritual to do this before an opening. This type of gallery exhibition is one of my favorites. I get to show all kinds of new artists in my gallery, upcoming and rising ones, who still need the boost in popularity to sell their work and to make a name for themselves.

It's how I originally made a name for myself. Now that I am a gallerist and gallery owner myself, I want to give back and help these upcoming artists.

On my way outside, my phone rings. One glance at it notifies me that I have several missed messages.

They won't leave me alone, so I may as well pick up now. "Hi Oliver."

"Aden!" he exclaims, his voice joyful. "I am so glad you picked up. It's so hard to get through to you, little bro."

"I was at work," I tell him. Oliver is my oldest brother and the one I probably like the most. We don't have much of a relationship, though.

"It's almost midnight."

"Yeah, there is a lot to do," I say, keeping it vague. If I tell him it's a gallery opening tomorrow, he might get the idea to come, or one of my other brothers will. And I can't deal with family drama on opening night. That night belongs to the new artists, spotlight on them, not on the gallerist.

"You work too much," he says reproachfully. His voice drifts off as he waits for me to say something. God, this is awkward. When I keep silent, he clears his throat. "Are you coming home on Sunday? Mom managed to gather all of us. You are the only one she hasn't been able to reach out to."

One of the many messages and calls from today was probably from her.

"I can't," I say promptly. "I am swamped with work."

"Even on the weekend?"

"Yes."

A pause. "You are watching out for your health, aren't you, Aden?"

Sighing, I take the keys to my car, open the door, and sit behind the wheel. I put him on speaker before driving off. "Yes, I am. I am okay."

Another pause. "You barely visit home," he finally says the words I am always dreading to hear. Every once in a while, one of them calls and says the very same words.

You never visit.

You never come home.

Mom is missing you.

We miss you.

Why don't you visit more often, Aden?

I answer as usual. "I visit regularly," I say. "For the holidays for example."

"Not for all of them," he points out.

"Oliver,“ I sigh.

"I know, work," he mutters. "Is that truly the reason?"

I frown, glad he isn't here in person to see my expression. I do believe I have a fairly good poker face, but certainly not good enough to fool him. "What other reason would there be?" I toss the question right back at him.

"I don't know, Aden." He sounds soft, a stark contrast to the rough boy he was when we were growing up. "You tell me."

"There is not much to tell."

"Aden..." Another pause, this time longer than the one before. It sounds like he is about to say something. I prepare myself inwardly to rebuff anything he can say, but then his voice sounds lighter all of a sudden. "You are coming for Mom's birthday, aren't you?"

God, yeah, I have to.

"I will tell her you won't make it on Sunday," he urges. "But please come for her birthday."

There is no chance I could miss that. I hate family meetings. If it were just Mom, I would visit her or invite her out more regularly. I don't mind spending time with her, but I don't enjoy spending time with the whole family. It always makes me feel tense, like I don't belong.

"Aden?"

"Yes, I am coming for her birthday," I say. "I need to go now, Oliver."

"Aden—"

"Good night."

I feel a twinge of guilt, like always, after I have talked to one of my brothers. I got used to it, though, and am now able to shake it off. To distract me, I switch on some music, realizing that Cedric put on a pop music channel the last time he drove with me, and forgot to change it back to what I usually listen to.

Well, I can just as well listen to some upbeat music now until I am home.

Home is a townhouse I own. I used to have an apartment, but it felt too modern, too everything, so I rented it out and instead bought a small townhouse. The purchase was twice as expensive due to the area and size, but it feels more private and much more like me. I do have neighbors, but I don't mind. I prefer it to a single house; it would make me feel too lonely.

Once inside, I pour a glass of wine, grab a plate of cheese, and then settle down on my sofa to go through the artists and their works again. We have an interesting bunch covered this time, a good mix of varied art styles and techniques.

I don't sleep a lot, but I am used to running on low sleep for a gallery opening weekend. One glance outside shows me that the line waiting for admittance is already long, although we aren't opening for two hours.

Cedric is so excited, I am afraid he might bounce off the wall. "Please tell me, you won't be like that all evening," Lynn says.

Lynn is one of my longest and most important employees, responsible for accounting and sales. She is fantastic with numbers and a good negotiator when it comes to buying paintings and artworks for our permanent collection. But she hates the more personal contact with customers and clients. That's what I am good at.

"He will," I mutter more to myself than to her, while going through the notes of my speech. "TV coverage?"

"Yes," she says. "I invited the usual TV stations and a few influencers with the right target audience and content."

I groan.

"Don't be a boomer," she grins. "You are not old enough to be one."

"So, you are telling me you will deal with them?" I ask.

"No way!" she exclaims. "I am going to handle the press and TV coverage. As for the influencers, I was thinking of someone closer their age." She glances at me, making me chuckle. Nodding at her, I give her the go-ahead to go through with her plan. "Cedy," she says, "that's a task for you."

"What?" he blinks. "But I am a nobody."

"You are not a nobody. You are the personal assistant of the gallery owner. You're the perfect person for this," she argues. "You are young, pretty, and you smile like you shit rainbows."

He pouts.

"I mean that in the best sense," she says. "Aden and I don't shit rainbows."

We really don't.

"But Mr. Randall is the pro," he stutters.

"You just heard Aden," she says. She never addresses me by my last name, and I don't push it on her, not even in official situations. We are more friends than boss and employee anyway. "He doesn't want to deal with social media. He never does. That's why we have you handle our social media accounts. Just be your usual cute and bubbly self, and the audience on social media will love you."

"Really?" His head perks up. Apparently, he forgets to be anxious and instead is excited to prove himself.

I nod at him. "I think you are the perfect person for this."

He beams. "Then I will give it my all! Are they here already?"

"Yes, they came through the press-only entrance."

"I will head to them immediately," he says, already dashing off.

"He always bounces back so quickly. One minute he is anxious, the next he is"—she gestures at him, disappearing through the door leading to the press area—"like that."

"It's definitely his strong point," I say.

"I am amazed you can work together with him."

"Why?" I chuckle. "Because I don't *shit rainbows*?"

"You aren't exactly patient," she says dryly.

I shrug. "The guy just has a way with people and takes his work seriously. It's all I've ever wanted."

"And he doesn't mind that you are a workaholic," she adds.

"That's rich coming from you."

"Well, no matter how bad I am, you are worse." She playfully pats my shoulder before turning towards the same door Cedric disappeared through. "I am going to prepare for the press interviews," she says. "You okay here?"

"Of course, go ahead."

Silence engulfs me when she is gone. It's a unique feeling to stand in these huge halls alone with no one around yet. There is excitement lingering in the air from the crowd waiting, but also from the artists. Their hopes and dreams are gathered in these rooms, and the noise reaching me from outside, from the waiting crowd, sounds like the buzzing of bees.

My phone buzzes too, mixing with the sound from outside. Taking it out of my pocket, I see that Oliver sent me a message with a pic attached. *Boys' night out. Wish you could be here.*

The pic shows him with two of my other brothers.

I put the phone aside. Something in my heart feels heavy, but I can't deal with that right now. I have to focus on the night ahead.

Two

ADEN

The night went as planned. Lynn and I have developed a routine by now and know how to handle these evenings. I know she will eventually need her own assistant to help her with her work; it's something we have been discussing recently. I do have the funds to hire another employee, so it's definitely on my priority list.

Cedric hit it off with the influencers and has probably just sealed his fate: to be solely responsible for our social media accounts now. My speech went well, and the TV interviews went even better. Lynn always convinces me to do them, claiming my quiet, composed way of delivering my lines always gets to the audience.

She calls it an air of mystery.

I call it being bad at conversation.

But whatever helps. If it works, it works, and that's all that matters.

Now that the place is buzzing, not only with spectators and artists, but also potential clients are roaming the gallery to spot artworks they like and might want to buy from the artists, I have time to roam the halls as well. I've seen most of these artworks in print already, but it's different to see them in real life. It's always different.

There is a niche for each artist we are showing, each one getting to present a maximum of three pictures or artworks. It's obvious there are plenty of talented folks. On every new exhibition of this kind, I look around the paintings, not as the gallerist but as a client. It's been a while since I mentored an upcoming artist. When I spot a piece of art that just strikes me, I usually reach out to the artist or their manager and make sure to support them.

It hasn't happened for a while, though. All of these people are talented, clearly so, but nothing strikes my own muse. And for me to step up and truly support someone, beyond showing their artwork here, it has to be special to me.

I am about to go to the restroom for a break, because again, I don't find anything that jumps out at me, when I pass the last hall. It's a smaller one, for artists who only show one piece of art each. That's when I see *it!*

A huge picture, a single work of the artist, is presented in the middle of the room. I need to compliment my curator and coordinator for this; he truly knew how to put the spotlight on it. The sole color used in the picture in all its shades is blue, giving it a melancholic feel. The motive of the artwork is a young man sitting at the edge of a bathtub. His back is turned to the spectator, his fingers dangling in the water. He is naked, only loosely wrapped in a towel. We only see him from behind, but even without seeing his face and eyes, there is something vulnerable about him. What is he thinking? What is he feeling? Is he sad? Are tears dripping down his face? It's not posed. It's a snapshot, a glimpse of a moment. The man's back is slightly hunched over, and he seems to be thinking, pondering.

It's a glimpse into his soul. The model has a soul, so does the artwork.

My eyes move to the small plate next to the artwork, where the artists usually provide details and explanations of their work.

There are none, just basic information.

Title: Shades of Blue or Man From Behind

Artist: Sterling Thomas, 27 years old. New freelance artist.

The price tag below shows that someone else knows the artwork's worth, too. Probably Sterling Thomas's manager. It's high, but not unreasonable. But even if it were too expensive, I know I would have bought it nevertheless.

A couple of hours later, I officially hold it in my hands. I will keep it presented in the exhibition, but once it's officially over, I will be hanging it in my living room for everyone to see.

STERLING

"Hey, Sterlone, are you here?" my manager, Mateo, yells through the whole apartment until I put my brush aside and finally pay him attention. He is using that silly nickname again. A while back he was into action movies and thought calling me Sterlone would give me an edge. Mateo moved on from his action movie phase, but the nickname stuck.

"What?" I mutter, trotting out of my atelier and into the living area. I own a loft with an adjacent room that I have remodeled into an atelier. I was lucky enough to have inherited it from my grandma.

"Did you get my call?" Mateo asks. His dark hair looks disheveled, and he looks tired as fuck.

"No, sorry, my phone was on silent."

"Then you probably haven't read my messages either?"

"No."

Mateo drops down on the chair with a sigh, his legs almost too long for the chair. It's a recurring problem for him. He is too tall for everything. Tall and skinny, and he hates it. I think it suits him. Very modelesque from an artist's viewpoint. "You are driving me insane."

"Coffee?"

"Yeah." His gaze follows me. "You have been painting?"

"Recently, my muse seems to be coming to me. Noel is a great help, too."

Mateo stretches. "He modeled for you again?"

"Yes, he was in the mood. But you know him. When he is sulky or broody, there is no chance of getting him to hang around for hours. Or rather, he would and push through it, but it's not the same then."

"He has always been like that," Mateo chuckles. "Glad he is more grounded now, though. You helped him a lot to deal with his issues."

"We both did," I argue.

Noel, Mateo, and I have been friends ever since university. We didn't study the same major, but we just kind of started to hang out together. The three weirdos on campus. The three geeks. All three of us were obsessed with our own hobbies and bonded through that. It didn't matter that we only shared one year together before Noel and I dropped out for various reasons. The connection between us remained.

Just like me, Mateo is a freelancer. He does ads for companies and solo businesses. I guess he had pity on me for sucking at advertising my art, and took it upon himself to become my manager. I'm not sure if he truly knew what he signed up for.

With two steaming mugs of coffee, I return to the table and sit down opposite Mateo. "So, what's the issue? I bet you are not here just to chat."

"I am not. *Shades of Blue* got sold."

"What?!" I exclaim.

"Yeah, that was my reaction too," he grins. "It's so you, to hit it off so quickly. First real exhibition and you sell the only artwork you have there."

"But how?"

"You should rather ask who," he urges.

Furrowing my brows, I stare at him. "What do you mean? Who bought it?"

Mateo leans back, looking all smug. He obviously was waiting for me to ask. Two dramatic pauses later that fucking little tease finally spills it out. "Aden Randall."

Silence engulfs us. My brain works slowly sometimes. It's always been like that. I can only draw well, while everything else comes to me at a slower pace. "Care to repeat that?"

Mateo smiles now, his expression not teasing anymore but joyful. "Aden Randall in person."

At that shock, I almost drop my mug of coffee.

"That was my reaction, too, when I got the call from his assistant last night saying he wanted to buy your drawing. He already paid." He hands me a piece of paper from his bag. "This is the contract."

I gape while staring at the piece of paper. Mateo didn't lie. My drawing got sold to the god of all gallerists, in person. Everyone knows that Aden Randall has a perceptive eye, a feel for art. Everything he touches turns to gold. He has made several artists over the last couple of years, helping them to rise to fame. He used to draw too until a couple of years ago, but it's said he gets more joy in organizing his gallery and exhibitions now.

"He also mentioned that he wants to be informed whenever you draw something new and have it up for sale," Mateo adds, killing me all over again. "He also bought your second painting, the one you deemed not good enough for the exhibition."

"You are fucking kidding me?"

"No. So, chop-chop! Get productive and make us rich."

"After that shock, I need to recover first," I say.

"You are aware that this is amazing?"

"Of course! It's insane!"

"You deserve it, Sterling," he says seriously. "You have worked your ass off. You dropped out of Uni just to support your little sister. If anyone deserves the fruits of his labor to pay off, it's you!"

"I have you to thank for this," I say.

"I know," he grins. "Which is why I hope you keep me hired."

"Are you kidding? I need you," I chuckle. "I could never do all that advertising and bureaucracy without you. Don't leave me!"

"Aw," he says gleefully. "Aren't you cute? Pity you aren't my type."

"Cute *is* your type," I grin.

"Yeah, and you aren't. Not usually," he smirks. "Weirdo."

"Says the right one," I retort.

"What's going on?" A voice startles us. Turning around, I notice Noel, who closes the door behind him and steps into my loft. He has a second key, so it's nothing unusual to see him around. "Mateo is here at such an early hour?"

"Yes, I came with good news."

"*Shades of Blue* got sold," I add.

Noel has a gentle face with beautiful features, soft brown hair, and freckles on his nose. Everything about him looks pretty, and yet slightly melancholic, which is why I love drawing him.

"Oh," he smiles. "That's good, isn't it?"

"It's fantastic," Mateo says. "Aden Randall bought it."

"That's the guy you talked about last week, right? The gallerist?" When Mateo nods, Noel turns to me. "Congratulations, Ster, you deserve it."

"What about you? Did you work all night?"

"Yes," Noel says, sitting down on the free chair. "I worked two shifts at the club."

Neither Mateo nor I says anything. We don't like him working there. It's a sleazy, sticky nightclub with all the gross dudes you'd expect to visit such a cheap establishment. But his father left him quite some debt. If Mateo and I could earn more, we would pay it off in a heartbeat, but at the moment, we can only offer moral support.

Well, maybe I will make it as an artist after all.

Mateo's phone signals an incoming message. "Work?" Noel asks.

"No, just my current flirt," Mateo mutters.

Noel's head perks up. "The cute girl you were dating. So, how's it going?"

Mateo's expression says it all.

"Oh," Noel says. "I am sorry, Mateo."

"Well, at the end of the day she just wanted to fuck, occasionally, and I wanted something stable. Not that the sex wasn't good."

I sigh. "This reminds me that I haven't gotten laid in forever."

"Me neither," Noel agrees.

"Seeing how I am free today because I just got ditched, I will cook us lunch," Mateo says. He points at me. "You, Sterlone, go back to work so you will become famous, and Aden Randall will stay interested. And you,"—he elbows Noel—"go and sleep."

"Be glad that I work well under pressure," I mutter.

"That's always been your strong point," Mateo says, making a shooing gesture towards me. "Do as I tell you. Lunch will be ready in two hours, by yours truly, Mateo."

Noel and I exchange a look. Both of us know better than to argue with Mateo. He is the nicest guy I've ever met, but he is also persistent. Once he puts his foot down, it firmly remains there until we oblige.

THREE

ADEN

Shades of Blue now has its proud place in my living room, giving me the chance to look at it every day. There is something about the intricate lines of his brush, the shading, and the emotions it captured. Sometimes, I just look at the picture, wondering what the man sitting on the edge of the bathtub is thinking or feeling. I wonder what his face looks like, and if his expression is as melancholic as the painting makes it seem.

During the last couple of weeks, I have bought every painting Sterling made. All of them have the same fascinating technique. None of them captures my heart like his first painting did, but that doesn't matter.

I am intrigued now. The artist has caught my interest.

With all due respect to his talent, though, I doubt he will be able to repeat the feeling the first painting struck in me. Paintings with a soul are too rare.

Then, however, Lynn calls me and tells me of Sterling's fourth painting.

'Yearning'.

It's the same young man, standing on a shore, the sea in front of him dark and unsettling, the light dim. From behind the man, shadows seem to be approaching. It hits right in the feels, again.

"Cedric." I march into the small adjacent office where Cedric is working. "Sterling Thomas has made a new painting."

"I have heard!" he beams. "It has to be good."

"Good doesn't even remotely describe it," I say. "I want it to be shown in the gallery."

Cedric's mouth drops open. "In... the regular exhibition?" He lowers his voice to a whisper as if he is scared anyone might spy on us. "Like for real."

I sigh. "Yes, Cedric, for real."

"Can I make a reel on Instagram for it?"

I have no idea what a reel is, but I assume he is going to advertise it. "Give it all the attention it deserves, and..." I furrow my brows. "Contact Sterling's manager. I want a meeting with him and his artist, preferably over lunch."

"Got you, sir!" He opens his notebook to scribble something down, a frown on his face while he purses his lips. "Maybe not too hipster..." he mutters to himself. "And not too fancy either..."

"What are you mumbling about?"

"Oh." He smiles brightly. "You, Mr. Randall, don't like hipster restaurants. And I assume a new artist won't enjoy a too fancy one. I am going to book something that caters to you both."

"That's not the worst idea you had today."

He beams. "Thank you!"

I stare at him, speechless at how happily he reacted to my random teasing comment. The golden retriever puppy vibe he gives off is truly a force to reckon with. Once I am back in my own office, Lynn comes over.

"Found your new toy?" she asks.

"It's an artist, not a toy. And I don't dispose of them, once I have supported them."

"It was a joke, Aden, relax. I know." She looks around, eyeing one of Sterling's pictures that I had put on my office wall. "So, you chose Sterling Thomas. Interesting."

"Why are you surprised?"

"He isn't your style usually. Don't get me wrong, I like his work, I just didn't know you would."

"His technique needs improvement," I say, getting up to stand next to her, looking at the painting. "But the way he paints has personality. He takes risks without forcing himself to do them. It flows naturally. He is able to capture a moment and make it seem alive, but he doesn't copy the moment either. What we see is what he sees through his tinted glasses at that time." I pause. "That's talent. It's raw and honest. Probably a guy who faced some hardships and who is empathic enough to see what's inside someone's soul."

"And you can tell all that while looking at his picture?"

I tilt my head, thinking of *Yearning* again, and the melancholy in it. Only his paintings with this young man have that unique feel to them. "Yes."

"You are a generous man, Aden."

"Where did that come from?"

"I am just saying," she shrugs. "You give back to the community."

"The community made me big. It's only logical that I would want to give back."

She chuckles. "If it were logical, everyone would do it. You are an altruist."

"You are silly. A true altruist would do much more than I do."

"Whatever you say." She shrugs before shifting the topic all of a sudden. "So, Oliver called me."

"No, he didn't." I pinch my nose in annoyance.

"He just wanted to know how you are."

"He can call me himself."

"That's what I told him, too," she says. "Guess what, I am not too fond of talking to my ex either. But apparently, he didn't get the memo." A pause. "He said you barely talk to anyone from home."

"It's nothing personal," I say shortly.

"It isn't?"

"No, I just don't feel close to them." I let my eyes wander over *Yearning* again. "Do you know the feeling that you don't belong?"

"Yes, sometimes, in certain situations."

I walk to my desk and pick up a folder to hand to her. "Here. You said you needed an assistant. These are the applicants for the job. Take a look at them and tell me who you want to see." I pause. "And next time Oliver calls you, tell him, it's not cool."

I wonder what kind of person I would meet who looks like a Sterling. It's intriguing that he has a combination of names that makes it hard to tell which one is the surname and which the first name. He has barely any online presence. Cedric dug through his social media, but his only account is on Instagram, and he only shows his art there, never his face.

Clearly, a man who shares my soul.

Unfortunately, despite my own feelings about social media, I have to agree with Cedric that he needs to advertise better.

"Thank you for taking me with you, sir!" Cedric looks so excited, I am scared he will bounce off a wall soon.

"You are aware, you are my assistant?" I ask. "I am not taking you along out of the goodness of my heart."

"I know," he chirps.

Well... I tried.

The restaurant Cedric chose is a smaller, more secluded place. Prices are mid-class, not too high to make Sterling and his manager uncomfortable, but still indicating we will get something decent. They have a wine card, which I appreciate.

"They have a smaller menu here," Cedric explains happily. "But they offer both veggie and meat options. Plus, it's not too specific."

"Not a bad choice," I agree.

He beams at me, as usual, perking up slightly when we approach our table. "Oh, they are here already!"

"I can see that."

I give myself a short moment to scan the two men as quickly as possible. In my career, I have learned to read those around me effectively. As we approach, the two men stand up. They look to be the same age. One of them is dark-haired and tall, easily hovering above us all, while the other is smaller in height with short brown hair and a calm expression. He has a tattoo on his forearm, it looks like a signature of a name—interesting—and is clad in simple clothes.

He looks slightly out of place.

"Sterling Thomas?" I ask, as I reach out my hand towards him.

"Yes," he says politely, shaking my hand. "I am honored to meet you, Mr. Randall."

He doesn't seem shy or insecure, but that's no surprise. His paintings carry a tone of confidence.

I turn to the man next to him, shaking his hand as well. "You must be Mateo Wheeler?"

He nods, smiling. His expression is more open and friendly. "Yes, thank you for inviting us, Mr. Randall."

"This is my assistant—"

"Cedric Nichols," he proclaims before I can introduce him, happily shaking hands with both of them. As usual, he looks like he just won the lottery, his expression open and happy.

Sterling doesn't bat an eye at Cedric's display of joy and affection, but Mateo looks amused. He tosses me a curious glance but doesn't say anything, and I don't feel like explaining Cedric, or my reasons for hiring him, to them either. It's no one's business but mine.

When we sit down, Mateo hits his knees against the table, cursing slightly. "You okay?" Sterling asks him.

"As always, Sterlone."

"You know each other well," I conclude.

"Yes, we are friends from college," Sterling explains.

"I didn't know you studied," I say.

"I didn't," he says, openly and honestly, which I appreciate very much. "I dropped out after one year. Uni just wasn't for me."

"That's okay," Cedric chirps. "I sucked at my classes as well. I have no idea how I finished my degree."

I hide a groan, not sure if I should smack the back of his head for acting as if he didn't have a job others were dying to get, or pat his back because he is just being his golden retriever self.

"Are you friends too?" Mateo asks.

"No," I say. "We only met three months ago."

"Fate's funny sometimes," he jokes.

I have nothing to retort. He is just right.

One of Cedric's strengths is not to be bothered by what anyone says, so instead of indulging in that conversation, he pulls out a folder and a notebook. Once the waiter takes our order, he is ready to go into business.

"As I said on the phone," I start. "I want to have an exclusive contract with you, Mr. Thomas—"

"Can we stick with first names?" he asks. "No one has called me Mr. Thomas in ages."

"Fine with me," I say.

"Really?" Mateo asks skeptically.

"Yes."

"Mr. Randall is far less stuck-up than everyone makes him look," Cedric comes to my defense, though I have mixed feelings about what he just said. Cedric turns to me. "But the distanced, cool CEO image works too well for you," Cedric analyzes. "Our followers on TikTok eat it up."

I decide to ignore him. "If I decide to support an artist, of course this means it comes with benefits." I gesture towards Cedric to take over, leaning back and sipping at my wine. It's also his chance to show off. He never does it arrogantly, I don't think he is capable of being arrogant, but he easily switches into business mode. He tells Mateo and Sterling in detail what an exclusive contract means, what kind of say they will have, and what we offer in return.

No artist needs to sell their soul to me. I am not Mephisto. I want them to keep their own style, their muse and their pace. But I invest in them and, in return, I get the first bid on their art, allowing me to put it into my gallery and sell it for them. It's part of the business.

"It's fine with me," Sterling says.

"Don't you want to sleep on it for a night, Sterlone?" Mateo exclaims.

"No, it's not like there is any better offer coming through anytime soon." He nods at me. "He has a reputation."

"Well, sure, but—"

"Thank you," Sterling tells me. "I will happily take the offer."

I can barely hide my amusement when I see the frown on Mateo's forehead. Seems like I am not the only one with difficult work relations.

To ease his mind, however, and to show him that I am genuine, I hand the two men four VIP tickets. "This is for a private dinner party that will be held at my gallery this weekend," I say. "I would be happy to see both of you. It will give you a chance to network, Sterling."

He groans. "I have to, don't I?"

"I can help with your social media accounts," Cedric offers before frowning and turning to me. "Am I allowed to do that? Is that part of my work?"

Another sigh leaves my lips. "Yes, it is."

He smiles happily. "Leave it up to me, Sterling, I am good at this stuff."

"There are four tickets," Mateo says. "Are we allowed to bring friends?"

"Or family or a date," I offer.

Mateo's eyes light up. "That's a cool thing, Sterlone! There will be other artists and potential buyers there. You can get your name out there."

"That's the plan," I verify.

Mateo seems to be fully on board by now. I know that he is a business major, and I am sure he researched me beforehand and is well aware of how the business works. He might not be experienced yet, but he has the drive to pull it off.

The two men discuss who they want to take along for the event, while I text Lynn to prepare the papers. On my phone, I can see the notification of a missed call and a message. It's not Oliver this time, but one of my other brothers.

They really are persistent.

Four

NOEL

"And why do you want me to come along?" I ask. "I am completely out of place there!" Not that it isn't great that Ster got this deal, but I don't belong to this crowd at all.

"For moral support," Sterling says.

"You can flirt with someone there," Mateo offers.

"What, you want me to grab a rich, sugar daddy?"

"No," Mateo curls his nose. "That would be too dangerous, but you could still flirt."

"You could try your luck with Aden in person or his assistant. Both are handsome."

"Maybe his assistant," Mateo says. "But do you think Aden Randall is gay?"

"I don't know. He doesn't give off specific vibes either way. He could be."

"Earth to Sterling and Mateo, I am not coming." They both look at me. Mateo, through huge, puppy eyes, which he can pull off despite his impressive height, and Sterling just gives me a big bro look that's hard to ignore. "I don't have anything to dress in."

"Oh, I have you covered," Mateo smiles. "I got a suit for you."

The vein at my neck starts to throb in annoyance. Bad enough I have to work my ass off in the night club, but to join an evening activity in my free time?

"It's going to be something far from what we usually do," Ster says, suddenly all serious. "This could be good, couldn't it? All three of us have been stagnating for years. I am not a fan of such an event either, but we haven't done anything together in ages, and this is a chance to mingle with people we usually don't meet. Just something new, you know?"

"Fine," I grumble. "The suit?"

Mateo shows me a garment bag with a suit neatly stored inside it. "Here you go. Try it on, so we can have it altered in case it doesn't fit."

"Why would you get it altered? Don't tell me you bought it!"

"I did," Mateo says.

"Don't argue with him," Ster mutters. "He bought me a new suit as well."

"Obviously. You have to look like a star," Mateo argues.

"You know he is right," I admit. "In a way, this is your party." I pause. "I *am* very happy for you, in case that didn't come through properly."

"I know you are," Ster says, smiling. "But thank you for saying it. And you did help a lot already."

"Right, it was *Shades of Blue* that caught Aden Randall's eye," Mateo muses.

"Any art of yours would have," I point out.

"I think it struck something in him," Ster says. "And as an artist, that's what makes me happy. I mean, how high are the chances for one of the most popular gallerists and art patrons to discover one of my paintings, fall in love with it, and then decide to mentor me?"

"I agree," Mateo inspects his own suit. As usual, he got it tailored. His legs are just too long for anything you can buy in a normal shop. "But you *are* good, and you worked hard."

"A lot of artists are good and work hard," he argues. "And yet they will never be able to make it big. Part of it is luck. And I know I got lucky. There is no need to pretend I made it on talent alone. I am very thankful for the help I received."

"At least show me that Randall guy," I say. "I need to know who you are dealing with."

Mateo takes one of the art brochures he has been carrying around, because they feature Ster's art, too, as he was part of that huge opening exhibition. "Here," he says, opening a page and showing me the man.

I was expecting an older man. "Just how old is he? I thought he would at least be in his fifties!"

"I believe he is in his late thirties," Mateo says.

True, Aden Randall looks like he is in his 30s. He is wearing a suit, he's neatly combed his hair, and his expression is serious.

Ster was right. He *is* handsome.

"He looks neat," I say instead.

Mateo snorts. "Right."

Furrowing my brows, I inspect the picture closely. Something about this dude rings a bell. "Are there more pictures of him?"

"He is pretty private," Mateo says. "But his gallery has a social media account. He is in some of the pics there. Wait..." He searches for something on his phone before handing it to me. Most of the pictures are of artworks and artists, but there are some funny reels, too.

Occasionally, though, there are pictures of the staff working for Aden Randall.

And...

"Here, he is wearing a suit again, but the quality is better." The comments seem to fuss over him. I am not surprised. He looks composed and well put-together, a tad mysterious even. A person who doesn't give away too much. I zoom in on the pic, staring at the face now. "I know him," I mutter.

"What?" Mateo stares at me.

"I have seen him somewhere before... but where..." I search for another pic with Aden Randall in it, and stare at it again. This time he is wearing a long, elegant coat, and his hair is styled, but not as neatly as for the official picture. "OH MY GOD!" I blurt out, tossing the phone away in shock.

Ster catches it last second. "What now?"

I throw my hands in the air, pacing up and down the room while hiding my face. "Fuck, it's him!"

"I have no idea what you are talking about," Mateo mutters. "And next time, please don't throw my phone."

"So, who is he?" Ster urges.

"The guy!" I say, turning to them. "The macaroni guy!"

It takes a while to sink in, but once it does, realization dawns on my friends' faces. "No way," Mateo exclaims.

"He is the guy who saved your ass?" Ster asks. "When you shoplifted?"

I was seventeen back then, and my situation was getting worse every day. My father had used me for shoplifting before, so I knew some techniques. I was just hungry. But this time, the shop owner spotted me. If it weren't for Aden Randall, who was coincidentally at the same place, the shop owner would have called the police.

"It's really him," I say in disbelief. He has been living in my mind, rent-free, for a while now. For him, it might have just been a small kind thing to do, but for me, it was more.

"Your crush!" Mateo exclaims.

I press my lips together, annoyed. "He is not my crush."

Mateo ignores what I just said. "See, even more reason to join the party," he grins. "You can finally thank him in person."

"It's been a couple of years, I am sure he can't remember," I say. "I looked different back then, and it was just a moment."

"Well, you remember him," Ster points out. "So, why shouldn't he?"

"Because it was a meaningful moment for me. A turning point. I am sure for him it was just a fleeting moment."

"You never know." Ster shrugs. "So, I assume you are joining us?"

I look at my suit, trying to play it cool. "I guess I have to, now."

ADEN

Lynn and I go through all the details for the dinner party. Everything is already set, but it's always good to take a last look at everything. We are almost done when my phone vibrates.

A message?

Hey little bro!

I frown.

Lynn tosses me a look. "Oliver?"

"No, Francis."

I just met Oliver for a couple of cocktails. Why don't you join us? We'd love to see you!

Francis works a corporate job; he is in finance and is doing very well. He and I are the only ones with more traditional jobs.

I curse myself for having read the message immediately. Now he knows I've seen it.

Can't. I type back. *I am at work.*

That's technically not a lie, though Lynn and I are about to wrap things up.

That sucks. But join us next time!

I don't know what to answer, so I leave it at that. Shortly after, a new message from Francis comes through.

Oh, forgot to tell you: We saw the coverage of your opening exhibition. Congrats!

At this, my fingers almost twitch with wanting to send a reply. In my family, I am the only one with an interest in art, I always have been, and I know that the channels that covered the interviews about the last exhibit aren't those they'd usually watch.

I stop myself from replying, deciding to leave things the way they are.

"Everything okay?" Lynn asks.

"Yes."

"You don't look okay, though."

"No, it's nothing. Just didn't expect a message from Francis. He wanted me to join him and Oliver for a drink."

"Why don't you?"

"I don't know," I admit. "I would feel out of place."

She looks at me thoughtfully. "I don't know, Aden. It looks to me like they'd want to hang out with you."

I shrug. "But why? We weren't close as kids. It makes no sense."

"Why wouldn't it? They grew up, too, and now probably want to be close to their little brother." She pauses. "You know Oliver and I dated in college."

"I know." Lynn was always nice to me. Pity that Oliver and she didn't work out. I was over the moon when we coincidentally met years later and began working together.

"He never said anything bad about you," she says. "In fact, he was always overthinking what to gift you for your birthdays."

"Yes, Oliver isn't too bad," I admit. At least he didn't bully me, but it's not like he cared a lot either.

"Maybe you are overthinking it."

"Maybe, maybe not," I say. "But for now, I want to keep the status quo."

Family just tires me out. Not so much Mom, but everyone else does. University was the first time in my life when I felt truly like I belonged and could flourish. I just don't like returning home, even for a brief visit.

I pack my things up and squeeze Lynn's shoulder. "Make sure to get some sleep."

"I will. Has Mateo told you yet, how many guests they will be coming with?"

"Yes, they will bring a friend and one sibling. I believe Sterling's sister will be attending."

"Great!" She nods contentedly. "I will bring a date too. Is that okay?"

"Of course! The guy from the fitness studio?"

"No, the one I met for my marathon training," she says. "He is in IT."

"Good. I am happy for you!"

She grins. "Now we just need to find someone for you. You have been single for too long." Before I can open my mouth, she continues. "Occasional hookups don't count. What's with the guy you met in the park?"

"There were no sparks," I admit. "I just want there to be an attraction, too."

"Yeah, I get it." She moves her fingertip over her lips in a thoughtful gesture. "Maybe it's the type of guys you are looking for."

"What's wrong with them?" I ask.

"You tell me! What do they all have in common?"

"Well, they are well-dressed, they are quiet and serious," I say.

"Yeah, like you," she says bluntly. "You never take any risk, Aden. You just go for the easiest solution. You know more than anyone else how to get one of these men, because they are like you. You talk about sparks and feelings, but you are very rational about how you pick them. Now, rationality can be good if that's your thing, but it clearly isn't."

"Are you saying I am self-sabotaging?"

"I am saying you go for guys who you know won't interest you on a deeper level. Because then it means you won't need to engage with them, you won't need to get to know them, you won't need to open up, you will have it easy and boring, and it will be zero effort to dump them."

"That was blunt," I mutter.

"Sorry?" she offers, clearly not meaning it. "Just think about it."

Am I really doing that? Flirting with a guy I am only remotely interested in and not allowing myself to date someone I actually find intriguing? For years now, I've only had loose affairs. My last actual relationship was years ago, and it was a disaster.

So, maybe she is right.

For a moment, Lynn stays silent before picking up the folder with Sterling's name on. Cedric and I have been collecting his data and his plans for the future. "Looks like he and his manager are decent guys. From what I have seen and heard so far, I like them. They seem genuine."

"Sterling's art is genuine, too," I say. "I would have been surprised if he appeared arrogant."

"You have a good eye for artists," she says. "I don't know how you do it."

"You can see it in the way they paint and form an idea into reality, how they approach their motives, where they take inspiration from."

"You say that as if it's easy to read them," she chuckles. "That's why I keep to our finances. You and Cedric do the rest."

I groan. "Sometimes I feel more like a babysitter for Cedric than a boss."

"Don't complain," she grins. "He is the first one you've worked well with. Don't chase our golden retriever away! He can handle your perfectionism."

"Shut up," I chuckle. "I will take that as my cue to go home now. I am working from home tomorrow. Cedric has his day off."

"I will be here," she reassures me. "In case something urgent comes in, but I doubt it will. Fridays are slow."

I nod. "See you on Saturday for the dinner party,"

FIVE

ADEN

The dinner party I host in the gallery, once a year, is for a limited audience. The main artists shown in my gallery are invited, some artists who usually apply for the event, some of my most loyal customers, some art enthusiasts, and of course, my employees.

It's a fancy event, but also an intimate one with people I appreciate and trust. And it's an opportunity for new artists to network.

"This is amazing!" Cedric gapes. He doesn't even hide how happy he is. From all my guests, he is probably the most in awe.

"Close your mouth or you will catch a fly," Lynn teases, before introducing the man at her side. He is tall and athletic, pretty much like Lynn herself. He has a kind, open face. "Patrick, meet my employer and friend, Aden Randall, and his mascot, Cedric."

"I am not his mascot," Cedric says seriously while shaking Patrick's hand. "I am his assistant."

"It's nice to meet you," I say, shaking his hand as well.

"The pleasure is all mine." Patrick puts his arm around Lynn's shoulder and smiles at us.

We make a bit of small talk, but neither Lynn nor I are big on it. Knowing her, she just wants to drag her man to the buffet and eat something, and flirt with him. I wholeheartedly understand that. She works enough, and this evening is for her to switch off working mode.

I decide to retreat politely. "I am going to greet some of my guests. Enjoy the evening, you two."

"We will," Lynn says. "Thank you."

"I just saw one of the influencers from the opening night of the last exhibit," Cedric says. "Time to network!"

I shake my head, amused, when I see him walk away. He walks with so much energy, and almost like he is dancing. On my own now, I walk through the gallery and talk to whoever I walk by. A lot of these people are friends, too, or at least acquaintances. I also make an effort to talk to the artists who are here for the first time.

Sterling and Mateo are here also.

"Aden." Sterling addresses me in his natural, calm and confident manner. It takes me by surprise, but then I remember we settled on a first-name basis. "Thank you so much for the invitation."

"I am glad to see both of you here." My gaze falls on the young woman next to Sterling. "You must be Sterling's sister?"

"Yes." She smiles shyly. "I am Roxana, Sterling's younger sister."

She looks a lot younger than him though looks can deceive.

"Roxana has just started college," Sterling explains to me.

"I couldn't have done it without you," she says, smiling at her brother. Then she turns to me. "Sterling has been supporting me for years now."

That makes a lot of sense. There is some sort of melancholy in his pictures, something real and heart-wrenching aside from his confidence. If he is the one supporting his sister, it makes me wonder what their parents are doing or if they are still around.

However, it's not my position to ask, and certainly not the right time for it.

"I am happy to see you here, Roxana. I hope you will enjoy the evening."

"I'm sure I will." She smiles happily. "Thank you."

"And your second guest?" I ask.

"Oh, he is grabbing something to eat," Mateo says, gesturing towards the buffet. I follow the direction he is pointing at, my eyes falling on a young man with wavy hair and a slender figure. My heart almost stops beating.

"Shades of Blue," I mutter.

Mateo and Roxana haven't heard me, too busy chatting, but Sterling has. He stares at me, his mouth dropping open. "How could you tell?" he asks quietly.

"You captured him too well for me not to recognize him."

"No one else can," Sterling muses. "Aside from those who know us well enough. He is one of my best friends, like a brother to me."

"I am going to say hello to him," I say.

"Are you not afraid it will shatter your illusion?" Sterling sounds curious, not upset or worrying.

"No, not at all. Do you know why?"

"I have no idea," Sterling admits.

"He is your muse, not mine," I explain. "For me, however, your picture scratched on a surface I want to know more about."

Sterling purses his lips and nods. "I guess I understand." He smirks. "He has claws, be careful."

His words make me chuckle. "I figured as much."

I leave the small group and walk towards the buffet, grabbing a plate and putting some pieces of food onto it before I approach the young man. He looks to be the same age as Mateo and Sterling.

"Hello," I say.

The young man startles, raising his eyes to look at me. He looks surprised first, then nervous, before a new expression spreads over his face. Defiance? Curiosity? It's hard to tell, but very intriguing. Sterling was scared it would shatter my illusion to see him or talk to him, but in fact, seeing his face makes me even more curious. "You are the young man from Sterling's paintings."

The guy gapes, his face turning red like an overripe tomato. "How could you tell? Ster never shows my face!"

"He caught your core," I say. The core of his soul.

"So, you know me already?" he asks defiantly.

"Not at all," I say. "I just recognized the man on the bathtub and the man at the beach. I have no idea who you really are."

Though something does strike me as odd, have I seen the man somewhere before?

At that, he blinks. "Noel," he finally says. "That's my name."

"Aden."

"I know," he says. "See, I know something too."

"Are you interested in art?"

"No," he says, so honestly that it makes me smile. "I mean, I like Ster's art, but I don't know much about artists and paintings," he hurries to explain.

"If you don't know much about it, how did you know me?"

"Mateo showed me your picture," he admits. "And..."

"And?"

"We met years ago, briefly," he admits.

So, I do know him! My gut feeling didn't betray me. I scan his face, trying to place it somewhere. Noel is watching me, before he shrugs. "It was just a brief encounter," he reassures me. "And you probably meet tons of people daily."

"Won't you tell me how we met?"

"No," he says bluntly.

Goodness gracious. That guy does have claws! I try to remind myself that he is not my usual type and that flirting with him will probably just lead me to be disappointed at best and heartbroken at worst, but damn it, I feel weirdly drawn to him. It's his eyes. His deep, soulful eyes. Sterling captured his very essence so well, it's even more mind-boggling now that I am talking to him in person.

"Care for a glass of wine?" I ask him.

Noel blinks at me, eyes wide. Then he nods. I take two glasses for us, walking to the balcony with him following me. "Why don't you push me for an answer?" he asks after I hand him a glass.

"You said you wouldn't tell me," I say. "So, what's the use in pushing you?"

It has the wanted effect because Noel's eyebrow starts twitching. "You are kind of infuriating," he says bluntly. He obviously doesn't mean it, though, or he would have left me by myself. Instead, he keeps sipping at his glass.

"Do you like the wine?"

"Yes, it's a good Cabernet Sauvignon."

This does take me by surprise. I didn't think he would so easily be able to tell what we are drinking. "So, you are a wine connoisseur?"

"Not really," Noel says. "But I know the most important wines."

"How come?"

"I am a bartender," he explains. He looks flustered as if it's embarrassing to admit.

"So, you can mix cocktails?"

He perks up visibly. "I can, but I don't like alcohol much." He gestures at his glass. "I only occasionally have a glass, but usually stay away from heavy stuff."

"Wait, you are working as a bartender, but don't like the drinks there?"

"Yeah, I don't. It's a long story."

I wait a moment in case he wants to tell me more, but he doesn't. Understandable, I don't waltz around, telling random strangers my problems either. I let my gaze wander over Noel once more. He is nothing like Sterling's paintings, but at the same time, he is. It's the discrepancy between the melancholy around him, which Sterling catches in his pictures, and his confident, slightly prickly personality.

I am fascinated.

"Mr. Randall?"

I raise my gaze to look right into Noel's eyes. Warm-toned, brown eyes, hidden behind his wavy bangs. He looks beautiful.

Not what I go for usually.

My God, what am I even thinking? Lynn didn't do me any good.

"Yes?"

"Are you hitting on me?" he asks.

I snort at his bluntness. "I don't know yet. Am I?"

"I don't know either," he says.

For a moment, we just look at each other. I can't deny an initial attraction to this guy, but at the same time, I am not sure if he is the challenge I want. Is it true that I am always choosing the easy way? Was Lynn right with what she said?

"Maybe you are just obsessed with Ster's paintings of me," he adds.

"Maybe," I admit.

Noel looks surprised. "You are honest," he mutters.

"Is that a problem?"

"No, in fact, I prefer it that way." A pause. "And now?"

For a moment, I consider my options. I have no idea what the fuck I want, and what I am even doing here with Noel, but somehow Lynn's words still echo in me. She is right. What I have been doing the last couple of years has been utterly sad and bordering on pathetic.

"Here," I say, taking a business card out of my pocket. On the back, I scribble down my private number. "If you ever feel like going for coffee or a drink—a type of drink you like—text me."

"You are leaving it up to me?" Noel asks. "The ball is in my court, huh?"

"Maybe it is," I admit. "But I gave you my private number, didn't I? I barely hand it out."

"Not even to hook-ups?" he asks.

"No, not to anyone. Barely anyone has my private number. I mostly use my work phone. Feels less personal."

Noel looks at me in awe. "Then it's special," he says, neatly placing the card I just handed him in his wallet. Then the sass is back in his eyes. "Don't believe I won't contact you!"

I chuckle. "I am curious to see if you will."

SIX

NOEL

For all my bravado the other night, contacting Aden is much more difficult than I thought it would be. The card with his private number on, is safely secured in my wallet. It feels so heavy. Every time I take my wallet out, I feel like it burns my hands.

In my job, I usually know when a guy flirts with me, and I get hit on a lot. Had Aden hit on me, it would have turned me off immediately, but he just talked with me, and while he seemed interested, he didn't look like he was about to jump into anything either. He didn't look too certain that he wanted me *that* way.

"You look like you are trying to solve a really difficult math problem," Emma says while pouring herself some coffee.

She is one of my roommates. I live with three guys and two girls in a quite cramped apartment. I can't afford more with my dad's debt dangling over my head, but at least they are nice people. Mateo and Ster hate that I am living here. They think the area is unsafe, and they keep begging me to move in with one of them temporarily, but I can't rely on them all the time. I can't take advantage of their kindness, and frankly, Ster has been supporting his sister for so many years, so it's not like he isn't swimming in money. And Mateo is still paying off his student debt.

"It's nothing," I mutter.

"Sure," Emma laughs. "Tell me."

"Man, Emma, don't you have your own problems?"

"Nope," she says.

"Don't you need to study?" She is currently in college, and most of the time, either studying or working to support herself.

"I had my exam yesterday," she says.

"And how did it go?"

"Well," she says. "But don't change the subject. What's wrong?"

Sighing, I sit down, accepting a cup of coffee from her. "You are not going to let this rest, are you?"

"I won't."

"Okay, so, I was at this event last weekend, remember?"

"The high society art event, right?"

"Yeah." I pause. "The owner of the gallery, who is sponsoring Ster, held it. I met him there."

"Okay," she says while dragging the O out. "And he is a weirdo?"

"No." I feel my cheeks flush. "He is calm and serious, and... nice."

Emma stares at me, before a wide grin spreads on her face. "Ohhhh, that's what this is about! He is also very hot, huh?"

"I can't deny that," I admit. Aden looks exactly like I would imagine a businessman out of a magazine. He is tall with a toned body, dark hair in a fashionable cut that sometimes falls into his forehead, and dark brown eyes. But that's not all. "He is hot, but he is also... There is something about him. He has that thoughtful look in his eyes sometimes. You know, that gaze of an artist like Ster has... Aden has it too. Like he sees something, and truly sees it. He must be loaded, but he isn't waltzing around showing it off. No show-off brands, no golden watches, just a normal handsome guy in a suit."

"You should go into sales," Emma mutters. "Because now I am curious as fuck about this guy. So, you talked?"

"Yes, he was instantly able to tell that I am the one from Ster's paintings. No one else can usually tell." It was a shock to have Aden be able to tell, at first glance, that it's me. A surprise that made him all the more intriguing.

"Was he flirting with you?"

"I am not sure," I say. "That's the problem. I think he was interested in me, maybe because I am in the drawings, but I don't know if there is more than that. Usually I can tell."

"Yeah, you can tell because you are used to these sleazy assholes in your club hitting on you. That's not how normal guys approach someone in a normal situation," she explains.

"He gave me his private number, but he didn't make it clear if he wants to... you know... fuck me."

"Right, Noel," Emma snorts. "Like I said, there are people out there who are not just after you for a quick fuck. He gave you his number so that you can talk or meet, not to get you into bed immediately. If he wanted that, he would have gone about it differently."

I stare at her. "You think he wants to talk?"

"Yeah, if what you said about him is true, then I guess he wants to get to know you better."

"Why?"

"Noel, baby, you for sure have dated before, haven't you? Then you know—"

"I haven't," I admit.

"What?!" she exclaims. "But you meet guys—"

"Yeah, to fuck."

"Are you kidding? But then, you do have a pretty face, I get why they are attracted to you."

She is right with what she says. I can't even count the amount of times I have heard a guy tell me he wants to slap his cock against my *pretty* face and cover it in his cum, or fuck my *pretty* mouth. I know I am pretty, and I wasn't ashamed to use it to my advantage as a teen when Dad forced me to do shady shit for him, or when Mom needed drugs or alcohol.

I am a pretty face, but not much more.

"Usually, no one is truly interested," I say. "I am exhausting."

"You are not exhausting," she says. "You are just used to meeting losers. If you were exhausting, I wouldn't be your friend. And Ster and the tall, hot guy wouldn't be either."

The tall, hot guy? I have to hold back a chuckle. Mateo is usually the tallest person wherever he goes. He used to be insecure about it, and a bit of his insecurity still remains, but he doesn't care as much anymore. And he is a hot guy. Ster and I make sure to tell him all the time.

"I just don't think I have much to offer."

"Why do you say that?"

"My debt, my lack of time because of two awful jobs, I have roommates despite not being a student anymore, the sleazy bars I am working at, my shady past. And—"

"Noel, you are overthinking this. You have a lot to offer. Instead of shooting down the possibility of a hot, decent guy being into you, why not just message him and give him a chance? Get to know the dude! You always complain how everyone just wants to get you into bed. Now there is a guy who actually wants to know more about you. That's what you were always waiting for."

I take Aden's card in my hand, looking at it. It doesn't help that he is the guy who saved my life. He can't remember, so maybe that's good. But I have definitely put him on a pedestal, and now I am supposed to reach out and sully this perfect person with my presence and with my shitty problems.

"You will regret it forever if you don't do it," Emma adds. "You are into him. Anyone with a brain can tell. It doesn't matter if you are insecure or not. Give yourself a chance. Talk to him, meet him, see where it leads you. Maybe your feelings were wrong, maybe he just wants to be friends. No one can tell that. But if you won't even try, you will have to live with that forever."

ADEN

I guess I have the ball now.

I look at the message, my amusement growing when Noel sends a GIF, immediately afterwards, with a little animated blob hitting a tennis ball.

"What are you grinning at?" Lynn asks.

"Nothing."

"Nothing? You are staring at your private phone. You never grin when you receive a message there."

"Yes, because usually it's family."

Originally, only Mom had my private number, but eventually my brothers got it too. I guess it was inevitable. The only other person who has this number is Lynn, and now Noel.

"Exactly! Which makes me wonder what it is that makes you grin like an idiot. Can't be me, because I am sitting here, and unless you haven't handed out your number." She pauses. "Wait a moment, you did!"

"Lynn—"

"You gave someone your number, and it can't be one of your shallow affair partners, because you never give them your private number." She gapes. "Unless you are sick, and this is your doctor writing to you."

"Would I grin then?"

"If he has good news, maybe."

"It's fucking weird how your brain works, yet somehow it makes sense. But I am not ill, and this is not a doctor." I pause. "It's a guy."

Lynn stares at me. "No way!"

"It is."

"I don't believe you," she says. "It's been years since you let anyone sneak into your phone. You are absolutely anal about your phone number. The only two people you handed it to are your mom and me, and then your mom spilled it to one of your brothers, and you got even more private with it. You are the only person I know who usually handles everything via work phone."

"Maybe you are right," I hear myself say.

"About what? You being anal about your phone number?"

"That too, but maybe also about what you said the other day. Me and my dating, and how I don't seriously try for a relationship, but just go for men who I know won't interest me enough to give them a real chance. Shallow relationships, you know?"

"And this guy is different?"

"He definitely is different."

"But?"

"I don't know yet," I say. "I don't know if I want to pursue him. He is interesting, though."

"Okay." She looks at me. "I am still waiting for the 'but'."

"He is my type," I admit quietly. "My real type. Like Emil was my type."

"Aden," she says. "I know Emil left you burnt. He was a problem, not because he was your type but because he was Emil. If you go into every potential relationship with the thought of the guy being like Emil, then how is that fair? So, let me guess. You said he might be your type: melancholic, sassy, direct, maybe a bit loud?"

I nod.

"A lot of people are like that. It's not like all of them are like Emil. It just so happened that Emil was one of them, not the other way round."

"I know," I say. "Fuck, I know. Which is why I gave him my number."

"Who is it?" she asks curiously. "Do I know them?"

"Yes, and no." I sigh. "You will have a field day with this, once I tell you."

"Now I am even more curious."

"He is the model from Sterling's paintings."

Her mouth drops open while she stares at me, dumbfounded, then she bursts into laughter. "I can't fucking believe it. How small is the world! This has to be fate, Aden!"

"Is it not weird?"

"Absolutely, it's fucking weird, but it's so you. The universe is giving you a sign, obviously."

"You don't believe in fate," I chuckle.

"I do," she says. "When it's convenient. And now it is! You are not going to shoot him down now that he messaged you, are you?"

"I won't, which is why I told you." I scrunch my nose. "If I want to run, you need to stop me from going anywhere without giving it a real shot."

She smiles. "Get to know him, Aden. You deserve someone at your side, someone you can love and someone who loves you."

Seven

NOEL

I can't fucking believe that I did it. I wrote Aden Randall the most unoriginal, pathetic message. What's even more of a mindfuck is that he replied. It's funny because he writes exactly the way he talks, exactly how I'd imagine him to. Polite, in full sentences and with perfect grammar. He doesn't use any emojis or GIFs either, but he hearted my silly football GIF, so I guess that's something.

"A friend's going to drop by, Cal," I tell my co-worker, while we prepare the glasses we will need later.

"Here?" Cal asks.

"Yeah."

"Why would anyone come here?" he queries.

He isn't wrong. I don't even let Ster or Mateo come. They only dropped by once to see how I was doing, obviously hated it but didn't want to butt into my business too much. We set the rule that they are allowed to complain about where I work and live, but aren't allowed to come and visit.

"Because I invited them."

"And why would you do that?"

"I want him to see where I am working and what I am doing," I say. "Maybe that's pathetic, but the earlier he sees the better."

Cal looks at me thoughtfully. He is a young guy, younger than me, and equally trying to pay off a debt. "It's *that* kind of visitor," he mutters.

"What do you mean?"

"It's someone you want to test," he adds. "Means he must be important to you."

"I don't know that yet," I admit. "But in case he becomes important, I want him to know now, so I won't get disappointed by him later."

"I am not judging you," he tells me. "I would do the same. Give him the chance to run now, before getting too invested and ending up broken-hearted."

"Exactly! Plus, this is still the safer place to meet, not like the nightclub. I wouldn't go that far. But when he sees this here, it's easier to tell him about the other."

Aden Randall.

I try not to have my hopes up too high. I don't know the man behind the handsome face, and the image I have had of him since I met him years ago. It was a fleeting encounter, yet it meant so much to me. If he sees me now, here in this bar, and runs, it will break my heart and ruin the image I had of him. But it will be worse if I let him in first, trusting him and falling for him, and then have him run when he sees my reality. That's why I need to do it now, before I invest too much of my emotions into this.

The evening starts slowly as usual, but from 9 p.m. on it's getting more and more crowded. I have so much to do that I barely notice who is coming and going. It's good, it takes my mind off Aden Randall.

That is, until Cal approaches me with a plate of empty glasses.

"He is here," he tells me.

"What?" I exclaim. "You mean Aden?"

"I don't know his name, but it has to be him." Cal puts the glasses aside and hands me a fresh plate with drinks. "Go and take a peek."

"How do you know it's him?"

"It's the only one who doesn't look sleazy," Cal says. "Someone like him who dropped by accidentally would be gone again in a minute, but he sat down at the bar and is still sitting there five minutes later. I get why you are so freaked out, though. The guy is hot."

My heart freezes in fear. "Oh my God."

"Go, and face reality," Cal tells me. "Get it over with. That's why you made him come here after all."

"Yeah... yeah... You are right." Now that it's getting real, though, all my confidence and fearlessness seem to disappear. Maybe I should have prepared him a little. Maybe he will run now because I forced him in at the deep end instead of meeting him first and explaining my situation to him.

But it's not like I can change it now. Maybe Cal was wrong, and it's another guy, and Aden will have cancelled because some super-important appointment came up.

I try to cling to this hope for the five minutes it takes me to shuffle in front of the counter again, just to have it shattered immediately. There he is, like Cal said, sitting at the counter, our sticky menu in his hand. He looks at it thoughtfully. I am not sure what he feels right now, at least he doesn't look downright disgusted.

It's no surprise that Cal instantly knew he was my date. Aden sticks out like a sore thumb, or rather like a well-groomed thumb with perfectly done nails. He is his usual elegant and stylish self. He has changed his dress pants for some dark blue jeans and is wearing a more sporty casual blazer. He still looks exactly like the CEO he is, but he obviously made an effort to dress for the occasion. Something about this makes the ground open beneath me, trying to suck me into a whirlwind of emotions.

He is so handsome. It's more obvious now next to the other dudes here than it was during the art event.

"Hello, Mr. Randall," I greet him, barely able to fight back my anxiety.

Aden looks up and smiles. "I thought we'd be on a first-name basis by now."

"Right, I forgot!" Count on me for making this even more awkward. "What can I bring you, Aden?"

"What can you recommend?"

I sigh, feeling my cheeks heat up in embarrassment. "Nothing," I whisper towards him. "Sorry for making you come here."

Aden snorts. "Do you have whisky?"

"Yes, but it's not a good one."

"Make it whisky sour for me. It will burn off any weird taste."

I can do that. However, our booze is cheap, and someone like Aden will immediately recognize it for the garbage it is, which is why I am surprised he orders anything at all. He also doesn't seem upset, and he doesn't look at me with disgust. The only time he looks annoyed is when one of the other men here starts hitting on him.

"Fuck, what did I do?" I mutter towards Cal.

Cal shrugs. "He is still here. He didn't bolt."

"Yeah, but now I feel bad about it."

Cal tosses a glance at Aden. He is sipping at his drink, not minding anyone around him. He looks a bit tired, which worries me. Probably came here from a long day at work and now has to hang out at this shithole.

"Okay," Cal takes a deep breath. "You have a short shift today anyway."

"Yeah, only one and a half hours left."

"I will take over for you," he says. "I still owe you one for jumping in for me last week."

"What?" I exclaim. "Are you for real?"

"Yes, today is a slow evening. So go, grab your handsome guy and leave. He is still here, so obviously he is interested in you. He is hot and has rebuffed any advances from other people here. He looks like he could become something for you, and I don't want you to fuck it up on your first date already."

"Thank you," I blurt out. "Thank you, Cal!"

"Just make something out of the remainder of the night, so that he won't bolt for real."

"I owe you one!" I proclaim.

Cal smiles. "Don't worry. It's a give and take. The next time I have a promising date, you can do the same for me."

"Got you." I give him the thumbs up before hurrying to our small staff-only area. I freshen up swiftly so I don't reek of alcohol and sweat, change my clothes, and then dash out into the bar area again.

Aden looks up when he notices me next to him.

"Sorry for letting you wait so long," I say, my anxiety skyrocketing. Please don't let him bolt now. "Shall we leave?"

Aden takes a sip from his drink. For what feels like an eternity, he doesn't say anything at all, then his thoughtful gaze lands on me, looking through my eyes right into my soul. Fuck. I have never noticed his eyes. They are a dark shade of brown, almost piercing now. "Did I pass your test?" he says.

I feel my cheeks flush in embarrassment. For a moment I consider pretending it wasn't one, and that I never intended for him to come to this shithole. "A bit pathetic, huh?"

Aden gazes around. "I guess you have your reasons," he says, much to my surprise. "It doesn't necessarily mean I am happy, but I'll let it pass if this was the one and only test you will put me through deliberately."

"I promise. I just... had some bad experiences."

"I thought so." Aden puts his glass to the side and gets up. "So, what's the plan now?"

"How about we grab something to eat?" I offer. "Or... you know... have an actual good drink?"

Aden's lips curl into a smile. "Then lead the way."

EIGHT

NOEL

I have decided to take Cal's advice seriously. It's only 11 p.m. and we still have time for a date. The bar is in a shady corner of the city, so obviously, our choices here are not top-notch, but I know my way around.

"I know this doesn't look fancy," I tell Aden when I lead him to my favorite bar. It looks cheap and run down, but the inside is well looked after. "They also have some nice food choices. Nothing special, but for this area..." I break off. "It's one of my favorite places," I finally admit. "Even if it isn't great."

"I'd actually like to see your favorite place," Aden says. "I am sure it won't scare me away."

"It's run by drag queens," I say quietly, realizing that I have put him through a lot this evening. "It's not a test, I promise. I am friends with the owner, and it's—"

"A drag queen place sounds good," he reassures me. "I am frequenting one, too."

"Really?"

"Yes, one of our patrons runs it. She loves the more extravagant art and buys from one of my artists. The guy is almost exclusively painting for her."

I feel my heart taking a leap. He is actually frequenting such a bar himself? I suddenly feel much lighter. I know from Ster and Mateo that the art scene is much more free-spirited than other fields of work, but Aden is still a CEO. Maybe not the typical CEO, but he could fit into their world easily. He is rich, owns his own business, and looks the part.

I gaze at him. Maybe he wouldn't fit one hundred percent. He dresses a tad bit more casual despite always looking proper, and obviously he knows how to wear jeans as he proved tonight, but still...

Aden chuckles. "What are you thinking about?"

"I just tried to imagine you in a drag queen bar," I say with a frown.

"And?"

"Doesn't work," I say bluntly. "You always look so perfectly classy. Wouldn't a fancy high-end bar suit you more?" I pause. "Oh fuck! I said that out loud, didn't I?!"

"Yes, you did," Aden says, furrowing his brows. I am so doomed. "But I appreciate this version of you much more than the one who wants to test me."

What? Is he serious? "I don't hear that a lot."

"That your date doesn't want to be tested?"

"No, that someone doesn't hate my bluntness. I am not really..." I think. "I have an attitude, okay? I know it."

"Have I complained?" Aden asks in return.

His words take the wind out of my sails. "No."

"Alright," Aden nods. "Then let's go to this bar of yours. And for the record, I do like to visit a fancy bar here and there, but tend to avoid those where I am forced to mingle with the typical CEO audience. Contrary to popular belief, I don't fit."

"Really?" I blink. "But I have seen you during the event. You can handle them so well!"

"Yes, because I have to, and it's my business. Also, the gallery is my territory. I know how to handle it well. But in my free time? I don't fit in at such clubs and bars, and more importantly, I don't feel comfortable there."

I let his words sink in. That makes sense, I guess. Just like Ster is an artist, and knows how to talk to his fellow artists during events and to potential patrons, but he doesn't like hanging out in such a stiff atmosphere, preferably.

~~~

The bar I am taking Aden to has a blinking pink sign above the door carrying the letters Paradise. It sounds and looks like a strip club at first glance, but the additional sign very much clarifies that it isn't.

The owner is named DeeDee, and fortunately, she is present tonight.

"Noel!" she exclaims with a smile when she spots me. Unlike the bar I work in, her place is actually crowded.

She comes over, giving me a hug before gazing at Aden, a bright grin on her face. "And who are you, handsome?"

"Aden," he says, reaching out his hand to shake hers. "It's a pleasure to meet you."
~~~

She shakes his hand, starstruck. "DeeDee," she says. "My, how polite." She turns to me. "Your date, or are you stupid enough not to grab the chance?"

I feel my cheeks flush in embarrassment again. "DeeDee!" I groan. "Can't you not embarrass me?"

She frowns while looking at me. "You are also looking way too skinny. Are you not eating properly?" Before I even so much as say anything, she already ushers Aden and me to a small empty table in a cozy corner. "Here, sit down there. I had a feeling you might come by today and saved this place for you." She grins. "Didn't know you'd come with such a hot date, though."

Since Aden doesn't say or do anything to correct her, that we are technically meeting casually as friends, I don't either.

"I will bring you something to eat. Anything you would like, handsome? We don't have many fancy choices, but what I offer my guests at least tastes good."

Handsome, aka Aden, just smiles. "Whatever suits a gin and tonic would be nice."

She winks at him and nods before turning to me. "For you, the usual?"

"Yes, please. Thanks, DeeDee."

She blows me a kiss before shuffling off. At the bar, there is her co-worker, Crystal. A relatively new drag queen. She is very sweet and always makes an effort to talk with the patrons of their bar. She waves at me and smiles.

Aden takes his coat off, stretching slightly. He looks more relaxed than I've ever seen him. What he just told me must be right. It also means that taking him here wasn't the worst choice.

"This is not a bad place, Noel," he tells me. "The atmosphere is relaxed. It gives off good vibes."

I beam. "I am so glad you like it here!"

"Thank you for taking me to this place," he says. "You said it's your favorite, and I guess you don't just take anyone here."

"That's true," I admit. "But I didn't want this evening to be a complete fuck-up, so, I took the risk."

Aden looks at me, amused. "So, first you took a risk by asking me to go to the bar you work at to see how I'd react. And then, to make sure I am not too upset, you take the risk and take me to your favorite place? Are you aware you over-complicated this whole process?"

"I know," I groan, brushing my fingers through my hair. "Why are you not running?" I ask bluntly.

"Why would I?"

"You just saw where I work! And you also saw how difficult I am."

"I did," he agrees.

"The place sucks! It's sleazy, and with equally sleazy patrons. And did you know I work at a nightclub too, running around in a skimpy outfit and serving drinks? And it's not one of the good clubs either. Actually, the one you came to is the better option."

"It's true, the place is sleazy," he says. "But I assume you are working there because you have to, not because you love the place."

"True," I mutter.

"You wanted to show me, didn't you? To see how fast I'd run and if I am worth the effort."

I feel my cheeks flush. "I..."

God, why does he so easily look through everything I do?! It's exhausting, it's embarrassing, and also kind of hot. He has his life put together, but in a way that it isn't patronizing or intimidating.

"It's also true that you are complicated," he adds. "But not unreasonably so."

DeeDee brings our drinks, giving me some time before I have to reply to what Aden just said. He takes a sip of his drink and nods contentedly. "Thank you. That's a good one!"

"Gin is my favorite," DeeDee explains. "I always make sure to have something decent around. We are not high-class, but there is a middle ground, you know?"

"Absolutely," Aden agrees. "I see now why Noel likes this place."

"Oh, did you tell him that you love it here?" she beams and pats my head. "That makes your momma happy."

"Who are you calling my momma?" I snap.

She grins. "He is a sassy one, but you know what they say about dogs that bark..."

Aden smiles. "Yes. I figured as much."

"Please leave us alone," I groan.

DeeDee laughs and moves away.

"She is nice," Aden chuckles.

"Easy for you to say, as you are not the butt of her jokes," I mutter, annoyed.

"She obviously sees you as her son or her little brother," he says. "I find it endearing."

"If you say so," I mutter before gazing at him. "It's a long story."

"Are you talking about you and DeeDee or you and the place you are working at?"

"Both, I guess." I pause. "I don't like the bar I work at, and I hate the club even more. But at the moment, I don't have many other options. It brings me the most money, and I need it." I pause. "I am sorry, I am not sure if I am ready to talk about it all."

"You don't need to," Aden reassures me. "What you said is all I needed to know."

Mateo keeps telling me that whenever I fuck up a potential relationship my pride is what gets in my way. Ster keeps saying the same, just with less words. I realize I did the same tonight, I was just lucky enough to have met a guy who is polite and respectful, and apparently sees a little more in me than just the pretty shell I am. Taking a deep breath, I gather all my courage. "I am sorry, okay?" I blurt out.

Yeah, that came out convincing. Good job.

Aden looks at me with his usual thoughtful eyes.

"For dragging you around," I add. "And for my weird stunt earlier tonight. I know others call me complicated and dramatic, and it's true. So, fuck it, thank you for not running tonight." I feel my cheeks heat up again. Why the fuck is this so difficult? And why does it look like I am making it worse?

Probably should have kept my mouth shut.

Aden's gaze turns to one of surprise now, then a smile curls his lips. "Thank you for apologizing," he says, his low voice warm now.

My god! I did it! The world's worst apology, but hey, at least it worked.

"DeeDee is coming with our food," I say, waving at her. I notice she doesn't just bring the usual finger food, she also made some dips and brought fresh bread. That's not on her usual menu; she did it for me.

"As I said," she tells Aden. "It's nothing fancy."

Aden smiles at her. "It's perfect, don't worry."

When DeeDee turns around to wink at me, I can't help but roll my eyes at her. This is either the worst night of my life or the best. I am not sure yet.

NINE

ADEN

For half of the evening, I've asked myself 'what the fuck I am doing here'. I came to the bar Noel wanted me to meet him at, just to realize it's the place he works at. If there is one thing that's a dealbreaker for me, it's mind games and tests. I have enough drama in my family, I don't need the additional one in my private life. However, it seems that 'usual' is not the fitting word for how I am handling things with Noel.

Any other guy, I would have politely told him I am leaving, and then never contacted him again. But one look at Noel when he approached me and asked me what I wanted to drink, one look into his eyes, and I couldn't bring myself to leave.

From the first time that I met him, there's been this vulnerability in his gaze, the one Sterling so perfectly captures in his pictures. But there was more than that... there was fear. Noel looked scared, and it stopped me from doing the *usual* thing. Instead, I stuck around and watched him handle the patrons and his job. He is diligent, I know that now. Despite his sass, he obviously works hard.

Now I am glad I didn't leave.

"DeeDee's food is pretty good," I say.

Noel's eyes light up. "Right? It's not the fanciest stuff, but she knows what she is doing!"

"She does."

He looks so happy now, munching on his fries. The gloominess around him is gone suddenly. This place must be one of his favorites, yet he decided to take the risk and bring me here. It means something to him. He opened up a little by introducing me to DeeDee and this place.

"Aden, can I ask something?"

"Of course."

Noel stares at me through his deep blue eyes, but furrows his brows. "Why exactly did you decide to meet me? It's because of Ster's painting, right? You must know by now that I am not like the guy he draws!"

I shake my head. "You are like the guy he draws."

"What?! I am nothing like the guy in the picture! You and Ster need to get your eyes tested, or you are completely delusional."

I snort. "Argue all you want, but what Ster sees when drawing you, it's there. But it's not all there is to you."

Noel has opened his mouth, probably to argue some more. But, he just looks at me, surprised. "What do you mean?"

"It's just part of you that he draws, not all of you. You are still a whole person. There clearly is more to you than Sterling draws."

"And that's bad, right?"

His words take me by surprise. "Why do you think that?"

"Because you are only interested in me due to the drawing. Meeting me in person must be a huge disappointment."

My God. I pinch the bridge of my nose, wondering once more what I got myself into. For a moment, I see Emil through my inner eye; he had a similar sass, but was much meeker. Something about that realization puts me at ease.

"See, I annoy you already?" Noel mutters.

"A little," I admit. "But that's what makes it interesting."

"Me being a pain in the ass is interesting?"

"Yes," I say. "For years I have only dated guys..." I pause. "Guys like me, I guess. Obviously, I wasn't interested in any of them. Until my best friend pointed out I was just running in circles."

"So, that's why you are here?"

"No, it's just what made me brave enough to finally escape the loop I am in." I pause. "And to answer your previous question: Just being my artist's model would not be enough for me to meet you in private. I was intrigued by 'Shades of Blue' because Sterling captured something deep and real. It's not been you who pulled me in, but his raw talent."

"Really?" Noel asks curiously. "He is good, isn't he?"

"He is fantastic. An unpolished diamond with lots of potential."

"So, if it's not because of the drawing... and not just because of your friend's comment..." He frowns.

"I approached you in the gallery because I was curious about the man Sterling drew. I gave you my number because you are the first person, in a long while, who I find interesting enough to engage with. I agreed to this date because I wanted to get to know the real you, and I am still here because you showed some honest vulnerability with me." I pause. "There is just something about you that makes me throw all reason aside."

I almost expect him to get upset. I am very much aware that not everything I said is a compliment, however, Noel surprises me by nodding thoughtfully. "I guess I am throwing away a lot of reason, too."

"Is that so?"

"Yes." He pauses. "Maybe part of me wanted you to run tonight."

I figured that much. Tests like these are usually a way to keep their distance. "You wanted me to be the one to run and prove to you that no guy will stick around."

"Maybe. But then you came and stuck around, and fuck, suddenly I felt so stupid. And weird, like I wasn't sure anymore what the fuck I am even doing. Does that make sense?"

"It does."

"Why did you run in circles?" he suddenly asks. "What you said earlier, about always dating the same type of guys..."

"I had an ex-boyfriend years ago, who..." My voice trails off while the usual whirlwind of emotions and anxiety grasp me whenever I think of Emil.

"Sorry for asking," Noel says. "I didn't tell you all my secrets either. It's okay. You don't need to answer."

"Maybe when I know you better," I muse.

His head perks up, hope in his eyes, as he widens them and smiles nervously. Suddenly, he looks so incredibly adorable. I didn't know he could look like that. "Does that mean you want to meet me again?"

"There is an exhibition next Saturday," I say.

"I am free next Saturday! I will accompany you."

His words make me laugh. This guy is unbelievable! "Why do you think I will take you along?" I tease.

"Why would you mention it otherwise?" he retorts. "I am obviously going to be your date!" He frowns. "Or am I?"

My amusement just grows at his attitude. He is truly unlike anyone I've ever met. "Yes, you are going to be my date."

Noel grins. "I know that look. You think I am insane."

"A little," I chuckle. "But—"

"In an interesting way?" he interrupts. "I guess for an artist or gallerist, this is not the worst thing to say. Aden, you were an artist too, right?"

"Yes, I originally made it in the scene as an artist thanks to the help of a mentor and sponsor. Then I inherited some money and decided to open my own gallery."

"That's amazing! It must have been extremely risky, at that time, to start something new."

I am surprised by his insight. "Yes, it was, but at that time I felt truly lost and just decided I needed to distract myself and do something I loved."

"And it worked," Noel muses. "Mateo says you have a very good eye for talent, and everything you touch turns to gold."

I grab another piece of bread to try the second dip DeeDee prepared. "Now he is exaggerating."

"Mateo is good," Noel says. "He knows what he is doing. He would never say something like that if he didn't mean it. He says you have a good eye for people and their art, and that you see beyond things, whatever that means."

Lynn keeps saying the same. I am not sure if it's true. "I am just doing what I do," I say. "I am not sure if there is really that much behind it." I pause. "You have been friends for long, haven't you?"

"Ever since college," he explains. "Stef and I dropped out early, but we all remained friends. We were the three weirdos."

"It made you stick together," I muse. "But I guess something deeper made you bond. It's great to find friends like those."

Again, his head perks up, and there is a sudden soft smile on his face. Another expression of his I haven't seen yet. Emil sometimes reminded me of a canvas, too, but he never was as natural in his actions and reactions as Noel. It always seemed like he wanted to appease me, as with Noel... he just is the way he is. "They are great friends," he explains happily. "The best. Mateo constantly dotes on Ster and me."

"Obviously," I chuckle.

"Why is it obvious?" he pouts.

"Because I have met Sterling, and he is the type of artist who is clearly in his own world at times. As for you, you work at a dangerous place, and you seem to work a lot too. Obviously, a good friend would be worried about you two."

Again, Noel surprises me by not being annoyed at my words. It's a weakness of mine to just say things, unfiltered. Lynn keeps telling me I am direct by pretending I am not, and that she probably would murder me if she were my girlfriend. Cedric, on the other hand, doesn't mind at all. Maybe Lynn is right, and he *is* my mascot.

"Makes sense," Noel says. "But he can be a bit patronizing."

"Yeah, I can see that," I say. "But I bet you and Sterling know how to stand up for yourselves."

Noel smirks. "We know, yes."

DeeDee drops by at our table, a warm smile on her lips when she asks us what else she can bring us. Her smile grows when I order another drink, and Noel wants more to eat. I guess my first intuition was right... that he works a lot, and doesn't always look after himself well.

"What about you?" Noel asks. "Do you have friends?" He scrunches his nose. "I mean, you are obviously nice, so I assume people like you, but you also look like the type of guy who wouldn't let many people get close to him."

I rest my chin on my palm, eyeing Noel thoughtfully. Where does he pull these insights from?

"Too much?" Noel asks quietly. "I overstepped, didn't I?"

"If you overstepped, I did too, earlier," I say.

"I didn't mean to imply you have no friends," he hurries to explain.

"But that I look like the type of guy who wouldn't want too many friends?" I clarify. "Maybe you are right. I do have a best friend, though. You probably saw her during the exhibition."

"Oh, is she the one who handled the press with you?" he asks.

I nod. "Lynn. To be honest, she probably is my only friend, so your take isn't completely wrong."

Noel just shrugs. "Mateo and Ster are my only true friends. I like my co-worker and my roommates, but they are just acquaintances." He pauses. "Quality over quantity, you know?"

"That's one way to put it," I chuckle. "I do enjoy the silence," I admit. "And to just spend a quiet evening at home."

"Not the party guy, huh? Figured."

"And you?"

"I just work at a club, but I hate clubbing." He grimaces. "My dream place is a small cottage in the desert or at an empty shore by the ocean."

Here it is again, the slight melancholy around him. "Hm, I can see how that would be alluring."

At 2 a.m., DeeDee closes the bar, and we are forced to leave. It's about time anyway. "Well then," Noel says. "We are seeing each other—"

"I am not going to leave you stranded here," I say. "I am taking a taxi. I will make sure to drop you off at your place."

He furrows his brows. "Then you know where I live."

"I also know where you work and where you hang out," I chuckle.

Noel sighs. "You are right. I wasn't particularly careful, huh?"

"Technically not," I say.

"Sterling would kill you if you did something." He shrugs before getting into the taxi. "I guess it's okay."

And I guess we need to have a talk eventually, about being more careful around someone who is technically still a stranger. Well, at least I can drop him off safely now. Noel doesn't live too far from his workplace. The area of the city isn't as bad as where his bar is located, but it's not too pleasant either. I am glad he agreed to let me take him home.

I don't push him anymore, however. When he gets out, I decide not to be too overbearing and accompany him to his door. He doesn't seem like the type of person who would want that.

Or is he?

Noel walks to the door of his apartment complex slowly, turning around to gaze back at the cab. There is this vulnerable look in his eyes again. Fuck, I am goner when he looks like that, totally under his spell.

I unbuckle my seat belt. "Please wait for me here," I tell the driver, before making it out of the car.

Noel's eyes widen when he sees me, stopping in his tracks. Once close to him, I take his hand, gently squeezing it.

"Did you have fun this evening?" he asks.

"It was a great first date," I say.

"So... it was a date, wasn't it?"

I smile. "I guess we can call it that."

To my surprise, Noel suddenly wraps his arms around me, leaning his forehead against my chest. I am not sure what made him act like that, but once again, he is being surprisingly vulnerable. I wrap my arms around him, holding him. I can feel him letting out a couple of shaky breaths.

When he draws back, he looks close to crying. I grab his face between my hands and look into his beautiful eyes. It looks like the doors to his soul are open right now. "Are you working tomorrow?" I ask.

"I have a night shift," he says.

"Tell me when you are home safely afterwards?"

A smile curls his lips. "Yes, I can do that."

"I am on a short business trip, but I will make sure to give you a call."

"Are you going to pick me up on Saturday?" he asks.

"Yes, I will pick you up. I'll send you the details later."

I cup the back of his head, gazing at him to know if I overstep any boundaries, but Noel just nods. It's all I need to lead forward to capture his plump lips. They are so soft, tasting slightly like the last drink he had. Noel is holding onto my arms. There is a joy in his eyes I haven't seen before.

I also can't remember the last time I kissed someone so softly without going into action immediately. It just doesn't feel right to do anything more tonight. I hold him for a moment longer, then I reluctantly let go, waiting for him to disappear through the door safely before I return to my driver.

What just happened?

Nothing I did tonight was like the usual me.

I came on this as a friend at best, not imagining wanting anything more than simply to get to know the guy behind the beautiful face. I was annoyed at his mind games, just to end up spending most of the night talking to him. I can't remember the last time I just talked to someone for hours.

And I don't remember ever following someone out of my car because I felt this suffocating urge to hold them in my arms.

My own actions are literally leaving me speechless.

Once back in the cab, my driver takes off. I am still trying to make sense of what just happened when my phone vibrates. It's the private one, so either it's Lynn or—I gaze at the display, seeing a notification pop up. A message from one of my brothers. Kayden. Sighing, I put the phone aside. It's too late to deal with this, and my evening has been too pleasant to ruin it now.

TEN

NOEL

Mateo and Ster look at me for long minutes, wordlessly just staring at me. "I know this is all kinds of weird. And I am weird, and the situation is..." I stop to think.

"Weird?" Mateo finishes.

"Well..." Ster shrugs. "I don't think it is weird."

"Of course you don't!" Mateo exclaims. "This is so you. Are you aware that Aden Randall is your boss?"

"Obviously, he isn't the typical type of boss. Plus, he is more like a mentor than anything else," Ster says, and once more just shrugs.

"I can't believe what happened," I mutter, rubbing my cheeks. My night out with Aden was nothing like I planned it to be. I originally just wanted to get to know him, yet also be sure that he wouldn't find me annoying and just leave me. But reality is, I found out that he isn't a complete and utter asshole like everyone else I usually date. I fucked up majorly, yet it seems I somehow won him over.

And then I end the fucking night by almost crying into his chest.

Almost!

It wasn't a full-blown meltdown. But at that moment, I just felt so insecure, so anxious, to leave and never see him again. He is so much more than I am, and he has much more to offer. I know that; I am not stupid. I just felt he would drive away and I'd never see him again.

And something about this just broke my heart a little.

Did he kiss me out of pity?

Oh fuck, I hope he didn't just kiss me because I looked like a miserable lost pup.

"I didn't even know you set up a date with him," Mateo mutters.

"We just met as friends... first," I admit. "He came to my bar."

"You made him go to the bar you are working at?!" Mateo asks in disbelief. "Oh, how I wish you would have told us beforehand. We could have stopped you from that insanity."

I scrunch my nose. "He wasn't too happy either, but I think I managed to smooth it down."

"Sounds like it," Ster says. "If he spent hours just talking to you, it certainly sounds like he had a good time."

"Do you like him?" Mateo asks.

"I don't know."

"Noel," he says with insistence. "Do you like the guy? This is not the type of person you date without having a clear goal in mind. He is Sterling's mentor and boss."

I feel annoyed at his patronizing tone, but I can't really hold it against him this time. I'd hate to sabotage Sterling's success. "It wasn't planned like this," I admit. "I truly just wanted to get to know him, but somehow he..."

"Struck a chord?" Sterling asks.

"Yes." My heart skips a beat when I recall the way Aden laughed. He doesn't seem to laugh or smile a lot, but when I met him yesterday, there was one moment in which he laughed brightly. And it was so raw and real and beautiful. It warms my chest just thinking about it, while at the same time, I feel my stomach clenching just thinking of someone else getting too close to him.

I don't have much to offer and am incredibly difficult on top of that. I only have my looks. But the world is full of handsome men, and I am sure there are so many guys out there who would suit Aden so much better.

Yeah, fuck.

I guess I broke my own rule not to fall for a guy too fast.

"Okay," Sterling says casually, pulling me out of my thoughts. "You like him. That's cool."

"You really don't mind?" I ask him.

Ster shrugs. "Couldn't care less. Also, I prefer him miles over any of the usual guys you hook up with." He tosses a look at Mateo. It's sharper than usual. "You do too, don't you?"

"Of course," Mateo exclaims. "He isn't a sleazy asshole."

I frown. "Could you not diss my dating life?"

"Sorry," Mateo says. "Don't worry, it's not like any of us has a great track record of successful dates. But Sterlone is right, Aden Randall looks like he is a decent guy."

"I am pretty sure he *is* a decent guy," Ster says while pouring himself more coffee. "I've heard some stories. Make him look good."

His words immediately pique my interest. "What type of stories?"

Sterling looks at his cup of coffee thoughtfully before getting up.

"Sterling! You can't ditch me now?" I exclaim.

Mateo nods. "He is right, I want to hear it too."

Sterling ignores us. He has that look in his eyes like he is somewhere far away. "I need to paint," he mutters.

I frown, ready to complain, but Mateo just takes my arm and squeezes it slightly. "Don't," he mutters. "You know how he is when he is like that."

"But mid-conversation?" I complain.

Mateo smiles. "That's how he is."

I lean back with a sigh, before eyeing Mateo thoughtfully. "You are mad at me, aren't you?"

"Not really," Mateo says. "I do think it was a risky move, though."

"To meet someone at a shady place or to meet Aden?"

"Both," he says.

"Yeah, not my smartest move," I admit. "I just... I forgot to think."

Mateo raises his brows. "Coming from you, that means a lot. You tend to overthink."

"Oh, come on, I am not that bad!"

"You invited the poor guy to that bar just for a test when you could have met him normally and told him you work there and why," Mateo points out mercilessly.

"And he didn't run," I say quietly.

"He didn't run," Mateo agrees. "Are you in contact with him?"

"Yes." I smile like a fucking idiot. "I promised I would write him whenever I come home from work so that he knows that I am safe. Oh, and he is on a business trip but keeps sending me messages." I grin. "He is the no-emoji type of guy, though."

Mateo laughs. "If that's his only fault, you are a lucky guy."

"He doesn't talk a lot about his private life, but neither do I," I admit. "Do you think that's a problem?"

"Why would it be? It's not like you are lying to each other. You are not obliged to share every single part of your life and problems with a guy you just started dating, and vice versa. Just promise you will try to open up to him, at least gradually."

It feels like a cold hand is being wrapped around my heart. "What if he doesn't accept me and what I did in the past?"

"Noel—"

"Please take my fear seriously," I beg.

"I do," he says. "But I don't think you need to be scared of his reaction. I bet he already knows things are off in your life. You did talk about the bar after all, he saw it, you even gave him an explanation and told him there is more to it. And he accepted it. He isn't an idiot, Noel. This guy has a way of seeing things," he pauses, "of just looking behind the façade."

I snort humorlessly. "So poetic."

"But it's true. It's why he is so good at what he does, and why he is so popular."

"He doesn't think he has a special gift," I tell him.

"Yeah, typical for people who are gifted," Mateo says. "Look at Sterling."

I turn around, my gaze wandering towards the small adjacent atelier where Sterling is currently drawing. He is so fucking talented yet acts as if all he does is *just* move paint across a canvas. "You have a point. But there is still no guarantee he will accept everything about me."

"There is always a risk," Mateo says quietly. "But it's worth taking. And if he is an asshole about it, tell us."

"How would that be helpful to Ster's job?" I ask.

"Sterlone can handle himself."

"Oh, he suddenly can?" I chuckle. "Didn't you just say that me dating Aden could ruin everything?"

"I didn't say it'd ruin everything, just make things more complicated," Mateo says. "Besides, you are more important than anything else.

Sterling would move the world for you. So, don't worry. He knows how to handle himself. My initial comment was stupid."

"Nah, I get it," I mutter. "Besides, I think Aden would be professional enough to keep supporting Ster when he dumps me."

"Why do you sound so sure that he'll dump you?" Mateo shakes his head. "Just five minutes ago, you were still raving about this guy and how he handled your date. Have a little faith."

"It's difficult to have faith," I admit.

Mateo is silent, then he sighs. "I know," he says quietly.

His phone rings just at that moment, disrupting our talk. "Sorry," Mateo says. "I need to take this one. It's Sterling's accountant."

"Don't worry," I reassure him.

Mateo steps out on the tiny balcony of Ster's apartment, closing the door behind him. Ster's apartment is ridiculous but fits him. It's all open space, minus said tiny balcony.

While Mateo is on the phone, I let his words sink in. Maybe he is right. Aden saw the sleazy bar and how the patrons hit on me and on him, yet he accepted that I worked there. He also accepted that I work in a nightclub. If it were a dealbreaker for him, he would have already run.

My own phone startles me by vibrating. Without thinking twice, I take it, opening my messages just to see...

My phone drops onto the table. "No way!" I exclaim. "Fuck, fuck, fuck!"

In one moment, all my rational thoughts have left me, everything except my heart beating so fast I am scared it will jump out of my chest. I try to pick up my phone again, my hands shaking so much, it takes a while for me to succeed.

Why did you block me?! Is this a way to treat your own mother, after I gave birth to you, you ungrateful little brat?

Another message.

Where is my money? How am I supposed to live?

And another one.

Come back, Noel, I promise I will be better. Please help me.

And:

You are reading my messages. Answer! I should have never had you, you—

A hand moves over the screen, covering it. I startle, as if I had been caught in a nightmare. When I look up, it's Sterling standing next to me. "Ster?"

He looks at me through those deep, thoughtful eyes of his. "Don't allow yourself to go there, Noel. Anywhere else but that mental space."

Mateo returns from the small balcony, putting his phone in his pocket. "What's wrong?" he asks.

Sterling just shakes his head.

I swallow thickly. "I thought you were drawing."

"I am drawing, but I am not that much out of the world that I wouldn't notice this type of emergency. Come, give me your phone, Noel."

I swallow thickly. "It's..." Tears fill my eyes. "Fuck! I had her blocked everywhere, but she always finds a way."

I hand Sterling my phone while he looks at me thoughtfully. "Say the word. I would never do it without your okay."

"Block her, please."

I always let Mateo or Sterling do it. It makes it so much easier for me, and keeps the distance I need to maintain. When Sterling hands me back my phone, the messages are gone. Just my rapid heartbeat remains.

Sterling pats my head gently. "You are strong. Fuck anyone who says something else."

ELEVEN

ADEN

As promised, I pick Noel up before I head to the exhibition. It's a smaller one, so I let Lynn and Cedric handle most of it. Lynn was skeptical at first, pestering me with questions as to why my *workaholic ass* suddenly decides to forget about its *perfectionism* and wants to delegate parts of the work instead of doing everything on its own.

She pestered me until I told her about having a date. She would have found out anyway. The shift in her mood, however, was mind-boggling. She even squealed!

Lynn never squeals.

I park the car in front of the apartment complex that Noel lives in, waiting for him to come out. I don't have to wait for long, because he is on time, something I truly appreciate.

"Hey!" Noel opens the car door, almost breathless.

I chuckle. "You didn't have to run."

"I saw you from the kitchen window and didn't want you to wait too long." Noel sits down in the passenger seat, taking a deep breath. "Do I look okay?"

He looks dashing. Obviously, he is a very handsome man and would probably look good in anything, but that aside, he also dressed well for the night. "Let me take a closer look," I say earnestly.

Noel nods, looking slightly confused when I lean forward. I grin, catching him completely by surprise when I pull him into a kiss. Noel recovers quickly, his hand moves to my neck, his fingers playing with my hair, while he opens his lips slightly, allowing my tongue to slip past them. He tastes like mint, so refreshing. He must have brushed his teeth right before he came down.

Something about this makes my chest tighten. I like this guy. I don't even understand why, I just know, I do.

Unfortunately, we are on the clock, or I would have prolonged this a little. When I draw back, Noel just stares at me wide-eyed. "I did not expect that greeting!" His cheeks flush, and he grins.

"Good to see I am able to surprise you."

Noel clasps his cheeks, smacking them slightly.

"What are you doing?"

"Obviously, I am still asleep," he deadpans. "You are too good to be true."

"Don't be ridiculous. I am just a normal guy."

"Yeah, totally." Noel rolls his eyes at me with his usual attitude. I should be annoyed, but I find it endearing. Maybe because his reactions are always so honest, he is being himself without being hurtful. It's cute. "Anything I should be prepared for?" he suddenly asks.

"No, don't worry. This exhibition is mostly for patrons. I won't drag you in front of the press with me."

"Thank god," he mutters. "If you ever do that, you need to tell me days in advance. I'd need to prepare myself properly."

"I'd need to be prepared for such an occasion, too," I chuckle.

Noel casts me a gaze I don't quite understand, but I don't feel it's the right time to enquire about what he is thinking. We almost reached our destination after all. If I hadn't been on this business trip until earlier today, I would have invited Noel to dinner first so that we could spend some time with each other. But as things are, we'll have to catch up on everything during the event.

It's still mind-boggling to me that I am taking him with me as my official plus one. That's much bolder than I ever was. When I was with Emil, he didn't like the spotlight, so I never took him along. And all my other hookups, well, they weren't important enough to me.

And now, here I am with this young man, whom I barely know. And it was me, who made the first step to kiss him.

Thinking about it now, it's no surprise that Lynn squealed. This is absolutely unusual for me.

"Now if you had chocolate, you would be truly perfect," Noel mutters more to himself than to me.

"Just open the glove compartment," I say. "Cedric keeps a stash there."

Noel stares at me. "Wait... you have chocolate..." he pauses, furrowing his brows. "Who is Cedric?"

He sounds a little off, but maybe I am just imagining things. "My assistant," I say. "You must have met him during the last exhibit."

"Oh," Noel nods. "The blond guy, right? Mateo introduced him to me. I completely forgot." He blinks. "Are you really working together with him? How does that work out?"

"Why is everyone asking that?" I mutter.

"I don't know." Noel grins, suddenly sounding more like himself again. "Maybe because one of you is a picture-perfect, neat businessman and the other is like an overexcited mascot?"

"And again, everyone keeps saying that," I sigh.

"Yeah, I wonder why," Noel chuckles. "But hey, if it works, it's great."

"I am said to be a perfectionist at my work," I explain. "The words demanding and strict fall a lot..."

Noel looks at me curiously. "Really? You don't come off like that to me. I mean, *perfectionist,* I get that, after all, you own a gallery and love what you do. I can see you trying to do everything as perfectly as possible. But you don't come off as demanding or strict to me. Maybe a bit serious, but that's not the same."

Again, with his honesty. Something about the blunt way he just said what he did, also *what* he said, makes me happy. "To be honest, I don't think I am easy to work with," I admit. "But I don't demand my assistants work themselves to the bone, or even to keep up with me. I just want to get a sense of passion for the line of work from them."

Noel nods, immediately understanding. "The passion for art..."

"You can easily learn the tools," I say. "Sure, someone with the job experience or with the right background would make things easier. Cedric has neither. But he is motivated and loves the work. He can learn everything else. I guess that's why we work well together."

Noel stays quiet for a moment. "You are an interesting man," he says quietly.

I eye him curiously, and he shows me a smile. He seems to be like he usually is, but something does feel a little off. Maybe my imagination.

NOEL

I promised myself not to let my mom ruin this date for me. She has ruined so much for me already, she can't ruin any more. Not when I, for the first time, met a man I really like. Aden is nothing like the stuck-up businessman I thought he would be before I went to that gallery opening. He also isn't anything like the arrogant, intelligent genius I thought he would be before I met him for our first date. I was sure that since his art and his gallery made him successful, he'd be full of himself, but he isn't. However, he is also not like the angel-like being who I'd put on a pedestal all those years ago.

He is just nothing like any of it, and it's making me fall head over heels for him. It scares me, but I can't help it. I like how calm and serious he is without being stoic or closed. He seems to have his boundaries, but he is patient and he listens.

He is fucking good listener!

He is also fun to talk to. I can't remember that I ever had a boyfriend, who I actually liked talking to, or who liked talking to me. Aden seems to be truly interested in what I have to say, how I feel, and what I think.

It's such a new concept to me that it makes me feel terrified as fuck.

I just can't fuck this up. I can't!

It's that mixture of joy to be here with Aden, and the feeling of doom that he will realize how much work I am, how much baggage I carry around, and that I am just not good enough for him.

"Noel?"

I raise my gaze, looking right into Aden's dark eyes. It sends a shiver down my spine. Man, he can look intense. "Sorry, did you say something?"

"I just asked you if you are alright?" He puts a hand on the small of my back, making my heart skip a beat. I am not sure if he notices, but this is such an intimate gesture, especially when we are out in public. "You seem to be distracted."

"I am sorry. I was just taking everything in."

"Is that all?" he asks, still looking at me through his thoughtful eyes.

I can't lie when he looks like that.

"I might not have slept well recently," I admit.

His eyes suddenly cloud with worry. "I am sorry. I probably made it worse by dragging you out here."

"I am actually so glad you did."

As if Aden couldn't get any more perfect, he reaches out his hand to touch my cheek softly. "I will fetch us something to eat. Maybe that will help."

"Are you not scared?" I ask. "Or embarrassed?"

"To eat? No, not really."

I feel my cheeks heating up, wondering if he is just teasing me or seriously that oblivious. "I mean, scared of showing affection"—I swallow thickly before I continue—"towards me."

"No," he says simply. "Everyone knows I am gay, and I invited you here as my official date. Everyone here knows it now. I would never invite a simple fling to such an event."

"We are official?" I ask. Wait... is he serious?! I am not just a random fling?

"Aren't we?" He purses his lips. "I guess it sounds weird to you, because we barely dated. We don't need to put any label on us yet, but as for me, I am not going to see anyone else. What do you think? Do you want to keep things open?"

"Yes!" I blurt out. "I mean, no, I don't want to keep things open." I can't help but beam at him. "What I wanted to say was yes, for me, we are official too."

"Then we are on the same page." He smiles. "As for showing affection openly… if you feel uncomfortable, I will make sure to watch out when we are in public. I am sorry, I should have considered that."

"No, it's fine." No one has ever taken my hand in public or shown me off as his boyfriend, or date or whatever. I am not sure if we are boyfriend stage, yet, but we definitely are official. Now that I am *official,* he won't get rid of me that easily! "I mean, you don't need to hold back. I like it."

"Alright." Aden puts his hand on the small of my back again, pulling me close in one swift movement. I am so close to him that my vision zones in and out. I am trying to look at his face and not think about how fucking close I am to him right now. However much I try, I can't help the twinge I feel in my groin. Fuck, that smooth movement of pulling me closer to him was hot.

So much about taking it slow.

Who am I even kidding?

Aden kisses my forehead. "I will get us something to eat. Anything you want or don't like?"

"Nah, I am not picky."

While growing up, I survived on so little food that being picky just wasn't an option. If it's edible and won't kill me, I will eat it. Aden brushes his thumb over my cheek before letting go. I can only watch him, dumbfounded, while he walks to the buffet.

Aden has two plates in his hands when he walks back to me. Halfway back to me, a young man approaches him. He is a cute one, rather small with a delicate body and a sweet face. I know I am pretty, it's my main selling point in my job, but it doesn't count much when I am difficult as fuck to be around and extremely prickly.

More than one guy has already pointed it out to me.

I probably shouldn't... I shouldn't...

"Mr. Randall?" The young guy sounds shy and nervous; however, he is not shy enough not to look him over. "I thought we could talk?"

I shouldn't...

Oh, fuck it, I should and I will!

Aden said we are official, and 'official me' is definitely not letting anyone flirt with my guy! Before Aden can even react, I walk over to them in a few strides, taking one of the plates out of Aden's hand, and then take his hand with my free hand.

"He *is* talking," I intervene, "with me." I pause to look at him, trying not to look anxious now, but I can't help it. I am sure my eyes give it away. I know I am too much sometimes. "Or are you?"

"I am," Aden reassures me. And then only for me to hear. "Behave," he whispers into my ear. It's not an accusing tone or reproachful, but rather teasing. It makes the hair on my forearms stand up. "I apologize," he tells the young man. His voice is friendly but also firm. "But I am here with my boyfriend."

TWELVE

NOEL

His boyfriend.

He is here with his boyfriend!

"Are you okay?" Aden asks me, amused, when we finally make it to one of the empty high tables.

"I still need to wrap my mind around the fact that you just called me your boyfriend," I say bluntly. "That came unexpectedly!"

"Really? After I said we are official?"

"That was a surprise, too," I point out. "I did not expect you to hit me with the second surprise so soon, especially after you said you weren't going to label us."

"I said, we don't need to put a label on us, not that I personally wouldn't do it," he points out.

He is right. He was talking about us, not how he individually would handle it.

"Noel, I told you already, if things progress too fast for you, then—"

"No, they're not!" I interrupt him. "I always cope better when I know where I stand with another person. If I am just an affair, I want to know. If I am a potential boyfriend, I want to know. I am just surprised because I thought you were the guy to let things progress much slower."

"I am," he says. "Usually."

"And what is different now?" I ask him.

"Obviously, the fact that I am dating you," he points out. "Maybe it's not smart to introduce you as my boyfriend so early, when we only went on one date, but whatever..." He shrugs. "It felt right."

Somehow, his words make me happy. It seems like he just claimed me as his new boyfriend without overthinking it. He felt it and then went for it. For someone who is so obviously an overthinker and a perfectionist, it has to mean something.

"Here you are," A tall, young woman approaches us. She seems to be around Aden's age, but it's hard to tell. She could be a little older or younger.

"Lynn!" Aden smiles. His stance remains relaxed, unlike when other people had approached him throughout the evening. With her, he doesn't slip into his professional mode. "She is my best friend," he tells me. "She basically does most of the marketing and HR related stuff."

"Oh, you told me about her a lot!" I smile at her. "It's nice to meet you."

"That's Noel," he tells her. "My boyfriend."

"So that's your name!" she exclaims while looking at me. "Every one is already talking about the beautiful guy with Aden Randall." She eyes Aden curiously. "Very unlike you, by the way. Up until five minutes before the exhibit, I thought you were joking about coming with a plus one."

"I know," he says.

To my surprise, Lynn looks happy. “Sometimes it’s worth taking a risk.” She grins. “Man, you must be a true minx,” she tells me. “Aden never introduces anyone to us. You are the first date he’s actually brought to such an event since,“ she pauses, “since ages, literally.”

Her pause alerts me. What did she truly want to say? Since when... or since who? Even I know, however, that there is a right time for such a question, and it’s certainly not now. Instead, I decide to be a good boyfriend and make conversation.

Boyfriend...

Fuck, even thinking of myself as a boyfriend gets me. No one ever treated me like that! I have no idea what to do now. How does a boyfriend act?

Well, there is no time to think about it now because his best friend is here, and ready to strike up a conversation with me.

“How did you two become friends?” I ask. “In college?”

“Not really,” Aden says. “Lynn is a couple of years older than I am and was pretty much already done with her studies when I started.” He pauses. “I guess our friendship just happened.”

He is being evasive. In my job, I have learned to read people’s expressions and tones, and I can tell there is something he is holding back. Once again, it strikes me that Aden is a very private man and is very closed off. He might have opened up a little to me during our first date, but he said so himself; he doesn’t like talking about himself or his past a lot.

Well, neither do I. So, I shouldn’t judge.

“What Aden isn’t *not* saying,”—Lynn grins, fortunately deciding to reveal the ‘secret’—“is that I am his brother’s ex.”

“No way?” I exclaim.

“It’s true,” Aden admits. “My oldest brother, Oliver, was her boyfriend back then, and I met her occasionally.”

"During family meetings," Lynn adds. "Well, Aden and I often fled to the terrace together. I'd have a cigarette, and he would just like the silence. Then, years later, we realized we pretty much are in a similar field of work."

I try to take in all she says, and also the things she didn't say. Aden must have more than one sibling if he emphasized that it was his oldest brother. And once more, he is awfully evasive right now. He lets Lynn talk, but doesn't add anything, and I don't feel like Lynn is saying an awful lot either.

"When Oliver and I broke up, Aden and I coincidentally met during a vernissage once. Aden was still painting, back then, but wanted to get into the business. And I was looking for a new challenge as well."

"To both of our surprise, we work pretty well together," Aden adds.

"Aden was surprised," Lynn tells me. "I had the feeling it could work. He is a perfectionist, and I am too, just with more sense."

Aden frowns at her words. "What's that supposed to mean?"

"Just that I know when to stop harassing everyone around me about the exact details," she grins. "Admit it, you need me and my people skills!"

"You have people skills?" he asks.

"Well, more than you do!"

I am in awe listening to their talk. Aden has his guard down around her completely. He must totally trust her. I feel a twinge in my chest. This time, however, not out of jealousy; there is nothing sexual between them, and Aden has been out as gay for ages, but it's the familiarity between them. The way he talks to her and answers her teasing.

With me, he is still much more formal. I have no idea how to make him drop his guard around me, and somehow this thought makes me sad while pissing me off at the same time.

Two hours later, Aden has introduced me to more people he is acquainted with, but it doesn't seem he is close friends with any of them.

"You know a lot of people," I mutter.

"Comes with the job," he admits. "But most of it is just loose contacts. Lynn is my only real friend."

"And your crazy assistant."

Aden blinks. "I am not sure if I would call him a friend."

"But he doesn't annoy you?"

"True."

"You feel like you can be a bit more yourself with him?"

"Again true."

When I stay silent, Aden looks at me amused. "Our bar for friends is pretty high," he says. "Seeing how you have three amazing friendships, I was expecting more."

"It's just..." I groan. "I don't know the guy. But he seems to be fun and quirky, and genuinely nice. Not that I want you to flirt with him, of course, and maybe you shouldn't hang out with him too often." Yeah, now I sound jealous. Either way I look like a complete nutcase.

"I have a hard time letting anyone in," Aden tells me. "I don't mind Cedric. He is a good person and a good assistant. But I am very careful about allowing someone to see more of me than I show to the outside."

"But you befriended Lynn."

"It's rather her who befriended me," he admits.

"And how come you let it happen?" I pause. "Sorry for being so curious. I just want to understand."

Aden is quiet for a while. "She saw something no one else could see," he finally says. I wait for more explanation, after all, Lynn was his brother's girlfriend. It's certainly unusual for the ex-girlfriend of a sibling to suddenly befriend the younger brother. There has to be a story behind it. But Aden falls silent again. It seems this is all I will get out of him for tonight.

I gaze around the room, noticing some guests occasionally eyeing me curiously. It only strikes me now that to them, I probably am like an alien. If it's true what Lynn said, then Aden has never brought anyone along since, whatever happened years ago. Neither she nor Aden clarified it.

"You brought me along to this event and introduced me as your boyfriend," I finally say. I am not sure if I understand why. We only met twice so far, and I feel like we connected, but I wasn't sure he felt the same.

"I did. But you heard what Lynn said. It was very unusual for me."

I can't help but stare daggers at him out of mere curiosity. "But why me?"

"I don't know," he admits. "I just felt like it. Believe me, I don't understand myself either. Seems like you just ticked a certain box for me I didn't know existed."

Well, that's not bad! He is obviously not sharing an awful lot about himself, rather the opposite, but when he says it like that, it makes me feel less anxious.

THIRTEEN

ADEN

Noel seems to suck everything up that happens around us like a dry sponge. I didn't expect him to be so interested in the whole event, in Lynn, and in everything surrounding me. Somehow, the realization makes me both happy and terrified.

"How about we get some fresh air?" I offer. "It's getting really crowded in here."

"Good idea."

Noel follows me through the two halls, still crowded with people, before we step out onto a broad balcony.

"Wow!" Noel stretches, sucking in the fresh air of the night. "I didn't realize there was a second balcony, and it's so big too!"

"Perks of knowing this place," I chuckle. "No one comes here. Everyone frequents the balcony on the front."

Noel turns to me. Against the moonlight, he looks so magical that my fingers twitch slightly, wishing I had a pen with me to draw a sketch. I need to ingrain this onto my memory and then put it to paper later. I haven't drawn anything or anyone in ages. The last one to stir that interest in me was Emil, but ever since he passed, I just didn't feel the motivation or the muse anymore.

The fact that Noel does that to me, so suddenly, is unexpected. I was intrigued by Sterling's paintings, but I know better than to insert myself too much into an artist's muse. However, meeting Noel in person changed everything. I was expecting to meet a melancholic young man, but instead I met someone fierce, sassy, and slightly mysterious. He pulled me in from the moment I talked to him.

"What are you thinking about?" Noel asks me, curiosity in his voice.

"I was thinking about how I need to draw this moment."

"What, me here?"

"Yes," I say. "It's truly magical. You are beautiful."

Noel's whole face seems to heat up, his cheeks turning pink, as do the tips of his ears. "How can you say that without sounding weird?!"

I shrug. "Because it's true."

Noel stares at me like I have lost my mind. I can't help but find him so adorable when he is confused. I take his face between my hands. "Certainly, you have heard that before?"

"No," he says. "Well, I have had my ass complimented a couple of times, but only if someone wanted to get into my pants. But usually no one sounds sincere when they say nice things."

"And I? Do I sound sincere?"

"You do, and that's so fucking confusing."

I don't loosen my grip on his face, but instead pull him closer, until our lips brush against each other.

"You are not toying with me, are you?" he asks, his voice so small it pulls at my heartstrings."

"I would never toy with anyone, let alone you," I say.

"Okay, because I pretty much like you."

"It makes me happy to hear that, because I like you too." I don't know the last time I told someone I liked them. Emil. I loved Emil and told him so. He was the only one I ever said 'I love you' to. But even back then, the words barely left my lips, and until now, I usually don't tell anyone I like them. With my hand at the back of his head, I tilt it up slightly before claiming his lips. Noel's fingers dig into my suit, holding onto me while he answers my kiss, almost hungrily so. I brush my thumb over his chin before gripping it to keep him in place, my teeth grazing his bottom lip.

Noel gapes, allowing my tongue to push past his lips. For a moment, we battle for dominance, until he just seems to melt in my arms.

Fuck, that's hot!

I loosen the grip on his chin and move my hand down to his ass, squeezing it through his soft pants.

Then my phone vibrates.

"Damn it," I mutter.

Noel draws back slightly, his lips damp and his pupils dilated. I don't know what I would have done if my phone didn't distract me, but I am sure it wouldn't have stayed at just kissing him. I put my arm around him to pull him against my body before I take my phone out of my pocket.

The name popping up makes me frown.

"Work?" Noel asks me.

"No, Kayden," I mutter more to myself than to him. Raising my gaze, I can see something flash in his eyes. He looks hurt all of a sudden, and once more anxious. Right, I should probably clarify. "He is one of my brothers."

Noel turns red. It's endearing how easy it is to read his expression. I switch my phone to silent, putting it back into my pocket. Noel looks at me curiously, but doesn't push for answers. Instead, he keeps casting me glances. It seems like he wants to say something, but the minutes pass by without him saying one thing.

"Okay, what's wrong?" I ask instead.

He lets out a frustrated sigh. "It's going to sound pathetic and weird, or creepy and pathetic, or—"

"Let me judge that and just ask."

"Aden, are you going to ask me to go home with you tonight? I have never been in such a situation where I actually dated someone. I don't know the cues. I know I said I want things to move slowly, but we obviously already... well..."

I eye him thoughtfully. I absolutely want to take him home. There is no denying that I want to fuck him, even if we barely know each other. However, he has a point when he says we wanted to take it slow. "Do you want me to take you home with me?"

He tilts his head. "I... it depends. Did I misinterpret things?"

God, what's wrong with me? I usually don't engage with this type of man. I like things simple, and easy.

It's easy to quit when it's simple.

Fuck, Lynn was right.

And who am I even kidding? Sassy, mysterious guys like him are exactly my type.

"If I sleep with you tonight, it means something," I tell him. "Only agree if it means something to you, too."

Noel purses his lips, his eyes looking at me defiantly. "Of course it means something! That's why I asked in such a weird way, quite literally. You are the heartthrob here, not me!"

"I barely date," I tell him. "You are the first guy in ages that I have introduced as my boyfriend."

Noel sighs and leans his forehead against my shoulder. He mutters something I don't quite catch, but I don't push him to repeat it. It probably wasn't for my ears anyway. Instead, I rub his shoulders. "Will you come home with me?"

Noel raises his gaze. "Obviously, the answer is yes."

NOEL

If there is one thing that annoys me about Aden, it is how evasively he answers sometimes. He is so fucking hard to read, and his words are not always that clear either. Maybe it's less annoyance and more anxiety, though.

Letting him fuck me is quite the step. Usually, I wouldn't mind. Guys only want me for sex anyway, but with Aden it's different. I want to sincerely date him. But I also want him to fuck me. Damn my primal urges!

"Noel," Aden opens the door to his house. It's beautiful. Tidy, perfect interior, and with artworks everywhere. I expected a cold, neat apartment, but not an actual townhouse. In typical Aden fashion, it is perfectly clean, but it still has personality.

"Noel?"

"Sorry!" I turn around to look at Aden. "I was just too much in awe of everything."

"I noticed." Aden takes his jacket off and places it in its designated place. Then he does the same with his keys.

I don't know why, but something seems to stir my nerves. What the fuck is wrong with me? This guy obviously likes me, or he wouldn't have introduced me everywhere as his boyfriend, even to his own best friend. He is still here although I fucked up once already. There is no need to freak out.

To my surprise, Aden comes over and takes my hand. "We don't need to do anything," he says. "We can just talk or sleep. And if you still feel uncomfortable, I will take you home."

Somehow, his words almost bring tears to my eyes. I can't help but throw my hands around him and hug him.

Aden hugs me back, gently rubbing my back. "Talk to me?"

"I just realized I really want you," I admit before grabbing his face and pulling him into a kiss.

"You are like a rollercoaster," Aden says, but it doesn't sound like he is complaining.

"And you like someone who doesn't give a flying fuck about that."

Aden's lips curl into a smirk. Ah, yes. Back in the mood!

I grab him by his tie, dragging him forward to... where I think his bedroom is located.

Aden looks equal parts amused and intrigued. "First floor, second door to the left."

He lets me pull him along until we reach his bedroom. Again, I am slightly surprised. I was expecting something like black satin sheets, but his bedsheets are actually turquoise with little strings of gold going through them. The walls aren't fully white either. The one behind his bed is painted in a similar turquoise to his sheets, with petals flying across it. It looks like a Sakura petal storm.

I am so stupid. I don't know why I constantly expect him to have bland taste when he is an artist himself.

"Did you paint that yourself?"

"Yes, all my murals here were done by me." Aden grabs me by my waist to spin around so that I am back to looking at him. "You can check everything later. Now focus on me!"

The tone he uses sends a shiver down my spine in the best way possible. It's low, hoarse and slightly bossy, making my cock stir immediately. Fuck, if he talks to me like that I might do anything for him.

Even more reason to push a little more! "It's not my fault," I say with what I hope is an innocent tone. "You are just not keeping me distracted enough."

One of Aden's perfect eyebrows shoots up. "Is that so?" he says.

Mateo sometimes talks in flowery words when he is in love. The last time, he told me something about a woman talking in a velvety voice, and I called bullshit on it. What the fuck is a velvety voice?

Now I know, this is it!

Aden tugs at my hand, forceful enough that I stumble forward and clash against his chest, his lips catching mine in an almost bruising kiss that takes my breath away, quite literally. One of his hands opens the buttons of my pants before slipping past them and into my underpants, squeezing my ass.

I can barely register what's happening when I find myself pushed onto his bed. With one tug Aden pulls both my pants underpants off me, freeing my cock. He doesn't give me time to react, suddenly pushing my legs apart and kneeling in front of me.

"Aden!" I moan. "You are not going to..."

Fuck he is!

His thumb brushes over the tip of my cock, before his lips close around it tightly.

No way! My first urge is to drop onto my back and just bask in the sensation, but there is a stronger urge that wants me to see how Aden's mouth swallows my cock. I don't want to miss it! He works methodically, going slow at first, almost excruciatingly, so that my erection is almost painfully hard.

"Aden," my voice sounds pleading. I would be embarrassed if I weren't so turned on. I have given plenty of blowjobs, but I have barely been on the receiving end. What does that tell me about my choice of dates?

"Patience," Aden smirks, blowing air onto the tip of my cock.

It sends a shiver down my spine. "Fuck!"

His lips close tightly around my shaft again, this time he doesn't go slow and soft, his head bopping up and down while I can feel my tip hitting his throat. "This... fuck Aden, this is too good!"

His fingers wrap around my shaft tightly, while he stops his movements, his lips wrapped tightly around the tip of my cock, hollowing his cheeks. His free hand tugs at my balls. I can't hold back anymore, my fingers digging into his hair for balance, a shudder going through me, swiftly followed by another.

"I am coming," I blurt out.

Aden just smiles, not letting go of my dick, instead he opens his mouth swallowing what I am unloading.

I drop onto my back, panting. He is good. The guy knows what he is doing! Now I can't wait to see how it will feel to have his dick inside of me. I push myself up on my elbows, my eyes searching for Aden. He is sitting in front of me, his hair not as neat as before, but not as messed up as it should be. We need to change that!

"That was fucking amazing," I say while tugging the remainder of my clothes off me and trying for a sultry and seductive expression.

Aden narrows his eyes, scanning me from head to toe. I am not sure if that's a good or bad thing. "Do you like what you see?"

"Yes," he says. His eyes have that look in them, the one Ster has sometimes too. "One day I will draw you like this."

"Naked?"

"Naked, and waiting for me to fuck you," he says.

Okay, maybe not *exactly* like Ster! I did not expect him to be that confident in what he wants. This guy is anything but stuck up! I am so glad he is showing me this side of him. "Are you done watching?" I tease. "How come you are still wearing clothes?"

"Time to change that," he says, taking off his suit. I keep watching him in awe while he slowly strips down until he is naked. I was not aware he would look like that under his suit. He is fucking ripped! He swiftly retrieves lube and condoms from his bedside drawer, and then he is back with me.

Before I can so much as utter a word, Aden is suddenly kneeling between my legs, pushing them apart. I lunge upwards to hug him, wanting to feel every part of his naked skin. He responds immediately. One of his arms is wrapped around me, pulling me down onto my back before his lips start to trail down my neck and to my nipples. He takes his time, sucking, twisting and grazing them with his teeth until they are sensitive and swollen.

His knees push my legs apart further. I can feel my cock stir again. Something about the demanding way Aden manhandles me, just turns me on so much. Aden draws back slightly, and before I can complain about the lack of contact, I can feel a slick finger pressed against my opening, pushing past the muscle inside me.

I gasp.

"Too fast?"

"No, not at all!"

Aden adds a second finger, stretching me more. I have had sex partners before, but it never felt like this. Maybe because I am crushing hard on this guy. I have never fallen in love with someone before, and somehow, the knowledge that I am falling for Aden makes me both anxious and excited.

Three fingers deep in me, Aden pushes them as far inside as he can, until a sizzling feeling runs through me, my cock stirring at the sensation. "Here," I moan. "Fuck that's good."

"You are so beautiful, Noel," Aden says, his voice hoarse and his eyes dazed. "If only you could see yourself like that."

"Now imagine how I'd look with your cock inside me."

Aden doesn't answer, instead he removes his fingers, and—

Oh fuckaluck! He plunges into me in one go, his cock so deep inside me, it takes my breath away and feels amazing. With every snap of his hips, a moan leaves my mouth. I am sure I sound obscene, but Aden doesn't seem to mind. It actually seems like my moans spur him on further. One of his hands is on the back of my head suddenly, before he pulls me upwards into a heated kiss.

Finally, his hair doesn't look as neat as before, and it makes him look so hot, as does the heated look in his eyes. I know he is a perfectionist and a very serious man, so seeing him so open makes my stomach do backflips. I cling to his neck, relishing in the feeling of his cock being thrust into me over and over again, so deep inside. Aden's fingers wrap around my hard cock. It's like I can feel him all around me now.

Aden's lips move to my ear. "Don't hold back, babe."

He fucking called me an endearment. No one has ever done that! I feel my walls around Aden's cock tightening, my cock pulsating in his hands while I chase my second orgasm of the night. Aden thrusts into me a couple of more times before I can feel his body tense up.

Aden doesn't pull out of me immediately, and it feels so good to be filled up by him. "Thank you," he says. "That was amazing."

I rub my eyes, contentedly exhausted. "I should be the one to thank you."

Aden carefully pulls out of me and gets rid of his condom. I can hear him shuffling around a little before I am suddenly in his arms again. I am sweaty and gross, yet he doesn't seem to mind. "You are nothing like I expected," I mutter against his chest.

His fingers brush through my hair and stop for a moment. "Is that good or bad?"

"It's great!"

FOURTEEN

NOEL

I am not sure how long I slept, but it's still dark when I wake up. Aden has his arm draped around me, his eyes still closed, and his chest heaving slightly. He is still asleep, and even in his sleep, he looks so handsome. Something about waking up next to him makes my head spin. I have never done that before, or rather, no guy ever wanted it with me.

It's so intimate. Maybe more so than having him fuck me. With the realization comes the usual sinking feeling in my stomach. I am getting used to this. Too soon, too fast. It's not even a week since I started dating Aden, though even calling it *dating* might be too much, and I am already *way* too attached to this guy.

This wasn't supposed to happen! I am not supposed to fall head over heels for someone I barely know. It's just going to get my heart broken.

Aden stirs slightly. "You are awake," he mumbles while sitting up and gazing at his watch. "It's 3 a.m."

I wonder if I should tell him that I just feel too anxious to sleep, but that would make everything more awkward. "I feel sticky," I lie.

Aden touches my arm softly. "Feel free to use the bathroom. It's the door on the right at the end of the corridor."

At least this gives me the option to remove myself from this intimate situation and my own vulnerability, and get my thoughts straight. A shower will warm me up and distract me a little. Aden looks at me for a while, his gaze thoughtful. He is pretty much like his usual self. The composed man who looks in control of every situation. He isn't exactly stoic, but very level-headed, very much in control of his emotions, and so fucking hard to read.

It seems like he wants to say something, but then just smiles at me. "You can find the towels in the cupboard in the bathroom. And there is a set of sweatpants and a sweater there, too. Take whatever you need."

I wonder what he truly wanted to say.

Oh, damn it! Why couldn't he just say it?

I am not any better, though. I just nod and smile like a dumbass and find my way out of his room, down the corridor and to the vast bathroom. It's... amazing! Beautiful tiles, simple decoration, tasteful furniture. There are tiles in a colorful mosaic on one wall of the bathroom, and the bathtub looks old-fashioned, like from an old movie. He also has a walk-in shower. Everything in this house seems to be intriguing, a mix between a modern style and a very individual one. I tend to forget that Aden is an artist too, but it's very obvious now that I see how he lives.

I wonder if he has an atelier.

He for sure does.

But will he show it to me?

I step into the shower, letting warm water dribble down on me. An atelier is very private. I know that from Ster. He is very particular about who he invites in and who he shows his drafts and private paintings to.

Will Aden let me in?

I don't know how long I spend in the shower, but when I finally step out of it again, my skin is warm, the stickiness washed away, and the soreness smoothed away. I feel a bit sad with the latter gone. There was something about feeling sore after Aden had fucked me that made me feel like I belong, like this is real.

And now it just feels like it was all in my head.

For a moment, I consider putting on my clothes from yesterday, but I am too grossed out to do that, so I grab a set of the spare clothes Aden mentioned. It must be his, because they are too large for me, especially around the arms and legs. Yet, it somehow feels comforting to wear them.

Comforting… and terrifying.

I slap my face a few times to wake myself up from whatever shit-show of an anxiety attack I am in. I just had an awesome evening with Aden, which ended in the best sex I've ever had. And I don't even know his body and preferences properly yet. How mind-blowing will it be once we have discovered each other's sensitive spots?

That is, if Aden even wants me for more than one night.

My head is going down the path of doom, as Matteo calls it. I thought he was exaggerating, but now I think he has a point. I feel I will have to knock myself out to stop from *thinking*.

I don't know how long I have been in the bathroom, but something tells me, if I stay any longer, Aden might come looking for me, and I really don't want to inconvenience him. Well, here goes nothing. The bathroom door opens and closes silently while I pat down the corridor back to the bedroom. It's still dark outside, but not pitch-black. Is dawn approaching?

I am about to open the bedroom door when I can hear Aden's voice inside, surprisingly loud and surprisingly angry.

"Kayden, why did you call so late if it's not an emergency?! It's far past midnight!"

For a while, it's silent.

"I am not avoiding you. Don't be ridiculous. I can't believe you are calling me so late. I thought it would be something with Mom!"

It might be something with Mom. Mom needs you. Do better for Mom.

Don't be so useless!

I shake my head to will the thoughts away. The last thing I need now is to slip into an actual panic attack. Fuck, why did my mother have to reach out to me again? She fucked with my brain, like she always does when she finds my whereabouts and tries to drag me down with her.

"Kayden, I truly don't want to talk about it now. You are drunk, I am not arguing with you."

Drunk...

Again, I shake my head, deciding I need to stop lingering in front of the door and step inside. My chest clenches, and I don't understand why. I don't know what's fucking me over so much now. It doesn't make sense!

"I am going to hang up on you now." He says, when I step inside. Aden is leaning against the window, his phone in his hand. "Oliver, is it you now? What is going on?"

To my surprise, Aden's expression is upset. I thought he would be angry, but he actually looks hurt.

"I know, I figured he had one drink too many. Please leave me alone for now."

Aden hangs up and puts his phone aside. He rests his hands on the windowsill, his face turned away from me, while he takes a couple of deep breaths.

"Aden," I whisper. "Is everything alright?"

No, it's not. Obviously! Why am I even asking?

It's almost like I can watch the blinds going down again, and Aden's whole expression becomes more distanced. "It's nothing, don't worry."

"It's not nothing. You were really upset. It was your brother, wasn't it? Kayden?"

"Yes, it was my brother, but it's nothing important." The blinds go down completely, and Aden's expression is suddenly almost blank. It's such a stark contrast to how he was with me when he took me to bed.

I wonder if he will ever trust me.

But why would he?

You are nothing.

I am nothing. I have nothing to offer.

...useless...

I didn't want you.

Why did you ruin everything?

I don't want you, Noel, not like that.

Don't make things complicated, Noel.

"Noel?" Aden's voice startles me, pulling me out of my trail of thoughts. "Is something wrong?"

When I first stepped into Aden's home, I wondered why I felt so off. Aden's place is beautiful and warm, yet something spiked my anxiety. Now I know what it is. Everything in this place is perfect, but me. Everything belongs here, but I am completely out of place.

"I need to leave," I blurt out.

Aden looks at me, confused. “Now?” he asks. “Why don’t you stay the remainder of the night? I will drive you home in the morning.”

“No, it’s fine.” I grab my remaining things. Fortunately, I don’t have a lot with me, and I dash out of the room. Behind me, I can hear Aden calling my name and saying something, but my ears don’t seem to pick anything up. It’s a constant ringing that I hear, that blocks everything out. That, and a dull ache in my chest.

I am not sure how I made it home. I ran until I finally found a way to the subway. My mind was completely switched off. Once back home, the ringing in my ear has stopped, but the ache in my chest remains.

FIFTEEN

ADEN

I skim through the information Cedric has put together, scribbling down notes on the parts that need improvement. Overall, he takes direction and feedback well, and this project he is working on is already so much better than he did two weeks ago.

I hand him back his folder. "You can work this into the presentation for next week," I tell him. "Take a look at the notes."

He gazes inside the folder. "Still so much to improve," he sighs.

I smile at him. "You have already improved a lot."

"Really?" He beams as if he just wasn't bummed two seconds ago. Then he balls one of his hands into a fist. "I will get even better! Thank you, sir!"

I don't even manage to utter a reply before he has already dashed out of my office. Outside, I can see him bump into one of the female employees. He profusely apologizes and then chats happily with her, sometimes pointing at my office while he does so.

I pinch the bridge of my nose, trying not to pay Cedric any more attention. This kid will be the end of me.

Talking about the end of me...

I gaze at my phone. Fuck, I should focus on my work, but Noel just doesn't leave my mind. He left almost immediately after we had sex and now, one day later, he still hasn't replied to my messages, not even the one where I asked if he returned home safely.

"Everything alright?"

I raise my head to look at Lynn. "How long have you been standing there?"

She raises her brows. "A couple of minutes. I called your name, but you were so distracted you didn't answer." She tilts her head. "Is everything alright? And before you answer, let me tell you, I know it isn't, so don't think about lying." I am still contemplating how to send her away when she folds her arms. "My date dumped me."

This catches my attention immediately. "You mean the guy you introduced to me during the exhibit?"

"Yes. Not that I was too involved already, but it's starting to annoy me. Somehow, I always manage to attract guys who turn around and leave the moment they see where I work."

Where she works isn't the problem, but I know what she is truly saying. "They are insecure assholes."

"Although I am always honest about me being a co-CEO," she says. "Somehow they don't believe it until they see it." She pauses. "Now, so much about me. I told you why my mood is terrible. Your turn now."

I sigh. "Close the door."

Lynn does what I told her and steps closer, sitting down on the chair in front of my desk. "The cutie, huh?"

"How do you know?"

"Come on!" She laughs. "You suddenly act unlike your usual self at work, right after you were at that exhibition with him, at which you also weren't like your usual self. That guy clearly is doing something to you. So, spill the beans."

I shift my pen between my hands. Maybe she is right. My normal reaction would be to leave it at that. Noel ran after our night together and didn't reply to me. I should probably take the cue and not reach out to him anymore, and take it as what it is.

But then I think of the vulnerable look in his eyes.

I don't know why, but he looked so anxious and hurt.

And somehow, I don't want to leave it at that, so I tell Lynn the short version of what happened.

"Man, Aden." She is clearly stunned. "I can barely believe it."

"I know, it's a mess."

"That's not it," she tells me. "Sure, it's a bit messy, but not worse than other stories I have heard. But you care for that guy!"

"Lynn—"

"I am so happy," she blurts out. "My God, Aden, I am so happy. You like the guy!"

"I think you are focusing on the wrong details right now," I say. "He literally ran from me."

"It's not the wrong focus. Finally, you have let someone in again, or you are starting to let someone in, and I guess that's where the problem lies."

Now, she has clearly piqued my curiosity. "What do you mean?"

"You have opened the door a little, but not fully. I don't know Noel well, but from what you told me, it sounds like he went through a lot."

"It does," I admit. "I don't know much, but the job at that sleazy bar gives it away."

"He is insecure, Aden," she says. "I can't believe I need to spell it out to you, but you are an intimidating guy to be with."

Her words make me laugh. "Now you are being ridiculous!"

"Well, you are not intimidating to *me*, but that's because I know you and you are my friend. But you have been intimidating to all your assistants—"

"Cedric isn't intimidated by me."

"He is," she points out. "He just knows how to handle it, and he likes the job, and he also likes working with you despite being intimidated." She pauses. "And as for your slightly anxious boyfriend? Definitely intimidated. You are extremely well-put together, very much in control, successful, and you barely share anything with anyone. It's extremely hard to read you. Noel is easy to read. I can tell already after only meeting him once. His emotions are all over his face, but you... You are like a closed book with a lock on it, and a super-strong, magical spell guarding said lock."

I let her words sink in, looking at her thoughtfully. "Is this how others perceive me?"

"Yes," she says. "It's not necessarily bad. For the gallery, it's pretty much a huge selling point how you are, but for a relationship, it can be scary."

"But you can read me well," I point out.

"Yeah," she says. "I also know you very well. I saw you through the eyes of Oliver's girlfriend first before becoming your friend. We go back years." She pauses. "You really like this guy, don't you?"

"Would I be as concerned as I am if I didn't?" I ask.

"You are doing it again." Lynn tilts her head. "You need to say it," she tells me. "Don't rebuff this question, don't deflect. I know why..." Her voice trails off. "If you can't even tell me, how will you ever tell him? And he needs to hear it sooner than later."

There is a lot Lynn is saying, but also a lot she isn't saying. She knows why I am so reluctant. Emil has messed me up. He broke my trust, my hope in a future together with him or anyone, and my heart. I try to push the image of him aside and replace it with Noel. There are similarities, but they are mostly on the surface.

Noel is different in the areas that are important to me.

I don't like mind games. Emil used to play them all the time, maybe not on purpose, but the outcome was the same. As for Noel, I don't think he is playing games.

When Lynn twirls around in her chair, she finally pulls me back into reality, into today. "I like him," I finally say. "But I can't tell if this relationship is going to be healthy for me or not."

"He runs when he is upset," Lynn concludes.

"And I don't like the chase," I admit. "Not anymore. You know that."

"Then tell him," she says. "Jeez, Aden, I get you. I don't like these games either. But you need to communicate with the guy. He doesn't know a thing about you. All he can do is guess, and believe me when I tell you, he for sure isn't a mind reader."

"Alright," I mutter. "It's not like I can get him out of my head anyway."

She smacks me with the folder she is holding. "That's the right spirit."

NOEL

I am such a lost case, completely and utterly lost. Aden took me to that exhibition. He was sweet and appreciative of me, and he was attentive. He took me home and didn't do anything against my consent.

He wanted me to stay the night.

He wanted me...

I groan. "Damn it!"

"When you have stopped hating yourself, hand me the new colors I bought," Ster says.

I do as he asks, careful not to get my clothes dirty. I have put on Aden's sweater today, after I spent the whole previous day panicking about what to do and how to answer Aden's messages. I was so petrified that I ended up not answering at all.

The sweater smells like him. It's comforting and terrifying at the same time.

I might have just fucked this relationship up before it even started.

"I fucked up, didn't I?" I say into the silence.

"You did," Ster says simply. "But it's nothing you can't solve."

"What am I supposed to do or say to him?"

"I don't know, but think of something fast, because he'll be here in a minute."

I stare at him. "What!" I squeak.

"He called Mateo an hour ago and asked him where you are." Ster looks at me, amused. "He has you figured out, Noel. He knows you will chicken out and not answer if he calls you directly."

"Am I that much of a wimp?"

"Yeah," Ster says mercilessly. "In this case, you are. The poor guy. Just imagine you take someone home, sleep with them and then the person bolts. And ghosts you afterwards. How would you feel?"

"Are you kidding me? I would feel horrible! It would completely shatter me and my non-existent confidence," I admit. "I had it happen to me plenty of times." I pause. "Oh, fuck it. I just did the same thing those assholes did to me."

"If you want my opinion," he says. "You are asking too much of the guy."

"I just want him to trust me," I admit.

"Trust is built. It's not magically there," Ster says. "You told me he seems to have issues with his brother. We don't know what kind of issues these are. He is not obliged to open up to you immediately. You need to give it time. You know better than anyone else how much your own past can have a chokehold over you."

"I didn't tell him anything either," I admit. "I am such a hypocrite."

"You are scared," Ster analyzes. "But normally not *that* scared. It was your mom, wasn't it? Her message..."

"Maybe," I say quietly. Whenever my mom reaches out to me, it usually is a huge trigger. It was the same this time, too. Ster and Mateo know how to handle me when it happens, but Aden has no clue. I didn't tell him anything, yet I expected him to open up to me, to soothe my anxiety. "How can I stop being scared?"

"You can't," Ster says. "That's the worst part about anxiety. It's always there, lurking in a corner and jumping at you when you have your guard down. The only thing you can do is take risks despite your anxiety being there. Roxana's therapist gave her the advice to use these worst-case scenarios she is imagining, just like you do, and try to overwrite them with a positive image."

"I could try," I admit.

"This could be something good," Ster says. "This thing with Aden. You deserve something good."

"I really like him," I hear myself say before I bury my face behind my hands. "Fuck, I like him."

Instead of an answer, I hear Ster's doorbell. And this time, I have nowhere to run to, although every inch of my body wants to just get away from here, too scared to face Aden and the possible rejection.

"Come in," Ster calls out towards the door. "It's unlocked."

When Aden enters, he is his usual neat self. It looks like he just came from work, but even then, he doesn't look tired. I watch him; how he slips out of his jacket, neatly puts it on the rack, and takes off his shoes. My God, he is so handsome. I feel something in my chest, a longing, so painful it takes my breath away.

"Thank you for allowing me to come over, Sterling," he says, before walking straight towards me.

Like a complete nutcase I am rooted to my place on Ster's chair, not able to say anything or to move. I must look like a deer caught in the headlights, because Aden's stoic expression softens visibly. "You look like I am about to bite your head off."

When he reaches out his hand to pat my head, it's like a dam lets loose. I can only wrap my arms around his middle, burying my head in his stomach. I love him. The realization makes my chest ache, the same dull feeling I have been battling with the whole day. It's a mix of longing and fear. My love for Aden hurts so much. It's scary, yet I want so much more of it.

Aden's longer fingers keep brushing through my hair. He doesn't say anything, but I guess if he wanted to dump me, he wouldn't be so gentle right now.

"Well, you obviously don't need me right now," Ster says. When I glance at him, he is already trotting back into his atelier. "Close the door when you leave. And invite me for dinner later. You owe me!"

Sixteen

NOEL

We left Ster's apartment half an hour ago to let him work on his newest painting, went to buy coffees and then to a small, empty playground. It's an old one that's been closed for a while because they are going to tear it down soon.

Somehow, that's sad. It was not a pretty playground, but I have gotten used to it being here. Just another part of my life that gets turned over completely. I don't do well when my sense of stability is shaken.

With our coffees, we sit down on two swings. For the most part, we only make small talk, but now Aden looks at me thoughtfully. "Tell me why you ran," he says. "Is it because of Kayden's call? Because I am not talking about my family? It's difficult for me to open up. You must have realized during our first date."

"I am the same," I say quietly. "Sorry, I snapped. That was stupid."

"What was the trigger?" When I stay quiet, Aden lets out a frustrated sigh. "Give me something to work with, Noel. Please."

My fear of rejection is huge, but my fear of upsetting him and fucking this up so that he walks away is worse. "I received a message from my mother a couple of days ago. I guess I haven't been myself ever since."

"Your mother?" Aden asks carefully.

"I have no contact with her," I admit. "For... many reasons. One is that she has been an alcoholic and drug addict since I can remember. And she..." I sigh. "It was not easy to be her son, let's put it like that."

Aden reaches out his hand, his knuckles brushing over my cheek. This gesture alone sends butterflies through my stomach like I am some silly teen in love.

"I have blocked her everywhere, but every now and then she manages to reach me through a different number or... I don't know how she does it. Sometimes, she actively searches for me and suddenly stands in front of me. This time, it fortunately was just a message. But it's always the same. The same old toxicity. The same old reproaches and guilt-trips." I pause. "It always makes me spiral."

Aden stays quiet for a moment. "You must have gone through a lot," he mutters. "As a kid, but also now. I am sorry this happened to you, Noel." He pauses. "And your father?"

I stay quiet, my chest clenching so painfully that it takes my breath away. "He passed away," I finally say. "And I wish I could be sad about it, but I am not."

Aden turns towards me as much as his swing allows him to. For a while, he is quiet, then he turns back, looking at a point in the distance.

"I don't have a good relationship with my brothers," he says into the silence. His words almost make me drop my coffee. I didn't expect him to share anything at all. "That's why I don't talk about them. Now that we are all adults, they regularly reach out to me. I think they want to mend what's broken, but I don't know if I want that."

"How many brothers do you have?"

"Five," he says. "I am the youngest."

I grimace. I don't know much about Aden, but from his online profile on the gallery's homepage, I do know he grew up in the countryside. "I can only imagine how rough it must have been to have so many older brothers."

"Yeah, but that was not the only issue," he continues. "I am their half-brother. Their parents separated, and after a while, our mother began dating my dad. They absolutely hated my existence. One of them outed me as gay, too, which was awful."

"No way," I blurt out. "That's the worst! Like, who the fuck outs someone? It could be so dangerous!"

"I know. I was fortunate that my parents didn't mind."

"Was it Kayden?" I ask. "He must have had something to do with it."

This makes Aden look at me, clear surprise in his eyes.

"Because you..." I feel my cheeks flush. I will just sound pathetic now. "You sounded upset when you talked to him. Differently upset than... I don't know... I don't have a comparison. But I felt like it was personal."

It's silent for a while. "You are perceptive," he says. "It wasn't Kayden per se, but he was the one who backed up the brother who did it and mocked me for being gay... more than the others did."

"Bitch," I mutter.

At that, Aden chuckles.

"It's true! He had no reason to do what he did."

"To them, I was the fault for their parents' splitting. You know, the affair baby, though they didn't even know if Mom and Dad had an affair. They hadn't, by the way. They met after my mom separated from her ex."

"Even if," I exclaim. "That's no reason to bully your sibling! What the fuck! And they were older than you. At least a couple of them must have known how wrong they were."

"When my dad died, only my oldest brother and I went to his funeral," Aden adds. "I guess part of me was never able to forgive the others for this. Oliver was also the first to reach out to me later on. I think he is the only one I feel some attachment to, or rather, I resent him the least."

"Didn't you mention your friend, Lynn, dating one of your brothers?"

"She dated Oliver," he explains. "That's how she and I became friends. She saw firsthand how fucked up our family was. I think a lot changed while she was dating Oliver. She must have said something to him, but I don't know for sure."

"And then?"

"I inherited quite some money from my dad. Once I was eighteen, I moved out to study, and now I am trying not to look back."

"But they don't let you," I conclude.

"Yes, and it's difficult to make the break, because there is still Mom. She is the only real family I have left, and I really love her."

I stand up, walking over to Aden, and wrap my arms around him. "Fuck them! When I see them, I will kick their asses," I say with emphasis because I suck at comforting someone, and this is the only thing that comes to mind, now.

Aden snorts. "I might take you up on your offer." He tugs at my sweater. "Just to clarify something: You are wearing my clothes, aren't you?"

I feel my cheeks heat up again, but my stubbornness outweighs my embarrassment, easily. "Yes, and I will never return them, just so you know!"

Aden looks at me thoughtfully. "The sweater is nothing special."

"It smells like you," I say.

An amused smile curls Aden's lips. He reaches out his hand, tugging at my sweater until I bend down. His hand clasps the nape of my neck, while he pulls me down into a kiss. The position should be uncomfortable, but all I feel is a flock of butterflies chasing through my stomach.

"Are you taking me home with you tonight?" I ask against his lips, my nerves almost painfully strained thanks to my anxiety.

Aden moves back a little, eyeing me again. "Are you going to run from me again?"

I shake my head.

"Then, yes, I will take you home with me." He pauses. "But you are aware that we promised Sterling we would meet him for dinner?"

I groan. "Oh shit, I almost forgot."

Aden smiles. "I am looking forward to meeting your friends properly. Besides,"—a smirk curls his lips—"we have plenty of time afterwards."

My heart stutters at the way he looks at me. The smile he just showed me is so beautiful. It's the first time he's looked at me like that. It feels like, little by little, he has come closer and let me in. But Ster is right, I am asking more from him than I am giving.

"Aden?"

"Hm?"

"I… I want to tell you more about me, but I am scared," I admit.

"You have told me plenty," he says.

"But you have said more."

At that Aden, just chuckles. "Noel, it's not a competition. I shared it willingly with you. And once you are ready, you will do the same."

"There are things I did in the past that I am not proud of," I say.

Aden tilts his head, his signature thoughtful look in his eyes. "I figured," he says, "when you mentioned your parents. It's okay, Noel. As long as you try to communicate with me, we should be fine."

"The same goes to you," I retort. Like, I am the only one who has communication issues.

Aden looks amused. "Yes, the same goes for me." He stands up too now, reaching out his hand to touch my hair. "But seriously, there are things I can't tell you yet, either. Let's do it at our pace."

I let out a breath I didn't know I was holding in. "Okay, we did it. Crisis averted."

"Noel..." Aden takes my hand, wrapping his fingers around it gently. "There is something I have wanted to ask you ever since our first meeting."

"And what's that?"

"Won't you tell me where we met before? I know we did. You said so yourself, and I know your face from somewhere. To be honest, I feel bad not knowing it. It seems to be important to you."

Fuck, he looked through me. I thought I could play it cool and pretend like it was just a fleeting moment. Well, time to put that new communication rule to the test. "I... It is important," I admit. "I am scared that if I tell you, I will need to tell you a lot more about myself, and I don't know if I am ready for that. But you helped me out once, years ago, when I was about seventeen. You were just a stranger, but you helped me. It made an impression on me."

I hold my breath, scared it won't be enough for him, but Aden just takes my face between his hands, planting a soft kiss against my lips. "Thank you for giving me a little piece of information."

"Is it really enough?"

"We can revisit it another day," he says. "Come." Aden puts his arm around my shoulder. "Let's meet your friends before we find ourselves in a new crisis."

ADEN

"Damn it!" Mateo blurts out. He had gone to stand up, but hit his head against the lamp. "Why do they hang them so low?"

"It's not too low," Sterling says in his usual calm manner. "You are just very tall."

"So, it's my fault now?" Mateo exclaims.

"I never said that," Sterling says. "They just design this stuff for the average person."

Mateo lets his head drop down onto the table. "Am I not average?" he asks, sounding miserable.

Noel furrows his brows. It's the look he has when he is about to show his claws. Somehow, it's a bigger turn-on for me than it should be. "Are you stupid? Why do you want to be average?! Obviously, you are great the way you are!"

"That's easy for you to say," Mateo mutters. "Not all of us are a beauty out of a painting."

"Fuck," Noel groans. "Ster, don't let him have another drink!"

"I am not drunk," Mateo mutters.

"That makes it even worse!"

"I can draw you too, Mateo," Sterling offers.

Mateo's head snaps up. "Who wants a pity painting?!"

Sterling's face carries an expression of confusion. "Why not?"

Mateo stares at him before exchanging a look with Noel. "He has a point, Ster," Noel says. "Who the fuck wants a pity-anything?"

"Yeah, you tell him, Noel!"

Sterling looks completely unfazed by his two friends' complaints and just shrugs.

When I agreed to join Noel and his friends for dinner, this was certainly not what I expected. Granted, I wasn't quite sure what to expect, but it still comes as a surprise to see the three of them this relaxed around each other. I can't remember the last time I was in a get-together where the whole atmosphere was so light.

Suddenly, I can't help but chuckle at the absurdity of this whole conversation.

Mateo looks at me as if he just realizes I am here, a look of horror on his face, while the tips of Noel's ears turn red. Only Sterling looks completely unfazed. "You must think we are so silly!" Mateo says.

"I kind of do," I say. "But in an endearing way."

Noel scoots closer to me, a frown on his face. "How can someone be silly and endearing at the same time?"

Instead of an answer, I put an arm around his shoulder and tug him closer. His eyes snap up at me in surprise. Good to know it is possible to catch him off guard, sometimes. "Some people can pull it off," I say.

Noel furrows his brows. "Sometimes I don't know if the things you say are meant as a compliment or not."

"It's like with Sterlone," Mateo says. "At times, I think I should actually be insulted."

"Must be the artistic gene," Noel says. "This reminds me—" His head snaps towards me. "You are an artist too."

"This would explain the whole, semi-insulting, without being insulting, attitude," Mateo adds.

I am not sure if I make sense of what he says, yet I kind of understand the sentiment behind his words. "I don't draw for exhibitions or patrons anymore," I explain. "Just in private."

"Why did you stop?" Sterling asks, his voice surprisingly serious while he looks at me thoughtfully.

Of course, he caught it.

"We're out of food and drinks," Mateo mutters. "I will order something for us." He gets up to walk towards the counter.

Noel jumps up to follow him. "Wait, I want to decide on my own food. You don't really have the hang of ordering for others."

Mateo argues something back, but I can't hear what he says.

"So, why?" Sterling asks.

I gaze at the whisky in my hand. "I lost my muse," I finally say. "Something in me just died that day. I don't want to say that I lost my spark, but it just wasn't the same anymore. My style and the whole atmosphere in my drawings changed."

"But is that bad?"

"Is it?" I toss the question back at him before turning my full attention to Sterling. "It shows a side of me now that I don't want others to see. It's too private."

Sterling remains quiet before he nods. "I understand."

We don't say any more, just sit in silence. Eventually, my phone vibrates. I am almost scared it might be Kayden again, or Oliver, but to my surprise, it's Lynn.

"Work?" Noel asks.

I look up, only noticing now that he and Mateo have returned. "Yes and no." I pull him to my side again. "It's Lynn. She just left work."

"Tell her to join us," Noel offers. "I'd love to get to know her better, too."

"Your friend?" Mateo asks.

"My co-CEO and best friend," I explain.

"We'd love to have her here," Sterling says.

"Well, if you truly don't mind." I swiftly send a message to Lynn, inviting her over. Deep down inside, she is a party gal, so I am not surprised when her answer comes soon, agreeing to join us and saying she will bring Cedric along.

Seventeen

ADEN

Lynn tosses her bag on an empty chair and drops down on the seat between Mateo and Sterling, with a loud '*umpf*'. "Just so we are clear," she says, pointing at Cedric, whose huge, innocent eyes look at me hopefully. "I truly just bumped into Cedric," She narrows her eyes to a glare, as if to dare me to tease her about it. "Don't ask! It was really just a coincidence."

"We don't mind," Mateo says. "The more the merrier."

"And we *have* met before," Sterling adds.

Cedric looks at me. "It's really okay if I join you?"

"You heard them," I tell him. "It's fine."

"Thank you, sir!" he exclaims before settling down between Lynn and Sterling.

What a funny group we are right now. I can't remember the last time I hung out with people like this, and with such a relaxed and genuinely fun group to boot. Usually, I only go to exhibitions or mandatory events, or I meet with Lynn for a drink. Both Lynn and I usually keep our dates away from each other, mostly because it's never been something serious.

With Noel, I have crossed a lot of new bridges, it seems, and I have only known him for such a short time. Mateo takes off once more to order drinks and food for Cedric and Lynn. He really seems to have a caring gene in him. From what I heard from Noel, he looks out both for him and Sterling.

"Your food should be here in a couple of minutes," he says once he is back. "Here are your drinks for now."

"Wow, thank you!" Cedric's eyes are wide.

"That was really kind," Lynn says. "Much appreciated."

"Don't mention it," Mateo says. "Besides, it's easy to order food for people who are not picky eaters."

"Excuse me," Noel huffs. "Spare yourself the dig! Sterling is not a picky eater!"

"How did you know I was talking about him then?" Mateo grins.

As if to prove his point, Noel grabs an olive from my plate and reaches it towards Sterling, until the latter takes it and eats it.

Sterling grimaces. "Yuk, how can you eat that?!"

I can't help but chuckle. "I didn't know you were a picky eater."

Sterling shrugs. "Well, if the others say it, it must be true."

"Don't let Mateo tease you," Noel exclaims. "You are a selective eater, not a picky one. Why has that become the main topic now?"

Cedric has been listening in awe. Now, however, he bursts into giggles. "You are such a meme," he says. "Actually, all of you."

Noel looks at him with a twitching brow. "You are one to talk."

"True," Cedric beams.

Noel looks at him, before a resigned expression crosses his beautiful features. His body goes slack while he leans against me, grumbling something under his breath.

"Don't worry about Cedric," I chuckle. "Been there, done that."

Noel rests his chin against my shoulder, looking at me through his soft brown eyes. I can't help but drive my fingers through his silky hair. He is just so breathtaking when he is close to me, but even more so when he is vulnerable and open with me. I feel a twinge in my chest, something I haven't felt in a long while. It's not uncomfortable, it's rather... a spark. It makes my fingers itch to grab a brush again and draw.

The feeling strikes me out of the blue, leaving me completely dumbfounded.

I want to draw?!

Noel leans his forehead against my shoulder, taking a deep breath as if he is inhaling my scent. By now, it must have dawned on Cedric that Noel is not just some acquaintance, because he stares at us wide-eyed, his mouth open.

"Close your mouth," Lynn says. "You are going to catch a fly."

"You knew?"

"Of course. How come you didn't?" she says. "Didn't you watch them at the exhibition?"

"I thought Mr. Randall was just being polite."

Lynn snorts. "If you think that was just a guy being polite to another guy, I feel like you need a babysitter at your side. Makes me worry for your overall safety."

"She is right," Sterling says. "Be careful not to get tricked, Cedric."

Cedric's cheeks flush slightly. "I am not that naïve," he mutters. "Okay, maybe a bit."

Before anyone can say anything, someone next to us clears their throat. "Lynn?" It's a guy's voice. He must be standing behind me, out of my view, but directly opposite to Lynn.

Lynn's gaze snaps up, staring at the person first, then at me, then back up again.

What was that?

"Wait... Aden, is that you?"

Noel startles slightly and moves his head from my shoulder while I turn to look right into Oliver's surprised eyes.

"Hello, Oliver," Lynn says. "I didn't expect you here. It's not your usual type of bar."

"I got invited over by a friend," Oliver says. "I am meeting Martin later somewhere else."

Martin? Fortunately, he is not meeting him here. It's bad enough to run into Oliver, but Martin is probably my least favorite brother of all. I decide to be thankful that at least it's only Oliver bumping into us.

"I understand," Lynn hums and nods.

It's silent for a moment. None of the others knows what to say or do. They don't even know who the guy is, just that it's very obvious neither Lynn nor I are particularly happy to see him.

This is ridiculous.

"Everyone," I say, trying to keep my voice calm and composed while willing all my emotions down. "This is my oldest brother. Oliver."

"Oh," Sterling nods.

Mateo regains his composure quickly and jumps right into his professional self. "It's nice to meet you, Mr. Randall."

"Oh, I am not..." Oliver says, before his voice trails off. "It's nice to meet you, too," he says instead.

"You are not what?" Noel wants to know.

It's funny. I can see it in his expression, he is so close to letting his claws out, but not in the humorous way, he does it with his friends. He looks a lot more serious all of a sudden.

"He is not a Randall," I explain in Oliver's or Lynn's stead. "We are half-brothers."

"Oh, I get it. I apologize," Mateo says politely.

"These are our friends," Lynn introduces the group briefly, without going into detail, who they are.

Oliver rubs the back of his head, slightly flustered. "Well, I guess I should leave you alone." He pauses. "Oh, before I forget, Aden, you are coming for Mom's birthday next weekend, are you? She is really expecting you."

That fucker. He knows I won't just turn him down when he asks me so openly in front of a whole group of people. I love my mother and do want to see her. Not even I can stay so cold-hearted and say no, when he brings her into the play and challenges me in front of my friends.

"I guess I will be coming," I say calmly. "Just for dinner though."

I can feel Noel's hand on my leg. It feels warm and soothing, calming my nerves down a little. If only I knew how to handle my family, things would be so much easier. Well, Rome wasn't built in a day either.

Oliver smiles, an expression of relief on his face. "I am so happy," he says. "I will tell Mom immediately."

Yeah, of course he will. So, I won't be able to take it back.

"Well, I apologize for disrupting your meeting," Oliver says with a smile. "I will take my leave. It was nice to meet you."

"Have a nice evening," Mateo says.

Lynn nods at him. "Bye, Oliver."

When he has finally left, silence engulfs us again, until Sterling breaks it. "Interesting," he mutters while he watches Oliver disappear into the crowd again.

"Not really," Lynn says dryly. "He is my ex."

"He and I aren't really close," I tell the group without going into detail. "I apologize, this must have been an awkward exchange to watch."

"Make it double awkward because I was there too," Lynn adds. "A drink, Aden?"

"Absolutely!"

Noel wraps his arms around my middle, snuggling against me again. I only realize now that he drew back earlier and didn't touch me openly while I was talking to Oliver. I guess he didn't want to embarrass me or out my relationship with him in front of my brother.

Lynn manages to organize a round of drinks for all of us. Only Noel sticks with a mocktail instead. He drinks very little. If he goes out and drinks at all, it's only one glass of wine.

"Lynn, you really were with Aden's brother?" Sterling asks curiously.

Lynn grins. "High school and later college sweethearts, but he obviously wasn't the one." She doesn't tell them why they broke up, and not even Cedric has the nerve to ask.

When our new drinks arrive, the group gets lively again, fortunately. Cedric is growing more confident, as well. "Say," He beams again. "Mind if I make a reel, Mr. Randell? Of you, casually sitting here? Maybe with Sterling?"

Sterling and I exchange a gaze. "What's a reel? A video?" Sterling mutters.

"Beats me," I say. "But it's for social media."

"And you think that will get views?" Sterling asks.

"Absolutely," Cedric is pumped with motivation. "Mr. Randall always sells well. Our viewers love his dignified, calm image. And I bet you, Sterling, will get quite the audience too." He turns around, gazing at everyone before his eyes land on Noel. "Please help me, Noel. You are the only one who looks capable of doing anything social media-related!"

Noel casts each of us a gaze, then lets out a sigh. "You might be right."

"Hey, what about me?" Mateo asks, while Cedric and Noel try to navigate Sterling and me into a position, they deem cool enough for their reel. "Do I suck at social media too?"

"You are not as hopeless as the others," Noel says. "But the bar is low."

Lynn and I exchange a glance. "I can't say anything in my defense," Lynn says shortly. "I barely post anything, ever."

"Me neither," I say.

"I only have an Instagram account because I have to," Sterling says.

"That's what you have me for now," Cedric exclaims. "I am going to be the world's best assistant!"

When Noel shifts me into position, he leans forward slightly. "Is he always that motivated?" he whispers.

"Yes."

"You truly are a weird combination of boss and assistant," he mutters. "But I guess I can see it work."

I smile. "You and I work well, too, after all."

Noel furrows his brows. "I am nothing like him!"

"I was just teasing you," I chuckle. "Don't make it so easy."

Noel mutters something under his breath, not gracing me with an answer. He is adorable when he is prickly, but I probably shouldn't tease him too much. Grabbing him by the back of his head, I pull him into a swift kiss. "Here, better?"

"I can't believe your sly tactics," Noel mutters.

"Well," Cedric proclaims. "I don't think we can use that one for a reel. Noel and Mr. Randall look like they are about to jump each other, and Sterling looks like the third wheel."

"I don't see anything wrong with that," Sterling points out.

"We are not going to have that on our social media," Lynn intervenes. "My God, guys, focus and take the damn video! It can't be that hard!"

Her words finally get us all into the right mindset, and a couple of minutes later, the video is done, and Cedric looks happy. "It's gotten pretty late," Sterling comments. "I want to get home and work on my newest drawing."

I nod, grabbing my credit card. "Allow me," I say.

"We can't possibly—" Mateo starts with Noel very visibly about to say something too.

"Of course we can," Sterling interrupts. "We are all broke."

"I can chip in, too," Lynn offers.

"You invited me last time," I say. "It's my turn anyway."

"True."

While I gather my things, I look at Sterling again. "Make sure to update me on your progress," I tell him.

"Will do," he promises.

"So," Lynn looks around. "Did I truly manage to find myself amidst a whole group of handsome, gay guys?" she asks dryly.

"I don't think you need me to answer that," I say.

"Yeah, sorry, gayer than anyone else here," Noel says.

Sterling nods. "Me too."

"Well, I for one am bi," Cedric says.

"Just like me," Mateo grins and wiggles his eyebrows at Lynn.

Lynn stares at him and raises her brows. "You are?"

He nods.

"And you are single? Because I am not hooking up with someone else's man."

"As single as one can be, and you?"

"My last flirt just dumped me."

"I am tall," Mateo says.

"I see that," Lynn says. "Who even cares?"

"A lot do," he admits.

"I will let you fuck me, if you promise you won't get all insecure because I earn a lot."

"Well, guys," Mateo grabs his jacket. "I obviously have a date with a beautiful woman now." When Lynn blinks at him, he grins. "I give a shit about how much you earn. Lead the way, Sugar Mama."

"Oh, my god," Noel groans. "Why are you so embarrassing?"

Mateo just grins and winks at us before following Lynn outside. I feel my phone vibrating. When I open my messages, I almost fear that it's Oliver again, or Kayden, or one of the others, but to my surprise, it's Noel.

Can I go home with you?

When I look at him, he looks away, his cheeks tinted a sweet, peachy color. I can't help but reach out my hand to touch his soft hair. "Yes," I say.

EIGHTEEN

NOEL

Aden and I make a brief detour to my place so that I can fetch some clothes and necessities.

The most tumultuous evening of my life is coming to an end. It was an up and down of emotions, or rather, a down and up, starting with me sulking in Sterling's loft, then Aden hunting me down and us talking, ending with us meeting our friends for that crazy get-together.

Aden unlocks the door to his house, letting me in. A repeat of two nights ago, just that this time my mind is much calmer.

"Aden, can I ask you something?"

"Of course."

"How did Lynn actually end up with your brother?" I ask. "She seems to be nice and fun."

"I guess Oliver can be like that, too," he explains. "Just because my relationship to him is strained, doesn't mean he isn't an outgoing guy.

From what I know, he was very similar to Lynn herself. That's how they connected."

"And how did it end?"

"She dumped him once she saw how strained our relationship was."

My mouth drops open. "What?"

"Lynn and Oliver started dating in high school and then continued in college. Don't forget that Oliver is my oldest brother. I am a lot younger than he is. At that time, I was very much still an outsider in the family. Lynn didn't like that at all. You saw her today. She was the same years ago, and she was very vocal about how terrible she found our home situation. It was not so much about Oliver himself, but about the others. Oliver himself was already trying to mend our relationship, but Lynn didn't like that he wouldn't stand up to our other brothers and just let them bully me. I guess her dumping Oliver was the wake-up call he needed."

"Crazy!" I exclaim. "I have a whole new respect for her! I hope Mateo takes his chance and doesn't fuck it up."

"I hope so, too."

"You are not mad that he is hooking up with her, are you?" I ask carefully.

"No, Lynn is very confident and knows what she wants. I don't meddle in her relationships."

I let out a sigh of relief. The last thing I want is for Mateo and Sterling to face any difficulties in their work, and I don't want Aden to be mad at them. They are all too important to me. "Can I take a shower first?" I ask, mainly to diffuse my own thoughts.

"Of course. I will take one after you. There are fresh towels there. You know the way, don't you?"

I wince slightly. "Yeah, I remember."

"Noel." Aden touches my shoulder. "If your anxiety overwhelms you again, promise me to give me a sign. If you need space, I will give it to you. If you need to be alone, then I will make sure you can have your privacy. If you need a hug, I will give it to you, too."

"What if you are mad at me and I need a hug?" I ask.

"I will never deny you comfort," he says. "Even when I might be upset or angry. So, please, promise me you won't run from me again."

I let out a shaky breath. "Okay."

With that, I finally manage to leave for the bathroom, almost scared I will spiral again just from remembering what happened last time. To my surprise, however, it's completely different this time. Instead of my body and mind remembering my last anxiety attack, I feel rather comfortable and relaxed in the bathroom, finally able to enjoy the intricate design of the place and the huge floor-level shower. I have always wanted one of those!

With newfound energy and motivation, I make sure to clean myself properly and even take my time to prepare and stretch myself a little. Fingers crossed for some action later.

Unlike during that fateful night, where I bolted, I take my time now, and once out of the shower and bathroom, look through Aden's place properly.

Meanwhile, Aden takes a shower himself, and once I am done looking at everything, I find him sitting in the living room, skimming through a notebook with a pencil in his hand. Is he writing or drawing something?

"I like how you live," I say when I finally join him in the living room. "It's elegant and suits you, but it's also surprisingly cozy."

"I am happy you like it. I wanted to have a place I could make my own, somewhere I could always retreat to."

"Say, Aden, do you mind if I look around?"

He blinks. "Didn't you do that just now?"

"Yeah, but more in detail."

Aden's lips tug in amusement. "You are the type of person to look into each of my drawers, aren't you?"

My cheeks heat up. "Only if you allow me to!"

He grins. "Just go ahead. It's fine."

He doesn't need to tell me twice. I dash off, this time snooping around a little. There are a lot of books and paintings, obviously. I have no idea if he drew them himself or if he bought them from somewhere. I do recognize Sterling's drawings, though. The one with me on the beach has a very prominent place in the living room, and the other one is in his bedroom.

"I didn't remember you hung the blue painting in the bedroom," I say, peeking into the living room again.

"I recently put it there."

"Why?"

"I didn't want anyone else to see it but me. It's too beautiful."

How can he say these things and not be embarrassed? "Does that mean that every time I stay over, I have to look at myself when you fuck me?"

Aden snorts. He puts his notebook aside and rests his chin against his hand. His gaze pierces me now. "Who knows? Maybe it's going to entertain me on nights you aren't here."

This fucking guy! "Are you never embarrassed?" I blurt out.

"You were the one who started it. I am just matching your energy."

"Are you?" I raise my brows, hoping for a challenging gaze. "How far are you willing to go to match my energy?"

"Far," he says.

I take a few steps backwards, happy when Aden rises from his place and follows me. The look in his eyes is dark, so much that it sends tingles down my spine. I decide to put on a show for him. On my way upstairs, I strategically get rid of my clothes until I have reached his bedroom and am only clad in my underpants.

Aden closes the door behind him, leaning against it. "Take it off," he commands.

Fuck, the tone of his voice goes right to my cock. For a man so neat and appropriate and polite, he sure knows how to make a guy all hot and bothered. But if there is one thing that doesn't embarrass me, it's being naked. May as well give him a show. I make sure to turn my back to Aden, while hooking my thumbs into the elastic of the underpants, slowly pulling them down inch by inch.

Too slow for Aden's liking, it seems.

He is suddenly behind me, one arm around my middle to press me against his chest, the other moving into my pants. "Fuck, Aden!"

"You were taking too long," he mutters against my neck while his hand clasps around my dick. His other hand moves up my chest, tweaking one of my nipples between his fingers while the grip around my dick tightens.

This guy makes me breathless just by touching me. It's almost like I am a teen again. I should feel embarrassed, but his thumb rubbing over the tip of my cock makes me forget any reservation. "You are nothing like one would expect in bed."

Aden moves us along towards his bed, until my legs knock against it and I am forced to crawl onto it. His hand prevents me from turning around, while I can hear him shuffling with his clothes. He is fast, soon pressing his naked upper body against my back again. "Is that good or bad?"

His slick fingers run down my back, squeezing my ass before disappearing between my butt cheeks. His first finger pushes into me easily. He halts for a moment, pressing his lips against my shoulder. I can almost feel his smirk. “You stretched yourself. And you are calling me a freak, huh?”

“I just wanted to be prepared,” I say. “Be thankful!”

“I am not complaining. Actually, that’s hot.”

Aden pushes a second finger inside me, making me moan. He takes his time until he has three fingers buried inside me, thoroughly stretching me. A shiver goes down my spine, sweat pooling on my forehead. I just want more, more, more, but Aden’s fingers move almost excruciatingly slow. My body is screaming for him, wanting his cock inside me, fucking me fast and relentless, but it seems Aden has his own plans in mind. By the way he looks at me, it’s obvious he is doing it with intent.

“You are being such an asshole tonight!” I groan.

“Is that really what you want to say to me right now?” Aden grins. “When you are at my mercy? How about you be patient for once?”

He curls his fingers, hitting my soft spot that way. “Aden,” I moan. I need more of this. The desperation makes me rest my forehead against the pillow while pushing back against Aden’s fingers. “Please.”

“Fuck,” Aden groans. His fingers are suddenly gone, but before I can mourn the emptiness, his cock plunges into me in one go. After being teased for so long, the relief of having him fill me makes me shiver.

One of Aden’s arms wraps around me from behind, pushing me back against him, while he snaps his hips forward. The sound of skin slapping against skin fills the room, mixed with my moans. My own cock is painfully hard, but when I go to touch myself for relief, Aden pushes my hand away. “Not yet,” he says.

“You are going to make me burst,” I groan.

Instead of an answer, Aden’s movements slow, almost making me sob. That’s when I feel one of his fingers against my rim, moving up to my entrance. Aden keeps the slow pace of his thrusts, while his finger probes me slightly.

"Are you okay?" he asks, his voice husky and low.

"Yes! Fuck, do it!"

When Aden inserts his fingers, I feel fuller than ever before. The stretch burns, but instead of being painful, it turns into something hot in my stomach.

"Please," I beg.

He stills once more, the sly bastard. "What do you want? Tell me what you want."

"Fuck me," I beg. "Make me come. Please, Aden, let me come!"

Aden removes his finger, and without pulling his cock out of me, he turns me over until I land on my back, then plunges into me with full force. I instantly wrap my arms around his neck and my legs around his middle, while his hips snap forward.

He easily finds my spot again, hitting it relentlessly with his cock.

"Fuck, Aden, you are so good!"

There is a glint in his eyes I haven't seen before. It turns me on more than I expected. He stills his hips, moving down to my ear. "Tell me no one else has fucked you like I do."

"Nobody has."

"Good." Aden's hand wraps around my dick, and while he thrusts inside me again, it only takes two strokes with his hand until I am pushed over the edge. I don't know what I am saying or moaning, I am a blubbering mess, when my release finally washes over me.

It takes a while for me to come down from my orgasm. I only remotely realize that Aden keeps me in his arms while he fucks me for a bit longer until his body goes slack too. He gives us time to calm down before carefully pulling out of me and getting rid of his condom.

"You are fucking amazing in bed," I blurt out.

Aden snorts before pulling me into his arms. "I hope this isn't the only thing you like about me."

"It's not. You can be assured. But I swear, I have never been fucked like that before."

Aden smiles while he turns his head to look at me. "You know how to stroke a guy's ego," he chuckles. "Just for the record, you are pretty amazing too."

"I need us to get tested," I mutter. "I want you to come inside me next time, without a condom."

"You won't need to ask me twice. I will make an appointment the first thing tomorrow morning," he promises.

NINETEEN

NOEL

When I wake up a couple of hours later, I expect to feel sore and sticky, but instead I am cleaned up and well-rested. Well, a little sore, but in a good way. Aden has also changed the sheets. I am not sure how and when he did that – I must have been completely out of it. Aden is not lying next to me anymore, and the house is filled with the scent of freshly brewed coffee.

It's 7 a.m., too early after a night out and some nightly action, but something about the fact that I am waking up in my boyfriend's bed and being able to spend the morning with him, makes me so happy that I drag myself out of bed. I have never experienced a moment like that with one of my former boyfriends, but then, they weren't boyfriends, more like flings.

This time I brought my own spare clothes, but make sure to pack Aden's sweater, the one I *borrowed*, into my bag. There is no way I will ever return that one! In the bathroom, I notice that Aden has prepared fresh towels for me.

I have known it all the time, but still, the realization hits me like a brick: He genuinely is a kind guy. The full package, actually. Aden is handsome and successful, yet kind to those he loves. He is interesting and a tad mysterious, quiet but not boring, and he definitely knows how to fuck a guy.

It gives me a stitch to know that I have no family I can introduce him to. *'Hi Mom, meet Aden, he is my partner',* are words I will never be able to say. That ship sailed long ago. My mother doesn't care about me, who I like or date, she never has. All she cares about is her addiction.

"Shut up," I mutter to myself, smacking my cheeks slightly. No gloomy thoughts!

I might not be able to introduce Aden to my family, but I definitely can proudly show him off to my friends!

And I have awesome friends who are incredible, generous, and who are very happy for me whenever something good happens to me!

With more positive thoughts, I finally make it into the shower. I clean myself up properly and dress in fresh clothes before hurrying down the stairs to meet my boyfriend.

Aden turns once he hears me approaching, smiling at me. I make sure to run over to him and hug him, like a lovesick puppy. He doesn't disappoint me and puts an arm around me, hugging me tight. "Coffee?" he asks.

I nod. "I can't go without one so early."

"I wasn't so sure what you wanted to eat, so I put out an assortment of different food."

He wasn't kidding. The table is full, with ham, cheese, eggs, some veggies, and he even made pancakes. "You know, if you asked me now, if I'd want to marry you, I'd do it on the spot."

Aden laughs. "Good to know I will get you with food."

It's not just the food. It's the act of service, the way he seriously considered me and my feelings. It's too cheesy to say it out loud, so I settle for kissing him. With cups of fresh coffee, we both sit down just as Aden's phone lights up.

He frowns when he gazes at it. "That's Lynn."

"Oh shit, hopefully Mateo didn't fuck up!" I exclaim. "You know, he normally wouldn't. He is like one of the sweetest guys ever. So, I am sure if something happened, then it's more a misunderstanding. Or maybe they didn't click. That could be possible too."

"Noel." Aden interrupts me. "Take a breath. Lynn isn't complaining."

"What is she writing?"

Aden takes a sip from his coffee. "She says: Incredible night! That Mateo guy knows what he's doing with his limbs. Finally, a guy who knows how to fuck me!"

I can't help but groan. "And here I was, worried for him! Why did I even ask?"

Aden raises his brows. "Do you want me to write something equally inappropriate back?"

I perk up. "Yes!"

Aden types something on his phone before putting it aside again and taking a sip from his coffee. The answer doesn't take long to come. When Aden opens the message, he just chuckles.

"What? Tell me?"

"I told Lynn that you are incredibly flexible and that I had the best fuck of my life."

I snort into my coffee. There is something about Aden talking dirty when not in bed that's just so contradictory to how he usually behaves. It's his proper appearance and his calm demeanor, paired with saying something like that. "And her reply?"

"She said she is happy for us, but that Mateo just made gagging sounds."

I grin while adding honey to my slice of bread. I used to love that when I was a child. There was a time in my life when things were good. Mom and Dad were clean for a short time, and Mom was happy, I guess. It only lasted a couple of months, not even a year. Bittersweet memories.

"That's fair," I say.

"How is your schedule this week?" Aden asks.

I wiggle my brows. "Are you asking so you know when to ask me for a date?"

Aden nods, business as usual, while he looks at his notebook, scribbling something down. "Exactly."

Okay, somehow, whenever I try to tease him, I am the one who ends up flustered. How is that fair? Well, I guess I can't help it. "I am free today but working a double shift tomorrow."

"Then how about you stay until tomorrow?"

I need to try hard not to stare at him, flabbergasted. Man, everything about this relationship is so different than anything I've experienced before. "Is that okay?"

"Of course, or I wouldn't have asked."

"Then I'll stay. Other than tomorrow, I think I will be working the whole week. I am jumping in for my co-worker at the bar, but also, have my shift in the club. I am only free on Wednesday evening."

Aden looks at me thoughtfully. "You work a lot, Noel."

"Yeah," I mutter.

"I don't want to pry," he continues. "But is there a reason for that?"

I shift around nervously, unsure if I should tell him or not. But then I remember how open he was about his family life. "My father left me quite the debt," I admit. "Technically, don't need to work that much, but I want to pay it off faster than the plan I set up originally."

Aden looks surprised. "You should not have inherited your Dad's debt, especially with your mom still being around!"

"Yeah, I know," I mutter. "It's also thanks to my mom and her committing credit card fraud and buying things in my name. I was not able to fight it after his death, because a lawyer and lawsuit would have cost me a lot." I pause. "Can we not talk about it, please?"

"Let me look into it," Aden offers.

"What?"

"You got scammed, and you probably were a minor when it happened. I assume Sterling and Mateo tried to help, but couldn't?"

"Mateo has his student debt to pay, and Sterling had to look out... rather, still is looking out, for his sister as well."

"Then allow me to help. You are my boyfriend, Noel. I do have the means and the contacts to help you."

I want to scream *yes*. Yes, save me. Please, help me! But how can I accept his help so easily? He barely knows me. Hell, I don't even know him properly.

Aden reaches out his hand and touches my shoulder. "You don't want me to help. Am I right?" he asks, tone deadly serious. "Talk to me, to help me understand."

"It's just... Fuck!" I brush my fingers through my hair in exasperation. "What if you have enough of me? What if I let you help me, rely on you, and then you are gone, and I am all alone and need to start anew... with my debt and with my life."

Aden looks at me, the look in his eyes unreadable, then something close to understanding crosses his expression. He looks gentle all of a sudden. "I understand," he says. "It's a trust issue, isn't it? Of course it is. I understand."

"No, yes, not trust alone!" I blurt out. "I don't think you are a villain at all. But sometimes things happen, people fall out of love, and then I need to be able to stand on my own two feet."

"I get that," he says. "Thanks for explaining it to me. But why do you think I don't want you to live your life?"

I blink. "Well, you are a gallerist and CEO. You are the embodiment of high society, and I am your bartender boyfriend, who also works in a sleazy club."

"So what?"

"I can't quit my job."

"Of course not," Aden says. "I wouldn't want you to quit your job. Granted, I am not overjoyed about where you work, simply because it's a dangerous place, but there is nothing wrong with what you do. I am your boyfriend and partner. I want to help you, but I certainly don't want you to give up your independence. I had that type of relationship once, and it ended as a shambles."

The last bit of information hits me like a brick. "Is that true?"

"Yes." Aden clenches his fingers around his cup of coffee before relaxing them again. "My ex-boyfriend was very dependent on me for various reasons and in various ways. It... it was not a good experience for me, Noel, and ended terribly."

Aden does not go deeper into it, but from the tone of his voice, it looks like the guy pretty much leeched off him somehow. He mentioned having had a very bad experience before.

"I like how much drive you have," Aden tells me. "I like how serious you are about your work, and how you want to stand on your own feet. I fully support that."

"You... you don't mind? That I am a bartender?"

"Not at all." Aden purses his lips, his expression thoughtful. "Let me offer something to you. How about I at least hire a lawyer for you? Someone who can help you with freeing yourself from your debt. It'll take more time to clear it than if I were to involve myself directly, but on the other hand, it will allow you to keep control over it."

My head perks up. With that solution, I would have a real chance of getting rid of this unfair debt. Granted, I wouldn't be able to have this chance without Aden's help. He is the one paying for the lawyer, and it probably will be a top-notch one. However, if I put my pride and anxiety aside and accept his help, it would also mean I could start looking for a better job, and maybe save some money for an actual course to take. I could find a better bar to work at.

But is it okay? Can I really ask so much of Aden?

"Noel, I am offering this to you because I want to, and because I like you. I know you are not in this relationship for money."

"How do you know?" I mutter. "I could be."

"I know. I have a good eye for people."

"But your ex..."

"I also knew back then," he explains. "The problem was not that I was naïve or didn't see the problem. The issue lay elsewhere. I wanted so desperately to help Emil, even when I knew he was using me."

Emil. So that's his name.

"If someone close to you willingly reaches out their hand, it's okay to take it. If it helps, I promise you I won't repeat the same mistakes I once made," Aden adds.

"I think I am completely and utterly in love with you," I mutter.

Aden raises his brows.

"Oh fuck! Did I just say that out loud?! What's going on in my head? You probably fucked my brains out last night. Forget I said that."

"I won't forget," Aden says. "Also, you must realize why I offer this to you. I wouldn't do that for just any person."

He hasn't said it, but does it mean he is falling for me too?

"So, I assume it's a yes. You'll take me up on my offer?" he asks.

I nod. "Thank you."

Aden looks equal parts relieved and happy. "I will immediately set you up with a lawyer." A pause. "So, Wednesday evening?"

"Yes, and since I work so much this week, I will be free on the weekend. That's rare!"

Aden's face falls slightly.

"Is something wrong? Are you busy during the weekend?"

"You were there yourself when Oliver cornered me. I have to visit home next weekend," Aden says.

"Oh shit, right!"

His whole expression is closed off again, but by now, I have figured it's a self-preservation thing. "I can't believe I couldn't manage to get out of it, but it's my mother's birthday."

"If you need help, I'd happily join you," I offer, before chuckling. "It was just a joke; in case you are freaking out now."

Aden stares at me.

"I was just goofing around," I mutter. "I know it's way too early for you to introduce me to anyone. Let alone your family!"

"But you would?"

"Huh?"

"If I asked you to come with me, you would?"

My eyes widen. "Are you serious?"

"The question is rather: Were you?"

"Aden, if you invited me to come with you, I'd do it in a heartbeat," I say.

"Are you sure? You know how strained my relationship with them is."

I don't have any money to give, but I certainly have my heart and support to give. And I definitely will do that. "I am coming with you next weekend. Make sure your mom expects one more person."

TWENTY

NOEL

When I arrive at Mateo's place, he is sitting on his sofa with Lynn, drinking tea with her. That's a rare view. I can't remember the last time he so casually hung out with a potential date. They must have clicked somehow.

Mateo's apartment is small, but he has a talent for using space well. It looks much more spacious than it is because he uses everything so well.

"I am glad you dropped by," Lynn says, taking out her notebook. "Tell me when you are free. Aden got in contact with a good lawyer. I am going to organize the first meeting."

I still feel guilty for bothering Aden and his co-CEO, but Lynn doesn't look like she minds. As for Mateo, he looks incredibly happy. Both he and Sterling were very vocally pleased that I decided to accept Aden's help.

"I think I could squeeze in Friday morning," I tell her. "Or is that too soon?"

"No, that should work. That way, you can kick everything off before the weekend. You are meeting Aden's family, right?"

I groan. "Yes, I am so nervous."

"Don't be," Lynn says, in her usual dry manner. "He barely visits them anyway. Even if you make the worst impression, it won't matter."

"Oh, I am not nervous about them! They hurt my man. As far as I am concerned, they can go fuck themselves," I exclaim. "I am nervous I won't be able to stand up for Aden. I have to deliver!"

"I don't think Aden expects you to defend him," Lynn points out.

"That doesn't matter. I am going to be his shield for once!"

Lynn blinks at me. "You have the weirdest sense of logic"—a sudden smile curls her lips—"but I can kind of see how that clicks with Aden. He can be weird, too."

"I take it that's a good thing?"

"It is," Lynn says. "He has been more his usual self since he met you. It's almost like the time when he built the company, and we started to work together."

"Do you have some intel on the brothers?" I ask.

"Why, you want to harass them?"

"Maybe a little."

Lynn smirks. "Well, Oliver is my ex. He is really trying to get closer to Aden again. He lacked a bit of backbone, though. Not sure if that's changed. Kayden was extremely mean to Aden. I still remember when I met the family for the first time, and thought, how much of an asshole he was. I ran into him a couple of years ago, and he had changed, but I don't think that really matters to Aden."

"But he wasn't the one who..." I pause. I am not sure how much she knows, and I am also not sure if it's okay to talk about it in front of Mateo.

"I will go and order us some food," Mateo says before getting up and giving us some privacy.

"Wow, the man can read the room," Lynn says. "I am impressed!"

"He has always been very aware," I point out, eager to talk well about Mateo, so that he will hit it off with Lynn properly. "Plus, he definitely has a backbone."

"I figured," Lynn says, smiling slightly. "So, you wanted to ask something about Kayden?"

"I am not sure if it's okay to talk about it," I admit.

"Let me think... the worst they did to Aden." She pauses. "There was plenty of bullying and harassment. But I think the breaking point for Aden was when he got busted for being gay." She looks at me thoughtfully. "Your lack of surprise shows me you know that already."

"But it wasn't Kayden, right?" I ask.

"I don't know. Could have been Martin. He is the second youngest after Aden, and he really looked up to the older brothers. He might have outed Aden just to impress them, but I can't tell for sure." She hesitates. "Listen, this family can be very kind. Aden's mom, for example, is a sweetheart, and the brothers really grew and changed. But Aden has a different reality. For him, that's probably the pit of hell. Just promise me you will be there for him."

"I told you already, I am there to have his back, not to kiss up to his idiotic brothers."

Lynn grins. "I had a feeling you would say that. Not one to shy away from a challenge, huh?"

"What can I say... I have learned how to kick annoying guys off me early on. I am not scared of his brothers. I just want to be there for Aden."

"You will be fine," she reassures me. "Thank you for doing this for him, Noel."

I try not to show it, but her words really mean a lot to me. Aden is picky with his friends, and he told me she is his only true friend, his best friend. I want her to like me, but I want her to like me for me, not someone who puts on a show. Fortunately, she seems to approve of the real me.

The only things helping me get through this awful work-filled week were my date with him on Wednesday, which we spent at his place with him cooking for me, because there is nothing this guy can't do, and my meeting with the lawyer. Anticipating the meeting kept me on the edge of a nervous breakdown for days, until the meeting actually happened, and it was so uneventful, even bordering on boring, that it blew my mind. The man was friendly and polite, and just collected all the data, plus told me what he would do, how he would go about it and what he needed from me. He also looked pretty pleased and confident, telling me it was a relatively easy case for him to handle.

Talk about boosting my confidence and helping me regain some hope for my situation.

Besides, there is also knowing I am seeing Aden for a whole weekend. It doesn't even matter that it's with his family.

"Did you bring everything?" Aden asks. "If not, I can lend you something." He pauses, angling for something in his pocket. "Oh, and I forgot this here."

I blink when he hands me a key. "What's that?"

"A key."

"Yeah, I see that." I grin. "I mean, what does it unlock?"

Aden looks at me, completely confused, before he gestures at his front door.

"Wait a moment?" I blurt out. "This unlocks your house for me?"

"Yes, obviously. What else would I keep locked up and you'd need a key for?" Aden puts his notebook into his bag, closing it safely, before grabbing two books. "You are often working late, and sometimes your shift ends before I come home. I want you to be able to come here and wait, if you want to."

While Aden seemingly is about to move on from this conversation, I can barely grasp it. "Aden..."

"Hm, anything wrong?"

"This is big," I mutter. "This is so big."

"Listen, Noel." He puts his books aside and takes my hand. "You don't need to take it if it's too much for you."

"No, I want it! It's just... isn't it too soon? Should you trust me that much? I could do God knows what when you are away and I am here."

"Would you?" he asks.

"Of course not!"

"Then it's fine," he says. "Listen, I know we are going fast, but we did that from the first moment on."

"True," I admit.

"I want you to have this key, so you are safe. You work two rather dangerous jobs in a dangerous part of town, and live in an equally dangerous area. I'll just feel better to know you are here, or that you at least know you have the option to come here. I am not asking you to move in with me.“ He pauses. “Yet. I just want you to know that you are welcome anytime.”

I can’t believe any of this. What is even happening? When I started dating Aden, I was so insecure about this potential relationship. I wanted to go slow, yet not even a couple of days later, he introduced me as his boyfriend, and I landed in bed with him.

And now he is handing me the key to his home.

A small voice in the back of my head keeps telling me it can’t be true. That he is mocking me or just doing this out of a mood, that a guy like him would never date someone as worthless as I am.

You are worthless. I should never have had you.

At least make yourself useful.

I shake the thought off, thinking about what Lynn said to me, and how she reacted to Aden and me dating. I think about our talk at the playground where he opened up to me. He obviously has his own demons, and he jumped into this relationship just like I did. It’s the same risk for him.

“Thank you.” I carefully attach the key to my keychain. “I would give you a key to my place in return, but I really don’t want you to hang out there.”

Aden chuckles. “If I want to wait for you somewhere, I will visit the drag queen bar you showed me.”

“That’s a great deal!” I beam.

“So, are you ready?” he asks. “We should get going. The drive takes us a couple of hours.”

“I am ready. Could you just lend me a second shirt? It was my roommate’s turn to do the laundry, but he got drunk instead.”

“Yeah,” Aden frowns. “And see, that’s exactly why I gave you the key. Do your laundry here instead.” He walks off only to return a couple of minutes later with a nice-looking shirt that's probably too expensive for me to wear. But I decide to for once not give a shit about it and just be thankful for his generosity.

"Aden, does your family know I am your sexy boyfriend?"

Aden smiles. "I told Mom. The rest can figure it out themselves."

My heart takes a leap of joy that he wants to officially introduce me to his mother. Actually, he already did that, but now I am going to meet her in person. "So, no hiding it?"

"No hiding it."

TWENTY-ONE

NOEL

Aden was correct in saying that it's a long drive, but it's also fun to hang out with him like that, especially because he gives me all the power over the radio.

"Can I really play whatever I like?" I ask.

"Of course. I'd love to know what you are interested in."

"What do you like?" I ask.

"I am a huge fan of classical music," he admits.

"Somehow that fits."

He smiles at my comment. "Maybe one day I will take you along to a concert and show you what I like about that type of music."

"I'd love to!" I beam. "It's not my type of music usually, but I still want to know." It might sound cheesy, but I want to know what he likes, I want to understand all the little details that shape him into the person he is.

"So do I," he says. "I want you to play whatever you like. I don't know a thing about any other type of music other than classical music."

"Then I got you covered!" I make sure to connect it to my phone to play all my favorite songs. I even sing along to some of them, just so happy that Aden is interested in what I like.

"You have a beautiful voice," Aden points out.

"Now you are just being silly." I grin. "You don't need to compliment me. I will let you fuck me without you sweettalking me." I pause. "Talking about *without*. Guess what I got?" I fumble with my phone until it opens the test results. Aden briefly glances at my phone and smiles.

"I got mine too. Just open the first drawer of my bag. It's in there."

"Then we can do it without a condom anytime!"

"Yes." He smiles. "Next time I come, it will be inside you."

I snort. "Good to know we are on the same page."

Aden steers his car away from the highway and down a more deserted road, leading us towards the small town his family lives in. "Back to the music... Why don't you consider working in a bar that offers karaoke or live music?"

I blink. "Would I need to be able to sing for that?"

"Not necessarily, but I guess it depends on the bar and what they expect you to do. If they want you to motivate the customers to sing along or if they want you to introduce an act, I guess it comes as an advantage if you are not a complete failure at singing."

"I have never thought about that." I muse. "I could talk to DeeDee." I stop, thinking. "Wait a moment! I could actually talk to DeeDee and ask if she can recommend a place. I'd love to work at a drag queen bar! It could be fun."

It's only when I say it that I realize I am actually considering changing my workplace. Yes, I do earn well right now, because I work more hours than I should, and because I work two jobs, but if my debt can truly be taken care of, I will be able to actually pick a job I like.

"Yes, exactly. And they probably pay better, and you would have the option to attend some courses like you planned to." He pauses. "What did the lawyer say? You met yesterday, right?"

"He took a look at everything and told me to leave it to him," I say. "He thinks I have a good chance."

"Of course you have," he points out. "It's fraud. You are a victim." He gazes at me. "You look conflicted. Does it not make you happy that you can finally get rid of this debt?"

"I am happy, but I also feel guilty," I admit. "Does that make sense?"

"It does," Aden says quietly. "I know the feeling."

"It means going against my mom. But at the same time, it's... I just want to be free, you know? I want to be free, so much!"

"Her mistakes are not your fault," he says. "She used you and took advantage of you, and now it's time she pays for what she did. Listen, Noel, I know it's hard, and I know part of you might be hoping to get your mom back, but—"

"But it doesn't work like that," I finish. "I know it. She has been gone for many years. In fact, I only remember a very short time when she was truly a mom. I need to let go. I also know I need to show some backbone finally. I... I might feel guilty, but I can promise you that my wish for freedom is greater than my feeling of guilt," I admit. "I want a new start, a new beginning, and I am ready."

I haven't had a mom for many years.

It's time to face the truth and take charge of my life.

"You are much stronger than you think you are," Aden says, much to my surprise. "The way you lived your life up to now, how you took charge of it and broke out of your toxic family. It showed a lot of strength."

"You think so?" I let his words sink in. No one has ever told me I am strong, not even Mateo or Ster. Or maybe they have, and it just didn't strike something in me. Somehow, when Aden says it, it's like a warm blanket that protects me. His opinion really matters to me. I don't know when it started to but I know it does.

"I wouldn't say it if I didn't mean it," he says.

And that's exactly why his opinion matters to me. He is very kind and treats me well, but he doesn't toss around compliments. So, when he compliments me, it always means something.

Maybe I should take him at face value about his comment on my singing voice, too.

A bar with live music, huh? DeeDee surely could recommend me to someone. She always hated where I work and has constantly told me to change jobs. I stick in these jobs for the money, but now I might not need to do that anymore.

"Almost there."

Aden successfully pulls me out of my thoughts, making my head snap up to check our surroundings. "I didn't even realize we arrived! Felt shorter than it was."

"I take that as a compliment," Aden smiles. "As in, you enjoy my company."

"I do! We should do this more often." I scrunch my nose. "Well, not visit your hometown, but go on a trip."

Aden looks surprised before a warm smile curls his lips. "I actually think that's a great idea. Let's plan something for the next holiday. What's something you have always wanted to do?"

"Go skiing," I tell him. "I never went skiing. Do you know how to?"

"Yes, it's almost mandatory if you grow up in a village close to the mountains." He chuckles. "We can certainly do that."

"You know what else would be great?"

"Tell me."

"Well, just the two of us in a cottage by a lake or the ocean. Nothing touristy, but a place where we could relax, just come down from the whole buzzing city, and have plenty of sex."

Aden looks thoughtful. "You mentioned that a while ago. Actually, that sounds exactly like something I need occasionally. I have always loved the calm of the water. It inspires me."

I don't say anything, not sure if this is something I am allowed to comment on or not. I know that Aden is barely drawing anymore. I saw some of his work when I was stalking his social media accounts, right before we started dating, and I wanted to check on what I was getting into. I don't know much about art, but I can tell that he is very good. I wonder why he stopped.

Not saying anything at all makes me look like an asshole, so I decide to be vague but honest. "I like your art," I say. "Granted, I only saw what's in your gallery and what Cedric posted to your social media. I can't tell why, but it strikes something in me."

"What does it strike in you?" he asks.

Yeah, awesome, now that's a question I didn't expect at all. "Sometimes, you really come off like a math teacher, you know?"

He chuckles. "What makes you say that?"

"Because you ask questions I don't expect."

"Lynn keeps saying the same. She thinks my brain is wired differently."

Just like Sterling, I think to myself.

"What you said piqued my interest," he adds.

"I don't know anything about art, but when I look at your drawings, it makes me feel warm and sad at the same time. It makes me linger and look at it, over and over again, because I am scared that I might miss something. I am not sure if I am supposed to smile or cry." I pause. "It's the faces," I add. "The expressions. You have that one drawing of a man in the sun, and everything looks warm and joyful, but his expression isn't." I sigh. "Sorry, that's all I can say. I know I suck at voicing what I feel or think."

Aden is silent. "Is this truly what you feel when you see my paintings?"

"Yes. And it's not just me. Sterling is obsessed with your work. He really looks up to you. And even Mateo, who isn't too well-versed in this area either, is drawn to it."

"Thank you," Aden says, much to my surprise.

His words make me blink in confusion. "What are you thanking me for?"

"I think you reminded me of something important. I will need to think about this for a while." He takes a deep breath. "Well, we are here."

He halts the car in front of a beautiful, three-story house, and for a while just sits in the car, staring at the house without moving an inch. I gently touch his hand. "You know, we don't have to do this. We don't have to stay. We are free to come and go as we please. In fact, we could just turn around now and leave."

Aden takes my hand, placing a kiss on it.

The tension in his whole body is so visible, it breaks my heart. I wonder how he felt growing up here, and occasionally returning for his mom's sake. "Aden, I want you to know I will have your back. And I will be on my best behavior. I know that's not my forte, but I will try to be."

"Don't," he says with a smile. "Don't be on your best behavior. Be like you always are."

"Is that really okay?"

"I want you to be yourself," he says, finally opening the car door. "Fuck my brothers!"

"That's the right sentiment," I exclaim. "I am ready."

"Then let's go."

Either his mom or one of his brothers must have seen us arrive, because we don't need to knock at the door as it is ripped open. "Aden!" A woman in her sixties opens the door, immediately wrapping her arms around Aden. "You really came!"

"Of course I did, Mom. I promised you after all." He clears his throat before gesturing towards me. "Mom, meet—"

"Ah, you must be Noel!" she proclaims, before he can finish his sentence, and comes closer to hug me. "I am so happy to meet you. It's the first time Aden has brought someone home! I can barely believe it."

She ushers us inside, her face full of joy. I am starting to understand why Aden feels so torn. It must constantly weigh on his conscience not to visit his mom more often, but at the same time, dread coming home and being reminded of his toxic household.

Aden and I take off our shoes and put our jackets into the wardrobe before following his mom into the living room. There they are, his six brothers. I only recognize Oliver, and Kayden from the picture Aden showed me. Two of the brothers have dates with them, or at least that's what I think the women next to them are, and one brother is wearing a wedding ring.

I let my eyes wander around. So, which one is the douchebag who outed him? Who's the fucker? Why did Aden refuse to tell me the names, and what exactly they did? I only know Oliver is the oldest, and apparently, the least douchey one of them. Kayden wasn't the one who outed him, but he must have been a major asshole, judging by the emotional way Aden reacted during their phone call.

Lynn mentioned Martin and believes he might be the culprit. So, who is the spineless douchebag named Martin?

Well, it doesn't matter who it was outed him; they were all terrible to him!

The moment the guys spot us, they are on their feet immediately, hurrying to greet us. They all introduce themselves to me, which means I finally know who Martin is.

"Aden, I can't believe it!" one of them calls out. "Oliver said you would be coming."

"It's close to a miracle," another one grins.

Yeah, shove your miracle somewhere else. How tone-deaf can someone be?

Oliver himself is holding back with his comments, just greeting Aden warmly. I guess he actually is the most aware of them all.

Funnily, they are all very friendly, also to me, I have to give them that, but I can feel Aden closing up next to me. It's like his whole stance changes, his expression turns stoic, the look in his eyes distances. It makes me realize that a lot of my anxiety about him not opening up towards me was in my own head. Seeing him now is proof of it. He is so different with me.

"I didn't know Aden would bring a friend," Kayden says.

"I remember you, Noel," Oliver says. "You were with his friends when I stumbled over Aden in the bar." He pauses. "We are very happy to have you."

"I am Noel," I say.

"Aden's friend?" Martin pushes.

"More like his incredibly hot boyfriend," I tell him before I can stop myself.

From the corner of my eye, I see how Aden's lips twitch. Okay, good decision to hit them with the truth immediately.

Oliver looks at us, stunned. "Wait... you are dating?"

"Yes," I say.

As if to underline my words, Aden puts his hand on the small of my back. "Obviously, we are," Aden adds, before turning towards me. "Come, I will show you around, Noel."

I can almost feel the eyes of his family on my back when Aden leads me away. "We are staying in the guestroom, right?" I ask.

"Yes." He leads me to the second floor and then to the end of the corridor, to the room prepared for us, where we leave our bags. "It's only the two of us staying, and Oliver. The others live close by. All but Francis and his wife, but they are going to stay with an old school friend," he explains. "I am sorry for all the tension."

"It's fine, don't worry," I reassure him. "Actually, I am starting to think I will have fun messing with them."

Aden pulls me into his arms, burying his face in my hair. He doesn't say anything, just keeps holding me. I return the gesture, wrapping my arms tightly around him.

TWENTY-TWO

ADEN

I can't believe I dragged the person I love into my family mess. The whole way home and up until Noel meeting my family, I was wondering if I was doing the right thing. It's selfish of me to take Noel along, I know that, yet I can't deny how much more relaxed I feel with him next to me.

Usually, on the rare occasions I join a family get-together, I sit around feeling awkward, like the outsider I have always been here. No matter how hard my mother tries or how many questions my brothers ask, there is always something inside me that recoils. An automatic tension, almost appearing immediately when they talk, as though I am expecting the worst. When we were kids, and they asked something, they would mock my answer at best, and downright bully me at worst.

I just can't trust them or myself in this house.

Home is a weird concept. I know from Lynn and from old acquaintances how it's supposed to feel. I have a vague idea of how I should feel when I come home, but unfortunately for me, home doesn't feel like much. It's the house I grew up in, but there is no lingering warmth, no comfort, nothing that makes me feel like I belong or that makes me wish to return here. While my mom fills the place with love with her presence, it only lasts as long as she stands next to me.

The only change this year is having Noel with me. It's like the sun is shining on me, giving me the energy and strength I need to get through this dinner without having to shut myself in completely.

"How do you like the food?" Mom asks Noel.

"It's fantastic," he exclaims. "I am usually not too big on roasted duck, but this is honestly one of the best things I've ever had, Mrs. Randall."

My mom's face lights up with his obvious honest excitement. "Please, call me Maggie, dear."

Noel looks so happy that it warms my heart. "Thank you for being so welcoming, Maggie," he says.

"See, your boyfriend obviously likes me," Mom tells me joyfully. "You need to bring him along more often."

"Maybe I should ask you to visit us and cook for us once in a while," I say, not ready to promise her to visit more often.

"That would be fun," Noel says. "Though I like your cooking too."

"You cook, Aden?" Linda, Kayden's fiancée, asks.

"I am trying to, at least," I tell her.

"Don't be so modest," Noel intervenes. "His cooking kicks ass. Must run in the family."

Linda and Francis' wife exchange a look and burst into laughter. "It doesn't," Linda grins. "Emily and I know from experience. Though from what I've heard, it seems Oliver is doing okay-ish in the kitchen."

"Francis can't cook to save his life," Emily grins.

"But I help," he says.

Emily smiles, kissing his cheek. "You do," she says softly.

"Martin is trying, too," Mom muses.

"Then it's just you who picked up cooking skills?" Noel asks me. It's so obvious he's using this chance to have a subtle dig at my brothers. It's hilarious. "Must be great to be a genius."

"I am not a genius," I chuckle.

"You totally are. The whole package, really." His cheeks flush slightly, as if he only just realizes what he said. "Well, it's true," he mutters more to himself than to anyone else.

Obviously, Mom is head over heels for him. She has always been worried about me never introducing anyone to her, and for barely sharing anything about my life. Now she looks like she is bursting with joy. I guess from her perspective, I can understand how she feels. She must be relieved to see how much Noel seems to like me.

"Wait till you see Mom's dessert," Kayden says. "She went completely overboard this time."

"Of course I did. It's rare that we are all together."

I turn to Noel. "Her desserts are fantastic."

"We used to fight over the last pieces of her cakes all the time," Martin adds. The others discuss this a bit further, while I can't help but fall silent. There is not much I can say about it. He is right, we always fought about dessert, though it was rather them fighting and me not even daring to make a go for it. I never had any chance.

I wonder how life is for siblings who receive love from their older siblings. I get why Martin saw me as a rival, as we were closer in age, but Kayden is ten years older and didn't feel the urge to protect me much either.

Under the table, I can feel Noel's warm hand reaching out and resting on my knee.

Yes, bringing him along was the best idea I've had in a long time. That and deciding to date him.

"Noel is a sweetheart," Mom says to me when Kayden and I help her with the dishes. She sent the others off to do some other tasks. Only refusing help from Noel, Linda and Emily.

"He is," I say.

"It's obvious how much he loves you," Kayden adds.

I stay silent at his words, but when Mom turns to me and smiles, I can't help but return the smile. "You are happy, aren't you?"

"Noel makes me happy," I say honestly. "He brings so much warmth into my life."

"How did you get to know each other?"

I don't mind telling my mother, but I don't want to have all my brothers know so many details about my private life. "Come and visit us," I tell her. "And you will get the whole story."

"Then I will come for sure," she beams. "Do you know when you have the next free weekend?"

"I don't have my schedule with me," I admit. "But I will tell Lynn to give you a call on Monday."

My mom rolls her eyes, but then looks at me, amused. "To think I need to go through a second person to set a date with one of my sons is unbelievable."

"You know how Aden is," Kayden says.

My eyes snap towards him immediately. "What do you mean?"

For a moment, Kayden looks surprised, but then he smiles softly. "You and your phone, dude. You are not made for each other."

I relax slightly. "Ah, right."

"You never have it with you," Mom sighs dramatically.

"Send a letter next time," I tell her.

Mom pouts while Kayden bursts into laughter. "Or a carrier pigeon," he grins.

"I'd also accept a message through Morse code," I add.

"You two are impossible," Mom exclaims. "Grab the dessert, Kayden, and bring it to the table. My God, you boys."

Kayden grins while he follows her back to the dining room. It's only when I follow him that I realize I just joked with him. I didn't notice. Now that I do, I am not sure how to feel about it. Usually, I jump to conclusions and expect the worst immediately, like when Kayden commented on my phone, but for a split second, I forgot to overthink my interaction with him.

Is this how things could be?

Well, technically, I understand that things could be like that, I am just not sure if I truly want it. Suddenly, there is a stitch in my chest. Kayden laughed. He laughed with me, but it's the same laugh he had when he laughed and mocked me for being gay.

Everything Kayden says or does always strains my nerves. Like when he called me in the middle of night, and Noel had stayed over for the first time. He was drunk and begging me to come over, and then complained that I never want to see them. Looking back at the talk now, it wasn't even anything dramatic; I just can't help but see the worst in him.

My gaze almost instinctively goes towards the table, hoping to see Noel there. My anchor. But he doesn't seem to be around.

"Linda, do you know where Noel went off to?"

"Oh," she smiles. "He went outside onto the veranda to catch some fresh air."

"Thank you." Overall, she is a very kind woman. I am not sure how Kayden won someone like her over, though, that might be unfair to think. Linda only knows the person Kayden is today, not the one he was when he was a teen.

Difficult. Everything about this place is exhausting.

"I am going to fetch him for dessert," I tell Mom, before turning around and walking through the living room to the veranda. The door there is leaning open, and I spot Noel standing, his hands on the balustrade, while he looks at the starry sky.

"The night sky here is particularly beautiful."

The voice startles both Noel and me. Noel turns his head, his stance stiffening slightly when he sees Oliver. The latter has two bottles of wine in his hand. He must have fetched them from Mom's storage, a small shed with a heater where she keeps some of her groceries.

"It's beautiful," Noel finally answers.

It might not be noticeable to many people, but I can pick up the strain in his voice. It makes it even more important that he came here for me today, to help me. I'll bet this is an exhausting evening for him.

Shaking my head, I reach out towards the door. I don't want to eavesdrop like a little kid, that is, until Oliver's voice stops my hand.

"You don't like me much, do you?"

Noel shrugs. "I don't know you. Just what Aden told me about you."

"And that's nothing good," Oliver adds.

"Would you?" Noel asks. "Tell nice things about yourself? Would you tell me that you were a great brother who protected his younger sibling?"

Oliver is silent. "Probably not," he admits.

Noel shrugs once more. "There you have it."

"Some bridges are hard to rebuild," he says quietly. "I know that. The others do too, but I don't think they are aware of how big the damage truly is."

"But you are?"

"Yeah, I am."

"It took for your girlfriend to dump you to realize, though," he points out.

Oliver flinches slightly. "I knew it all along, which makes it so much worse. I was a coward. When Lynn left me, it was finally the wake-up call I needed to truly make a change. But I guess it was too late. Or is it?" He looks at Noel like he has all the answers.

Noel pulls his hands away from the balustrade and puts them in his pocket. "I don't know. I am not Aden, so I can't answer that. But you are way too pushy in the wrong way. And believe me, I know a thing or two about being pushy."

"How am I supposed to reconnect with him then?"

"How about doing it his way, or in a way that's not forcing him into doing something he hates?" he offers. "This is ridiculous. You are a functioning adult. You must know that you are just forcing all of this on him, to make him reconcile with you quickly, probably to relieve your conscience. You need to do it for Aden, and not for yourself."

"You are saying I am being selfish."

"I guess I am."

Noel's words make me smile. Yeah, he can be merciless like that.

Oliver snorts. "You are one of a kind. So, what do you suggest?"

"I don't suggest anything. I am obviously on Aden's side and always will be, but, at least don't push him. You keep calling him and pushing him to meet you, while that is nothing he likes to do. Why don't you just start with, I don't know, talk? Through messages or emails."

"He barely answers."

"Yeah, because you always want him to come home or meet one of you. Of course, he doesn't answer. Just ask him how he is or what he is up to. Normal small talk."

"Like strangers," Oliver mutters.

"Yes, like strangers, and go from there."

From the dining room, I can hear voices that seem to approach. Yeah, I should probably make sure I am not caught listening to my boyfriend and brother. Besides, I have eavesdropped way too long anyway.

Taking a couple of short breaths, I step back slightly before approaching the veranda door again. I make some loud walking sounds, opening the door as if I just arrived.

"Oh, Aden," Oliver mutters.

"What are you doing here?" I ask. "Mom is waiting with the dessert."

"Oh fuck, right!" Oliver exclaims. "I am going!"

I nod, waiting for him to leave so that Noel and I can have a moment together. Noel keeps looking at me, his body tensing slightly. "You heard us, didn't you?"

"I am sorry, I was looking for you and couldn't help but listen."

I can see how panic crosses his features. "I overstepped, didn't I?"

For a moment, I can only look at him, scanning his deep eyes, which hold so many emotions, and his lips, which are quivering right now. He is proud, strong, and confident, while also vulnerable and insecure. Yet, he so openly told Oliver his opinion. No one ever did that for me before. "I love you."

"What..." Noel's mouth drops open before his cheeks flush a beautiful pink. "Do you... Do you really mean it?"

"Yes, I love you. I have known for a while, but seeing you stand up for me just made me realize I need to tell you."

"I am so glad you said it! Because I love you too! I mean, obviously, I already said it once." Noel basically jumps into my arms. "And you are not mad that I gave your brother attitude?"

I take his face between my hands, brushing over his cheeks with my thumbs. "Why would I? You were amazing. Thank you for having my back, Noel."

TWENTY-THREE

NOEL

"Okay, you were right, your mom's desserts are amazing." I smack the pillow to soften it up a little before putting it back onto the bed. I am positively surprised that his mom lets us sleep in a room, together. I thought maybe she would hesitate because her son introduced a boyfriend and not a girlfriend.

But she honestly doesn't seem to care about my gender.

"I believe her ability to whip up the perfect cake was how she kept six boys under control," Aden says. "Thomas and Kayden were both on their high school's football team, and Martin did track & field. Actually, they all did sports. They can eat a ton."

"You were the only artist in your family," I analyze. He must have felt so alone here. I can only imagine how his brothers bullied him for not being into sport, like they were.

"Like my dad," he explains. "I was lucky, he really supported me."

"He must have been a great person."

Aden opens his wallet and takes out a picture, showing it to me. It's as if I am looking into Aden's face, just an older version of it. "You really look a lot like him!" I exclaim.

"I hear that a lot."

Aden's expression is fond and sad at the same time. I can't help but wrap my arms around him. While I do know how it feels to lose a parent, I don't know the feeling of losing someone you love. My own father was a deadbeat, at best, and an abusive drug addict, at worst. It's not comparable to Aden losing a loving parent.

"I miss him a lot," Aden admits. He draws back a little to look at me. "I wish you could have met him."

"I do too," I say. "I really like your mom, and I am sure your dad was a great man, too. His son turned out very well after all."

Aden takes my face between his hands like he did before on the veranda. It's such an intimate gesture, one that sends butterflies through my stomach.

"Sorry, I probably ruined the mood, didn't I?" he asks

"The mood for what?" I ask, wiggling my brows. "Did you have any plans?"

Aden looks amused. "I can't say for certain that I did."

Does he mean it? Well, we are at his mom's house, so it would be awkward.

"Of course, I had plans," Aden says. "Don't make it so easy to tease you."

"Is this room soundproofed?"

"Not really," Aden says, leaning forward. His lips are almost touching my ear, sending goosebumps down my arms. "I guess you will need to try to be quiet."

The freak in the sheets makes a return, huh? Oh, I love how he can shift from proper and calm, to I will fuck your brains out, within seconds. But today I have plans too. Putting my hand on his chest, I push him back until his legs hit the bed frame.

My fingers open his belt, pulling it out of its loops, before unbuttoning his pants. Now it's my turn to give back a little. Aden's gaze is pinned on me, his eyes dark, spurring me on even further. "Noel," he says, his fingers driving through my hair. "Undress for me."

The look in his eyes is so intense that it makes a shiver run down my spine. Fuck, even now, when I want to be the one to lead and tease him, it looks like he is in control.

And I am so fucking there for it.

I take off my clothes in record time, before getting down on my knees again. Aden helps me by pushing down his own pants and underwear, then his hand is back on my head. I expect him to grab me and push me forward, but instead his fingers move towards my face and to my lips, forcing them to open. I let my tongue dart out, licking and sucking at his fingers.

"You look so hot when you are doing that," Aden mutters. "I wonder how you will look sucking my dick."

"Even hotter," I dare him.

Aden smirks. His free hand tightens its grip at the back of my head, before he pulls his fingers out of my mouth, replacing it with his dick. I take him all in one go, until he almost hits the back of my throat.

"Fuck!" Aden curses.

Yes! This was the reaction I was hoping for. I press my tongue against the shaft of his dick, keeping my lips sealed tightly around it, while hollowing my cheeks. Aden groans. I let his cock slip out of my mouth before targeting its tip, licking it with the tip of my tongue before using my whole tongue again. Wrapping my lips around his tip again, I take his cock in, moving my head. With each move, I take more of him in my mouth. When I look up at Aden, I can see his eyes pinned to me. The way he looks at me makes my own cock harden so much, I need to fight the urge to touch myself. I was never too keen on giving blow jobs, but fuck, doing it for Aden just feels different.

To distract from my own erection, I move my hand to his balls, squeezing them gently.

"Noel," Aden groans. "I am going to come."

I flash him an innocent gaze that's supposed to say '*And?*'

"If you want me to come inside you tonight, this is the moment to stop," Aden smirks. "Not that I mind coming into your pretty mouth."

I give his dick one last suck, before letting it slip out of my mouth. "I want you inside me."

Aden pulls me up on my feet, keeping me upright when they buckle slightly. Fuck! Being on my knees for a long time really isn't too comfortable. I forget all about it, though, when he smashes his lips against mine. A moment later, I find my back on the bed, with Aden's slick fingers between my ass cheeks, probing my hole before pushing a finger inside me. He hasn't even bothered to take off his sweater, and something about that is just turning me on so much.

I don't need much preparation. We've been sleeping with each other pretty regularly, and I have gotten accustomed to his size. Despite this, I still love it when he angles his fingers and finds my prostate.

"Aden," I moan, gripping some strands of his hair. "I want you inside me! Aden!"

"Quiet," Aden grins. "Or someone will hear us."

"Like I give a fuck now," I groan.

Aden pulls his fingers out of me, grabs my legs, and puts them on his shoulders. Fuck, yeah, I will feel him so deep inside me like that. He enters me in one go, capturing my lips with a kiss before I can scream his name. I grip the bed frame for balance while Aden thrusts into me, doubling me over with every thrust. He is so deep inside me, it makes my head spin, but I just want more.

"More," I beg. "Aden, harder!"

"Damn it," Aden curses. "Oliver will have to get over it."

With that, he gives in to my demands, thrusting into me fast, making it impossible for me to keep my moans quiet. When Aden wraps his hand around my cock, brushing his thumb over my tip, I can't help but tremble. My walls around his cock clench up, making him groan. "You are so unbelievably hot, Noel. I love you."

No one has ever said that to me before him. Hearing it in bed hits differently, though. It makes my walls break down. Letting go of the bedrest, I cling to Aden instead. "I am coming," I moan.

"Good," he mutters, moving his lips to my collarbone and sucking at it.

I feel my body tensing up, and my toes curl while my body finds its release. I try not to make too much noise, boring my nails into Aden's shoulder instead and biting down on my lips. My body still shivers when I feel Aden's hot seed fill me up.

I have never had a guy come inside me, and feeling how Aden's hot seed fills me up... just hits differently. It's like he is marking me as his completely.

We lay there, both panting, before Aden kisses my forehead and gently pulls out of me. He cups my cheek with his hand. "That was amazing."

"We are always amazing," I mutter.

"We are quite compatible, it seems." He smiles. "Wait here, I will clean you up."

I am relieved I don't have to wobble through the corridor to the bathroom and instead have him deal with everything. Aden is only gone for a couple of minutes. When he returns, he is wearing a bathrobe and holds a wet washcloth. I close my eyes, letting him clean me up the way he wants. Something about this makes me feel so warm and loved.

For a while, I just doze off in Aden's arms afterwards. Something he said before still lingers with me, about how compatible we are. I turn my head, pressing my cheek against his chest. "Isn't it funny how well we click?"

"Like I said, we definitely are compatible," Aden says.

"Aren't you surprised about that?"

"I don't know," he muses. "When I met you for the first time, on our first date, when you had me come to your awful bar—"

I scrunch my nose. "Sorry for that."

"Don't worry. I didn't mention it for you to apologize, but I feel as if that evening I got to know some important parts of you. We might not be similar to each other, but our personalities don't clash either."

"You think we complement each other?"

"I guess that's what I am getting at. I don't think I would have clicked that well with someone who had been the complete opposite of me. And I definitely wouldn't want to be with someone who would be exactly like me either."

I think his words through and he is right. At first glance, we might not share a lot, but essentially, there are a lot of connections we have. Similar values, similar dreams, similar expectations. From the outside, Aden looks like a typical CEO, but inside, he has never stopped being an artist. I don't think I would have fallen for an actual businessman.

Thinking about his job makes my thoughts run to my own problems. "Aden?"

"Yes."

"After our talk in the car today, I have decided to get a new job," I tell him. "Now that you set me up with that lawyer, I feel like it's time to take back control of my life. I was thinking about asking DeeDee for help."

His face lights up. "That's a fantastic idea."

"You really think so?"

"Yes, go and take back your life in whatever way you want to!"

"I guess I will." I turn onto my back. "Say, do we have any plans for this week?"

"I'll have a rather calm week," Aden says. "And was thinking about decluttering my attic. It's something I have postponed for years. It's time to let go."

I eye him curiously, wondering what exactly he is talking about. It certainly sounds like it's something positive, but I don't want to stir old wounds too much. So, instead of asking him, I decide to wait for him to come to me when he is ready to talk. "I can help," I offer instead.

To my surprise, Aden's eyes light up at my suggestion. "That would be great! I was thinking about asking Lynn for help, too. But with you around, I am probably more motivated to do it."

"Then it's set! When do you plan on doing it?"

"Thursday and Friday evening."

"Good, I will make that work."

TWENTY-FOUR

NOEL

"Don't you worry." Mr. Pierce, the lawyer Aden recommends, shaking my hand. He is an older man, serious and dignified, looking exactly like I would have envisioned a seasoned lawyer. "We'll have this dealt with in no time."

"Really? I thought it would take months or maybe even a year, or more," I admit.

Mr. Pierce nods thoughtfully. "Normally, it does, mainly because such a case doesn't have a high priority, but I am pushing for it to happen. I have already sent the first letters out. Your mother should have been informed also. At the end of the week, I will have an appointment at court."

"Do you need me to come?"

"No, it's just the lawyers and a judge," he says. "You are not suing anyone, and you don't need to be there as a witness. I am your representative."

"What if my mother decides to sue?"

"We'll see if she truly does it. She'll need money for it. Does she have money?"

I shake my head. "She is an alcoholic. She is barely making it."

Mr. Pierce looks at me warmly. "She doesn't have a case. You can rest assured about this. I will get you out of this."

I feel relieved at his calm confidence. "Thank you."

It strikes me once again that without Aden's help, this wouldn't have been possible. Or maybe it would have, with a pro bono lawyer or someone who costs less. Maybe I could have achieved this with Mateo's and Sterling's help, but I never found the courage.

Maybe that was the real problem.

I wasn't ready to face my mother.

I know, however, that it's only thanks to Aden that I am able to deal with this issue so quickly. It was something that was like a sword of Damocles hanging over me, a constant threat, a constant sorrow that made me almost give up myself and all my dreams for the future.

Part of me believed I deserved it for all the bad things I did as a teen. But now, I just want to break free.

All pumped and ready to tackle my life, I decide to meet DeeDee next and talk about a job. I take Mateo with me for emotional backup and meet him at DeeDee's favorite Italian restaurant. As usual, DeeDee is late, so Mateo and I sit down and order something to drink.

"Thank you, Mateo, I know you are probably busy."

"What are you talking about? Never too busy for one of my friends." He pats my head. "Sterlone wanted to come too, but he has to finish a painting."

"Right!" I beam. "Aden mentioned there will be a new exhibition in a couple of weeks."

"It's a big thing," Mateo says. "Aden wants Sterling to show a couple of his drawings this time around, and be there on the day of the exhibit, to talk to potential customers and explain his art. This is a huge chance."

"He'd better work his ass off," I say, my heart taking a leap of joy. "Things are really looking up for all of us, huh?"

"Looks like it," Mateo grins. "For the first time ever."

"How are things going with Lynn?"

"She is so cool." He beams. "We are going slow and haven't put a label on us yet, but there is no way I will just let her go, now that I know how fucking awesome she is."

He must have totally clicked with her. "I am happy for you," I say. "You deserve it. And from what I have heard, Lynn deserves it too."

Aden hinted to me that Lynn was disappointed by the men she dated. She is a powerhouse, strong, capable, and wealthy. However, I know that Mateo won't give a shit about any of that. He is just not an insecure person, not about that at least. Instead, he would be proud of her and what she accomplished.

"And you are truly ready to finally quit those shitty jobs of yours?" Mateo interrupts my train of thought.

"Yes, I am ready."

"Finally," Mateo exclaims, "you are seeing reason!"

"You make it sound like I am utterly unreasonable."

"You are stubborn," Mateo says. "You wouldn't even accept Sterling and my help whenever we offered. I am just glad that Aden got through to you."

I allow his words to sink in. My first instinct is to lash out at him for suggesting I needed Aden to get my ass up, but the more reasonable part inside me knows that Mateo and Sterling have just been concerned… for ages. "I wasn't ready, Mateo," I admit. "It wasn't so much that it was you and Ster offering help, and me being overly prideful. It's... I wasn't ready to let go of the guilt." I pause. "Aden made me realize that I deserve more from life and that it's okay to be selfish and reclaim my life. I probably worried you both a lot, and I am sorry."

"Don't apologize," he mutters, looking flustered. "We are best friends. Obviously, we'll have your back whenever you need it. We would have continued pushing you for as long as you needed it. You are a good guy, Noel. You are allowed to be happy."

You are allowed to be happy.

Can I honestly allow myself to be happy?

"One step at a time," Mateo says as if he just read my thoughts. "We are starting with quitting your job."

"I could not believe it when I heard it!" I hear DeeDee's voice right behind me. She pats Mateo's shoulder before pulling me into a hug and smooching the top of my head. When she lets go, she tosses three folders towards me. "These are all friends," she tells me. "One is a bar that shows live bands, one is another drag queen bar, and the third is just a normal bar, but a small fancy one. All of them are hiring."

I feel my chest squeeze slightly. It's getting real. And somehow, the thought is terrifying me. What if I fail? What if, despite all the help I am getting, I won't be able to deliver? I will disappoint them all.

You are such a failure.

Disappointment...

...useless...

"Sebastian, the owner of the fancy bar, would hire you in a heartbeat," DeeDee blabs. "He came with me once, to that shady shithole you work at currently, and saw you working. Said with your skills and looks, you belong somewhere else."

Her words chase my oncoming anxiety attack away, at least momentarily so. "Really?"

"Yes, he wants to see you as soon as you can. As for the other two, they are both interested and are hiring."

"Why don't you give Sebastian a call right now?" Mateo says.

"What, now?"

"Sure, why not?"

He looks at me with a smile that seems like he just made a spontaneous suggestion. But I know him too well to buy it, or rather, I know that he knows me too well. He is well aware I am about to chicken out.

"Mateo is right," DeeDee muses. "Sebastian hasn't opened the bar yet, but he'll be in the office."

I want to chicken out, I honestly want to. I just want to grab my things and run.

Run... run... run...

Are you going to run from me again?

I don't know why I think of Aden all of a sudden. He is not part of this conversation. I wouldn't even be running from him if I jumped up and left now, but somehow his words are ringing in my ears. Are you going to run from me?

How long do I want to run?

"Go get them!" Mateo exclaims in relief when I type Sebastian's number into my phone and dial it.

I called all three of them. The drag queen bar, unfortunately, had already hired someone today, but the other two both wanted to see me as soon as possible. With my newfound courage, I decide to tackle this immediately.

The bar with the live music looks amazing. It's quite big and clearly made for holding smaller concerts. It's busy with lots of young people visiting. The team look nice, and the owner is part of the whole concert scene.

As for the fancy bar, which DeeDee's friend Sebastian owns, it is nothing like I expected. It's a small place, very high-end. The customers mainly range from thirty years upwards. They serve all kinds of drinks, but mostly the typical classics. On top of that, the bar is also LGBTQ friendly, and very openly so.

"We have patrons who have been coming here for years," Sebastian tells me. "The location helps, as we are very close to two business districts. After work hours on weekdays can be busier than actual weekends."

"I can cope well with that," I reassure him.

"I figured. I saw where you worked," he says.

"I know it wasn't a particularly good place," I tell him. "But I have gained plenty of experience there, especially with stressful situations."

"DeeDee recommended you," he says. "And I know she doesn't recommend just anyone as trustworthy. Would you mind telling me a bit about yourself?"

I do mind, actually, but I also understand why he wants to know more about me. He is about to hire someone with a shady background after all. I could hide it, I guess, but at the same time I don't want my past, or rather my family's past, coming back and biting me in the ass later, so I don't hold back. I tell him about my parents' debt and how I struggled because of it, but how I am trying to reclaim my life.

"I know this is all a bit problematic," I tell him. "And I understand this is a high-end bar. I won't lie, my mother still is a problem. But I have strategies to handle her. However, I understand how I would be too risky for you to hire."

Sebastian looks at me, before an amused smile stretches his lips. "Yeah, I can see it." When I look at him, confused, he just chuckles. "Why DeeDee likes you so much." He pauses. "Yes, it is a risk," he finally says. "It's always a risk to hire someone like you, but it also comes with the advantage of knowing you will be able to handle a tough crowd, on the rare occasion things get rough. You probably know the signs of someone getting too drunk, and can step in, and you probably know how to kick someone out of a bar if they misbehave."

"Yes," I admit, feeling a bit flustered. "I am not so sure if all of this is good to know, but I do."

"We have a bouncer," he tells me. "So, your mother certainly won't be a problem to my place. As for you, I trust you to handle her yourself." He pauses. "Thank you for your honesty. Not many people are."

I guess I at least get some points for this.

"You can mix the usual cocktails?" he continues to ask.

"Yes. I can mix all the classics and some more."

"How come? From your previous job?"

"Partly. They served the usual drinks. But I like mixing cocktails, and I usually practice a lot at home."

"What about wine?"

"I am not a connoisseur," I tell him. "But I know more than just the basics about wine, and I usually know what to recommend if someone asks."

"If I sent you to an actual course to become a sommelier, would you be willing to do that?"

"I would love to," I admit, trying not to sound too excited. A job that gives me the possibility to educate myself a bit more just sounds awesome.

"What about preparing some edibles? Are you able to whip up some smaller snacks?"

"I didn't need to do that in the bar I worked at," I tell him honestly. "But at the club, we sometimes offered food options. I am a fast learner as well."

Sebastian smiles. He looks like he is in his fifties. A quiet, composed gentleman who looks exactly like I'd have imagined an owner of such a bar.

"I am looking for a full-time worker," he tells me. "The bar is getting too big for me to handle alone, and I'd need someone to help me with the paperwork, too. I only have two part-time bartenders coming in, but they only work a couple of hours a week, and it's just not enough."

My mouth almost drops open. A full-time employment?

"Would this be something you can see yourself doing?"

"Absolutely," I say, sudden excitement filling me. I would have never applied to a job in such a bar if it weren't for DeeDee. I just never saw myself in such a fancy place.

"We also have some artists frequenting us," he explains. "Would you be able to hold a conversation with them?"

My eyes light up at that. "My best friend is an artist," I tell him. "And my boyfriend, too. I am also pretty used to chatting about just anything from my previous job."

Sebastian doesn't seem to mind me mentioning that I am gay, he even nods contentedly. "I am not going to lie, Noel. You are pretty young. For the office work, I'd have preferred someone with more experience, but I need a young co-worker to mingle well with the younger crowd. You look like you would be able to get along with some of our patrons." He eyes me thoughtfully. "Would you mind working an hour or two just to see how you hold up?"

"Absolutely! I would love to give it a shot."

"When would you be free to do so?"

"I can take over a shift today," I tell him. "That is, if you even need anyone today."

He raises his brows. "Actually, today would be perfect. It's going to be a busy evening. Are you sure this is not going to be too much for you?"

I feel like this is the moment I need to be bold and confident, so I just nod. "I am sure."

He is going to test me to see how I cope. Hah, I am used to sleazy guys trying to grope my ass. I am pretty sure I can handle any crowd. I give Aden a brief call to tell him I am going to be home later, before letting Sebastian show me around and tell me the basics. I won't need to do anything difficult tonight. Just mix some of the more basic drinks and get orders.

He was right when he said it would be busy. The longer the evening goes on, the more patrons drop by, but as he said, the crowd is well-behaved and overall quieter. They are here to unwind from a long day at work, not to party, though I can see some subtle flirting here and there too. I have never been shy, so improvising and making small talk come easily to me in such situations. Maybe a couple of months ago, I would have still been insecure to actually take it up with this rather elegant crowd, but it seems like being with Aden has prepared me for such a task. One of the regulars is even an art collector, and I manage to strike up a conversation with him about an exhibition he is going to visit soon.

At the end of the shift, I know I aced it. And I also know that I love the place. It's not the loud, buzzing place I originally wanted to work at when I decided to search for a new job. It's more quiet, but I enjoy that it's not as loud as I am used to.

And the prospect of being able to actually learn more about this craft just makes it even better.

Sebastian shows me how to do the paperwork at the end of my shift and how to lock everything up. "Everything else can wait for later," he tells me. "I will properly show you everything once you start working here, especially the office work. I won't leave you all on your own at the beginning, don't worry. As for the sommelier course, I want you to work for two to three months first, but will sign you up for one then." A smile lights up his face. "Well, Noel, I had high expectations, but you just exceeded them. If you want to, you can start here on Monday. I know you are a young man, I sincerely hope you don't find this place too boring, because as for me, I can see you working here."

Something in my chest almost explodes with joy. This is the first actual job I am going to do, which I truly want. Sure, I never dreamed of becoming a bartender, but I quite liked the work even in the shady bar. But my previous work was just a means to an end, to pay off a debt that wasn't mine.

But today, I am actually able to choose.

And I want to work here!

"Not boring at all," I profess. "I had so much fun today."

Sebastian looks amused again. "Your excitement is contagious. You are really made for this type of job. So, is that a yes?"

"I would love to work here. I would just like to go through the contract first," I say. "Thank you so much, Mr—"

"Sebastian," he interrupts me before I can address him formally. "Let's stick with our first names."

"Thank you, Sebastian." I shake his hand. "I won't disappoint you."

TWENTY-FIVE

NOEL

I just can't believe it. I can't fucking believe it. I went through the details of my contract with Sebastian. To my relief, DeeDee actually joined us–I have an inkling that she and Sebastian might be more than just friends, but hey, I am not one to pry. I am just glad she is there to keep an eye on me for setting up my work contract.

Sebastian signs it and hands it to me. "Take it home with you," he says. "I am sure you want to give it a second glance."

"Thank you, yes, I want to look through it properly," I answer honestly.

"If you are content with it, bring it along on Monday. If not, give me a call at the weekend so we can discuss it in more detail. I know this is all on a tight schedule."

"That's fine," I reassure him. "I will write you a message on Saturday either way."

"That's even better." Sebastian laughs. "Then I hope to see you on Monday."

With that, I leave the place, almost skipping along. I decide to get all the necessary things done first, namely, quitting my other two jobs. The downside of working at such sleazy jobs is that basically, my rights as an employee are not exactly covered. It means I can get kicked out anytime. The plus side is that I can also quit anytime.

The club owner doesn't even give a shit about me quitting, but the owner of the bar isn't too happy, much to my surprise.

Once done, I make my way to Aden's place, finally giving him a call. "Aden!" I almost yell into the phone with joy when he picks up. "I have a job! I got the job in that bar."

"The one DeeDee recommended?" he asks.

"Yes!"

"Congratulations, Noel! That's a really good place! I go there sometimes too." I can almost hear the smirk in his voice. "I will make sure to frequent it more often from now on, to see my hot boyfriend at work."

"To your service," I chuckle. "Can I still drop by your place now?"

"I told you, you can come whenever you want. That's what I gave you the key for. No need to ask beforehand."

His faith in me makes it hard to breathe for a moment. When did someone ever...

"Then I'll come."

"Do you need me to pick you up somewhere?"

"No, I should be fine."

"If you change your mind, call me," he says.

"Thanks." I pause. "Say, would you look through my contract with me? DeeDee was there when the owner set it up, but I want someone with experience to look at it."

“Of course. We can look at it together later.”

“Isn’t it too late?”

“We are both free tomorrow,” he says in his usual calm manner. “I can take a look at your contract, send it to Lynn and then fuck you senseless.”

I should be used to the way he can be crude at times, but fuck, he gets me every time. “I can’t believe you still manage to surprise me with what you say!”

“You are surprised I’d help you with your contract?”

“No”—I glance around to check if anyone is following me. The last thing I need is to have someone listen in now—“I meant the other part.”

“Oh, you meant that I want to look at the contract before I fuck you? We can reverse the order of events, if you prefer that.”

I frown. “You are totally making fun of me now, aren’t you?”

He chuckles. “Do you want to know how I’d like to do you tonight?”

The smart thing would be to tell him to surprise me at home, but I was never known to be smart, so fuck it. “How?”

“I want you naked the moment you step through the front door. I want to bend you over the dining table with your eyes right on the painting of you. I don’t have a mirror big enough, yet, but I want to fuck you while you look at yourself.”

“A mirror...” I mutter.

“Just imagine you could see how I enter you from behind,” he continues. “The face you’d make, your pretty mouth open and gasping for air.”

I wonder what kind of expression he would make then.

“I hate you!” I huff.

“Why, are you getting hard for me already?”

"Yes, you asshole!"

"Ah, that potty mouth of yours. I expect you to put it to good use later," Aden chuckles. "Then hurry home, and don't let your boyfriend wait any longer."

I glare at my phone, not sure if I want to run to Aden's place to strangle him or run there to jump his bones. For a moment, I imagine how he would bend me over the table and fuck me. Well, jump his bones, it is. It will probably prove to be more fun than sulking.

Still, I need to find a way to pay him back. He definitely made sure to rile me up and give me that boner on purpose.

Fortunately, Ster pulls me out of my predicament by calling to ask me about the new job. It's way past midnight already, but it's Ster, and I am used to him calling during ungodly hours. The guy tends to get lost in his art at times. I don't think he always notices how late it actually is, once he is done with his work and ready to interact with friends and family. The only exception is Roxana.

There was a time when I used to be annoyed by how much of an airhead he could be.

But we all have our shortcomings. Ster is always truly interested in what the people close to him are doing and how they feel, and that's more important than being upset at being called at 1 a.m.

Besides, it's exactly the distraction I need to forget about what Aden just promised me.

"Mateo told me everything," Ster says instead of a hello. "I am happy for you, Noel."

"Eh, Mateo doesn't know I got the job. I was on my first shift to see how I'd cope," I tell him. "Then I quit at my other two places and called Aden."

"I knew you would get the job," Ster says simply. "No need to verify it."

"You are such a weirdo," I exclaim. "Why would you think that?"

"Because you are better than you give yourself credit for," he says. "Of course, they would want you. I bet the other bar you introduced yourself to today will want to hire you, too. You are extremely quick on the uptake, like to work at late hours, are a diligent worker, extroverted, and good at risk assessment and management," he says. "Plus, you are a handsome guy. You are a bar owner's wet dream."

"Way to make that sound weird."

"But it's true."

"Really?" I ask. "I never saw it like that."

"Yeah, I know, Mateo knows too," Ster says. "I am glad you are finally starting to see your own worth. And reclaiming your life, getting rid of that debt and all that."

"Took me a while," I mutter.

"I get why," Ster says quietly. "I get it, Noel. It's hard enough to let go of toxic friends, but family is a whole different issue. You don't need to be embarrassed or ashamed," he adds. "And you don't need to feel guilty."

I swallow thickly. Sterling is not one for big words, and he usually doesn't talk much at all, but when he says something, I always know he means it.

"I am terrified," I admit.

"I know," he says. "But you are still doing it and taking charge of your life. You are doing all of it despite your anxiety. That's the only way you will be able to do things: accept your anxiety as what it is, and take the challenges of life despite that. Like you did when you entered a relationship with Aden. You are much stronger than you believe you are."

"Aden said the same."

"Aden is an incredibly smart man," Ster says. "But that's not all there is to him. He sees the world in a unique way, through a lens only he owns."

"Like you do," I say with a smile. "At heart, he is and will always be an artist."

Ster chuckles. "Yeah, we are a special species."

"I am just scared the other shoe will drop eventually," I say.

"Things can't remain perfect," Ster says. "The other shoe will always drop eventually. You just need to figure out what you will do once it happens and how to deal with it. That's how life is. It's an up and down, and there are things you can't influence, so the more important it is to take charge of the things you *can* influence."

"Now you almost sounded like a fortune cookie," I mutter.

"Whatever. You know I am right."

"I guess you are."

"Now, go and meet your boyfriend," Ster says. "You were on the way to meet him anyway."

Not just *meet* him. I grin to myself when I hang up the phone. Who am I even kidding? I just love Aden's attention and his desire for me. It's obviously not my style to play hard to get. The moment I am home I want to ride his dick, or better yet, have him fulfil his promise.

The subway brings me close to Aden's place, but usually I'd need to take the bus for the last couple of stops. Obviously, it was impossible to catch the last one. It's way too late already. I could bother Aden with picking me up, but tonight I actually enjoy the walk. Maybe, once everything is settled with my debt, I will buy myself a small, used car, or maybe a bike.

I don't know yet.

Behind me, I hear some rustling, almost like footsteps. Turning around, I just look into the darkness of the night. Is someone following me? Not too far in the distance, I spot a group of young students, chatting and laughing with each other. Well, I am not alone.

And this is not the type of area where creepy people hang around.

I decide to pick up my pace, though. Better safe than sorry. The small fence around Aden's townhouse is already in sight. I can see the lights in the living room on, my heart taking a leap of joy to imagine that I have so much good news to share.

There is rustling behind me again, and footsteps, making me freeze. I don't believe it's a coincidence anymore–I am definitely being followed.

I turn around, studying the empty street. "Is someone there?"

Something moves in the shadow of some trees, before I can finally see a person step forward.

"No way," I mutter. "It can't be! How?"

My mother takes a few steps forward, her eyes narrowed, her expression grim. "I finally found you."

TWENTY-SIX

NOEL

I can't fucking believe she found me! How did she do it? It's impossible for her to track my phone, but she does know parts of my life. She knows I am friends with Mateo and Sterling. Maybe she stalked one of them.

The fuck, I don't know how she did it. I just know she is here now, and I don't want her to see me, or worse, see Aden.

Or even worse: Talk to him.

I told him a bit about my family, but it's always different to see the craziness in person. Aden means the world to me, and imagining him turning away from me because of the mess that is my family makes my stomach churn.

"What do you want?" I ask.

And why did she not announce her presence earlier? Was she waiting to see which house I'd be going into?

Mom staggers towards me, wavering, but it doesn't seem like she is completely shit-faced drunk. I want to turn around and run, but I have no idea where to, and I don't want to lead her to Aden's place.

Well, technically, we are right in front of it, but she doesn't need to know that.

My indecisiveness gives her the opening she needs, though.

"You," she screeches, grabbing me by my collar and shaking me. "How could you?"

Every time I am face to face with her, I just freeze. I want to believe that I am a fairly confident person, but when it's her, I turn back into my terrified, 7-year-old self.

"It's not my debt to pay," she screeches.

Her words rattle me awake. She must have received my lawyer's letter. "It is," I say, trying to keep my voice down. I am sure we've already alerted the neighborhood, no need to yell even more and have them call the police. "It *is* your debt! You cheated the system and put it on me instead, your child!"

"I should never have had you," she spits. "You and your useless father ruined me! You owe me that much!"

I take a shaky breath, trying to remember what I am fighting for, and that I can finally be free of my past. "I don't," I say. "I didn't ask to be born. You brought me into this world, and you and Dad fucked me over."

"Give me the money," she yells. "Pay the fucking debt!"

I take another breath, gathering all the backbone and strength I have. "No," I say.

She lets go of my collar, her eyes narrowed to slits. Before I can even fathom what's going to happen, she has slapped me so hard that my head whips to my side and I stumble backward. Fuck, that hurt. I can taste iron on my lips and a sharp pain on my cheek. She must have scratched me with her fingernails when she hit me. It's been a while since she lashed out at me like that. I am not used to it anymore.

"You ruined everything," she hisses. "You useless—" She raises her hand again, ready to strike. My mind screams at me to stop her, to fight back, or to at least run, but my legs don't move, my whole body seems to be completely frozen, and my mind seems to wander off like it always did when my parents beat me. But to my utmost surprise, the impact doesn't come.

"Let me go," my mom snarls.

My eyes finally focus back on what's happening around me, my gaze landing on my mother. Someone grabbed her wrist before she could hit me.

Aden?

I only know Aden as kind, maybe a bit too serious sometimes, thoughtful, and incredibly hot in bed. Now, he looks so cold I feel like I am going to freeze. "You have some nerve," he says to my mother, his voice low and dark. "To assault someone I care for."

"What do you know?" she snarls. "He is my flesh and blood, yet betrays me. He always did."

Aden's eyes are dark when he pins his gaze on my mother. "You have been scamming your own son for years. Take accountability!"

"He owes me for being born," she snarls. "He—"

"He owes you nothing!" Aden interrupts her. "Take responsibility for your own actions and pay your debt like you should have done to begin with."

"You don't know what he did," Mom hisses. "The things he did. He is not as perfect as he looks. Looks like an angel." She looks at me with so much venom, I feel the remainder of my heart break a little. "But he isn't. He stole, he betrayed others, he—"

My heart sinks. She is right. I did all that. It doesn't matter why I did it; the fact is, I did. I never wanted Aden to find out, at least not like that. I don't care for anyone else's opinion, literally everyone can judge me, but if Aden started hating me, it would fucking break me.

Aden lets go of my mother and puts a hand on my arm, pulling me to his side. "I don't care what he did to survive," he says, furrowing his brows. "How old was he when he started to steal, as you call it?" he asks. "Sixteen, seventeen?"

"Fourteen," I mutter quietly.

"And what did he steal?" Aden inquires further. "And why?"

When Mom stays quiet, Aden just nods grimly. "Your fourteen-year-old son was forced to steal to survive," he snarls. "Or worse, you made him do it. Are you not ashamed?"

"So, he got himself a rich guy, huh? But still can't spare his mother a penny. What is in it for you?" she snarls. "You know a guy like him is no good!"

"Love is in it for me," Aden answers. "A person who loves me with all my quirks. Someone genuine and kind. And he became that way despite his upbringing and his parents. Noel makes me laugh. He healed a part of me I didn't know needed healing. That's more than anyone else has given me, ever! I will be damned if I let him go!"

Before Mom can say anything, Aden shuts her up. "I need to ask you to leave Noel alone," he says, his voice icy. "If you strike him again, I will call the police. If you ever come close to him again, you will face a fucking lawsuit. This time from me, directly! And believe me when I say, you won't want to take it up with me!"

Mom keeps glaring at him, but when he takes his phone into his hands, something close to fear crosses her face. Finally, she turns around and runs off into the darkness of the night.

"I am so sorry," I mutter. "I... have had no contact with her for years. I don't know how she found me, and I almost led her to you. This is such a mess. My life is a mess. I can understand if this is too much for you."

Aden rests his hand against my cheek. His palm is cool from the outside air, yet so soft, making me burst into tears. "This is not your fault, Noel, and I am not going anywhere."

"Is it bad that I still love her? I hate her, but I also love her. I want her to see me, and hug me, and love me, but I know she won't."

"Oh, Noel," Aden says sadly. He wraps his free arm around me, pulling me close. I can't believe I have a full-grown meltdown in front of him; that's a new level of embarrassment. But somehow, I can't stop the tears from flowing.

Aden doesn't tell me to calm down, he doesn't say any fake reassurances about how everything will be alright. I know it will never be alright. Mom is Mom, and nothing will change that. And if she changes, it certainly won't be in the near future

"Thank you," I mutter against Aden's chest when I feel more like myself again. "I can't believe I cried on you."

"I am glad you did," he says. "I am your partner. I should be there when you feel down."

"I should have told you," I admit. "About my mom. I should have... I am so sorry you had to find out like that."

"I told you, you can tell me about your past on your terms, at your pace," Aden says quietly. "I am not mad, Noel. When you told me about your family and mentioned doing shady shit in the past, I took a wild guess that this is what you were hinting at. You did what you had to do to survive, and you did survive." He pauses. "Also, I remember, now, where we met for the very first time."

At his words, my eyes snap up. It feels like all the air leaves my lungs.

"No need to panic," Aden says quietly. "I am glad I remember. Let's go back inside. You are freezing and in shock."

"You remember?" I mutter my question while I take off my shoes and jacket. It's only when I follow Aden into the living room that I notice how cold I truly was. The sudden warmth makes me shiver as the cold leaves my body.

"First things first," Aden says, stepping closer to me. He cups my chin, tilting my head to the side a little. His eyebrows twitch slightly.

"It's okay," I hurry to reassure him. "It's..."

"It's not okay," he huffs. "I should have called the police after all."

"I prefer you didn't."

"I know," he says. "Which is why I didn't do it. But the next time she pulls up and even looks at you the wrong way, I won't let her get away. Her fingernails left marks on you. Let me patch you up." He ushers me further into the living room, to his sofa. "Sit down."

My mind is in a haze. I barely register what Aden is doing, and I can't help but replay the encounter with my mother, over and over again. Eventually, I realize that Aden has put a cup with hot tea in front of me and some sandwiches. He has also put a patch over the scratches my mom left on me, and he is on the phone talking to someone.

I didn't notice him doing any of that.

"Who was that?" I mutter.

"Your lawyer," Aden says. "I informed him of what happened. It will certainly help your case.

I nod. He is right. I didn't even think of telling my lawyer any of it. It hadn't crossed my mind at all.

"Hey." Aden touches my back. "Are you back with me?"

"I completely detached and dissociated, like back in the days when my father would come at me after he drank too much." It's still hard for me to grasp when I dissociate. It's like I am taking a backseat while my body acts on autopilot. "I haven't done that in a long while."

When Aden opens his arms, I snuggle into them. "It was due to the shock," he says quietly.

"Do you really remember how we met the first time?"

"The grocery store," he says.

"You really helped me back then," I admit. "I was so hungry. Dad had just overdosed, and Mom didn't give a flying fuck, and I was so hungry."

"You don't need to explain yourself," Aden says. "You did what you had to do to survive."

"You could have called the police back then, but you didn't."

"You know, I saw this young guy with a can of macaroni in his hand, and I just couldn't look away," he says after a while. "I just couldn't."

He saw me shoplifting that time, and instead of calling the police, he not only bought me the can of macaroni, he added a whole bag of groceries to it and handed me enough money to get through the next couple of nights. He even handed me an address for a shelter.

"You saved me, and it was my turning point. I stopped running away, and I guess I started to turn my life around." I look at him. "I know for you it wasn't big—"

"It was," he says, to my surprise. "It was my turning point, too. I didn't remember it was *you*, but I never forgot that years ago, I met this young guy who pulled me out of my depression. I was at my lowest back then, but just looking at you and hearing you thank me, so genuinely, really pulled me out of my slump."

"Really?"

"Yes, really."

I wait for him in case he wants to tell me more, but he stays silent. I guess he isn't quite so ready to share everything yet. Not so long ago, that would have made me insecure, but now I don't mind. He doesn't need to tell me everything immediately. I know he will eventually.

"What did you do afterwards?" Aden asks.

"I went to the address you gave me, the homeless shelter for young men. They helped me stay safe, and I got a job," I say. "I cleaned toilets first, then eventually got a job at a fast-food chain. I even finished school. I wanted to study too, but I just... You know, my dad's debt kept looming over me."

"You achieved a lot," Aden points out. "You need to be much prouder of how you turned your life around than you are, Noel. You had zero support at that time. Mateo and Sterling weren't in your life then, but you pulled yourself out of the pit. You are leading a successful life now."

"Well, I had a kind stranger reach out a hand to me, when I needed it the most," I say. "Sometimes that's all a person needs."

"I usually don't believe in fate," Aden brushes his fingers through my hair. "But this is almost too much to be a coincidence."

"You have a point," I admit. I never believed in fate either, because if I did, it would have made my situation even worse. But now, with Aden, it feels like it was worth the struggle. "Is it weird?" I ask.

Aden keeps brushing through my hair softly. "What's weird?"

"If we both hadn't been at our lowest, we might have never met. Maybe we would be entirely different people today. So, in a way, I am glad life brought me to you, as much as I hated the steps I had to take to meet you again." I pause. "Is it weird to think that way?"

"Not at all," Aden says. "I think the same."

Chapter 27

NOEL

I feel drowsy when I wake up, noticing that I am in Aden's bed. I have no idea how he managed to drag me up there, but apparently, Aden can just do anything. One look at my watch tells me it's 10 a.m. already–insanely late for me!

Aden is not in bed anymore either, but I take the hint of the smell of coffee coming through. Well, no time to waste!

Jumping out of the bed, I rummage through the half of the wardrobe Aden emptied for me to keep my stuff in. I don't want to wear any of my clothes, though, so I grab one of Aden's sweaters and a pair of boxers, and head to the bathroom. My face doesn't look as bad as I thought it would, or maybe it's just because Aden nursed me so well. There are only two ugly scratches from my mom, and some light bruising. Nothing makeup can't hide.

Ten minutes later, I am walking down the stairs, ready to tackle the day.

Last night was a disaster, but it does not detract from all the things I achieved beforehand. The altercation with Mom may have been unavoidable, so better to have it over and done with now, than waiting for it to happen.

"Aden!" I call out, and before he can turn around, I wrap my arms around him from behind. My man is standing in the kitchen, making breakfast for me again. "You are spoiling me."

"Well, you put up with quite a lot concerning me and my work, I feel like giving something back," he says.

"You feel like giving something back?" I blurt out. "After I am the one bringing all the drama to you?"

He touches my hand softly. "You did not bring all the drama into this relationship. Actually, I think you have dealt with some drama that wasn't yours. Remember my family and my brothers?"

"That's something else."

"Why?"

"Because your family isn't a drug-addicted alcoholic who assaults you and wishes you dead."

"Maybe," Aden says. "But it still eats at me, and you didn't even need a moment to consider. You just came with me and had my back. To me, it's not different just because our family drama differs." He pauses. "Are you feeling a bit better, Noel?"

"I do," I pause before I can finish the sentence. "I... I don't," I finally admit. "But not just because of yesterday. I think it will take a while to truly understand and accept what happened to me, and even more time to let go of it."

Aden turns around, taking my face between his hands. He doesn't say anything before he places a soft kiss against my forehead. "It takes a lot of strength to admit to needing some time to deal with a trauma, or to deal with it at all."

"I realized that I do have people I love in my life. Like you, Ster and Mateo."

"You are not alone," Aden verifies.

"I am not alone," I repeat. "I have my own chosen family."

"Do you want to move in with me?" Aden asks, surprising me with the boldness of his question.

"Like, completely?"

"Yes. We talked briefly about it, as in you can stay over as long as you want, but as for me, I'd love to have you here with me all the time."

My heart beats a little faster at his suggestion. Having this every day? Seeing him even on days he is busy at work, and always coming home from the bar to a warm bed?

I would love that, but I am also terrified of giving up more of my independence.

I know it's not like that. It's not quite my independence I am losing, because I still have a job and friends, but it's such a huge step.

"No need to decide now," Aden reassures me. "I know we haven't been dating for long, but in the future, I can't see myself with anyone but you."

"It's the same for me," I admit. "It's just such a big step."

Aden chuckles. "And I know you hate change."

"You said, you didn't like change either! Didn't you?"

"I did," he says. "But apparently, not anymore. Listen, Noel, I meant it when I said you don't need to decide now. We can keep the status quo as it is for as long as you need. I just want you to know where I stand in our relationship. When you feel ready, I'd love you to move in here."

I nod. "You know I need a bit of time, but I... I don't hate the idea."

"Talking about not hating an idea." Aden grabs my shoulders and pushes me back slightly. "Is that my sweater you are wearing?"

"That's a rhetorical question, right?" I grin. The sleeves of his sweater are way too long for me, and his sweater easily covers my butt.

Aden stares at me, his gaze scanning me from head to toe, lingering on my naked legs.

"Like what you see?" I ask with a smirk.

He pulls me closer again, his hand moving from my back down to my ass. The look in his eyes is tentative, though. "You haven't had breakfast."

"Don't care. Can eat later!"

Aden slips his hand into my boxers, squeezing my ass. "And you are really sure you are in the right mind space?"

"Yes, Aden," I snort. "I came here dressed in nothing but your sweater. I am in the right mind space. Now fuck me, or—"

"Or what?"

"I don't know! Just fuck me and stop asking questions. Don't make me beg. It's not cute."

His eyebrows shoot up.

Oh, damn it! I just gave him a new idea, huh?

Aden still looks slightly skeptical, but doesn't remove his hand either, so I wrap my arms around him, looking him straight in the eyes. "You can take my word for it," I say. "I would never initiate sex just to numb myself down. And if I wanted to do that, I would straight out ask you to do it for that reason."

"And I would probably give in to you," Aden says. "I just like to know what I am dealing with."

I grin. "You are dealing with me.

"Without any doubt."

"We had plans for the night, hadn't we?"

Aden hooks me up in his arms, making me wrap my legs around him while he carries me to the living room. Unfortunately, the dining table there is covered with folders and papers that look important, so the original fantasy has to make way for something else.

Something else is the smaller work desk he has. I don't even know what he usually uses it for, because he has a separate office after all, but I guess he will use it now.

Aden lets me down there, before digging his fingers into the waistband of my boxers. I hold onto him, lifting my ass up slightly so he can pull them down. When I want to take off his sweater, he stops me.

"I like the thought of you being surrounded by me completely," he smirks.

"You know that this will be yet another sweater you won't ever get back?"

Instead of an answer, Aden just chuckles and gets down on his knees. I am still processing what he is about to do, when his hot mouth is suddenly around my cock.

"Fuck, Aden!"

Aden lets my cock slip out of his mouth, looking up at me with what I can only describe as a teasing smirk. "I could retort with a boomer take, if you want that?"

"Oh no!"

"Fuck, Aden, huh?" he says. "More like fuck Noel."

When I groan, he just laughs. "That was lame!" I complain.

"That's what makes it good," Aden grins.

He pats my upper thighs before wrapping his lips around my half-hard cock again. It's then that I realize he has never joked like that before or said anything silly. The realization goes right to my heart, making it beat wildly. He does it in front of me. He is secure enough to joke with me and to be silly.

There is a part of his past that's still locked firmly behind a door, but I realize I don't mind it anymore, not much. He can be vulnerable and open with me, and laugh and make jokes; that means more.

I dig my fingers into his hair, closing my eyes while I feel his tongue pressed against the base of my shaft. One of his hands is still pressed against my upper thigh, while his free hand moves to my balls, his fingers circling them playfully before giving them a tug.

"Aden," I moan. "Fuck, so good!"

Aden hollows his cheek, taking my dick in until it hits the back of his throat.

"If you go further, I will come," I warn him.

Aden lets go of my cock and gets up. I jump down from the desk, turning over and grabbing the edges. For a while, nothing happens, making me stir slightly. What's taking him so long? Then he suddenly presses his lips against my shoulder, his wet fingers wandering between my ass cheeks and circling my entrance.

"Wait a moment," Aden licks up my neck and bites into my earlobe. "You are loose."

"Maybe... I may or may not have used my time in the bathroom well."

"You absolutely planned this, didn't you?" Aden snorts, moving back and smacking my ass.

I toss a glance back over my shoulder and blink innocently at him. "Just wanted you not to waste any time."

Aden cups my cheek and forces me to turn my head, kissing me before drawing back again. "Well, then, I won't."

"Won't what?"

"Waste time."

Fuck, yes, exactly what I need, and want! Aden doesn't make me wait any longer, the tip of his cock presses against my entrance before he pushes into me in one move. It still hits so differently to feel him inside me without wearing a condom. Just knowing we can do it bare turns me on so much.

"So good," I moan.

"Yeah?" Aden thrusts into me a couple of times before he pauses. "How good?"

"Don't stop!"

He just chuckles before picking up his pace again. He goes faster immediately, his hips snapping forward, every time burying his dick deep inside me. It feels so good when he fucks me like that. The table gives me the necessary balance and helps me keep an angle I couldn't otherwise hold. It's like Aden can go even deeper this way.

His hand is around my cock, stroking me while keeping up the thrusts of his hips. Then he stills again.

"Don't"—I let out a shaky breath—"stop. I am so close!"

"I know, babe, I know."

A sigh of relief leaves me, when he fucks me again until I feel like I am almost over the edge, but he still his movements for a third time, making me groan in frustration. "Stop being an asshole!" I complain. My insides are burning with need. I want him to continue, but at the same time, I want it to last forever.

His hand presses against my back to hold me in place while his head moves down, until his lips are right next to my ear. "I remember you mentioned something about begging, didn't you?"

"I knew it," I blurt out. "I did give you an idea! Deep inside, you have a real sadistic streak."

He smacks my ass again, making me moan. "I just love seeing you whimper and squirm beneath me," he deadpans.

I can't even deny it. I am fucking shivering with anticipation when he picks up the movement of his hips again, pulling out and pushing into me slowly. The minimum friction makes my mind go wild. "Fuck, Aden, give me more!"

He stills again.

"No, don't stop!"

His hand moves down my back to the cleft of my ass and back again, while his other hand moves to my dick. "Ask nicely."

When his fingers wrap loosely around the base of my cock, starting to pump me slowly, I have to admit defeat. "Okay, you won! I blurt out. Please, fuck me, please, Aden!"

"See, that wasn't so difficult."

I'd have a lot to retort to that, but my words get stuck in my mouth when Aden pulls out of me and plunges into me. He is obviously not playing anymore. Fucking finally! His fingers are wrapped around my dick tightly, pumping it quickly while he keeps thrusting into me relentlessly. With being bent over the desk I can feel him reach deeper inside me than ever again.

"You are so hot, Noel! Tell me how you feel!"

"Good, so good," I moan, not able to say anything else let alone form a coherent sentence. He kept me on the edge for so long that my mind is mushy and my body burning with the need to come.

Aden moves his thumb over the tip of my cock. "Then come," he says.

I press my forehead against the cold wood of the desk, while a shiver goes through my body. Finally, I feel the tension inside me subsiding, wave after wave of hot strings of pleasure rush through my body, until my body goes completely lax.

Twenty-Seven

NOEL

I lean my head against the wall of the shower. "That was good," I sigh.

"The shower or our little 'gymnastics' downstairs."

"Both," I chuckle. "But I was talking about the latter, obviously.

Second shower this morning, but I can't even complain because I asked for this. My legs do feel slightly wobbly, though, probably thanks to the long evening I had yesterday with the job applications, then the run-in with my mom, and my breakdown. I guess this is why Aden insisted on taking a shower together. Part of me thought–or hoped–he might have wanted some additional fun, but Aden wouldn't be Aden if he gave in to all of my whims.

I mean, somehow, he does, but not when he thinks it's doing me any harm.

"I am fine," I reassure him when we step out of the shower, and he towels me dry.

He looks me over with a frown. "Are you sure?"

When he looks that worried, I can only wrap my arms around him. "I promise, I am. I am going to get dressed and then come downstairs."

"Fine, I will go ahead and prepare our breakfast. Any wishes?"

"Pancakes with maple syrup and berries, and I need coffee."

"Alright." Aden kisses the side of my head before leaving the bathroom. It gives me a moment to unwind and realize how much has happened yesterday and today, and during the last weeks.

Maybe my relationship with Aden is a whirlwind romance. I know everyone else would tell me to take it slower, but I don't care for anyone's opinion. Being with Aden feels so right.

About time I didn't give a flying fuck what others think of me. I know that Mateo and Ster support me, and Aden does too. Everything else doesn't matter.

The scent of pancakes startles me from my thoughts and makes me hurry to get dressed. I thought I was equal parts tired and hungry, but after catching this heavenly smell, it's obvious hunger wins oversleep for now!

Once back in the kitchen, I notice that Aden has indeed fulfilled my wish. "You really are spoiling me," I say while sitting down at the counter.

Aden cups the back of my head and kisses me. "Maybe I like spoiling you."

"What if I feel bad about it?"

"Do you?" he asks.

"Not really," I admit. "But I feel like I should."

Aden blinks. "Who says that? I like spoiling you with little things. You are not taking advantage of me."

"Then... when you come to the bar, I will make sure to mix you my best cocktails."

He chuckles. "Deal." When he brings us our coffee, he also has some paper in his hands. "Here."

"My contract?"

"Yes, you left it out on the dining table," Aden says. "I took the liberty to look at it earlier this morning."

I eye him anxiously. "And?"

"It looks good," he smiles. "Congrats, Noel."

I jump down from my seat to grab the contract and put it away safely, when my legs suddenly buckle under me, making me drop onto the floor like a sack of potatoes.

"Noel!" Aden is instantly next to me, helping me up again. "Are you okay?"

I didn't even realize how nervous I was until he said the words *Congrats, Noel.* "I am fine, just overwhelmed." Aden takes me to the living room and makes me sit on the sofa, before bringing my plate of pancakes to me. I notice he has added some more to it. "And you think I can eat all that?" I laugh.

Aden doesn't laugh, though, he just looks deeply worried. "I feel like I overstrained you."

"No, you didn't!"

"You barely had any sleep, the fallout with your mother and then I jumped your bones." He shakes his head. "Your blood pressure is probably down. I should have been more responsible."

I grab his arm, pulling him down to sit next to me. "It's not that," I tell him. "It's more like the stress has finally subsided. I thought it wouldn't work out."

"You mean the job or getting rid of the debt?"

"Both," I admit. "It just all felt too easy, you know? And when it's easy and things are going well, I always wait for something bad to happen, for the second shoe to drop. And this here, in particular, it feels like I achieved it way too easily."

Aden looks at me thoughtfully. "You need to stop saying that."

"Huh?"

"Saying that it's all coming to you easily. It didn't. It never was easy. You fought for this, and you are winning now because of your hard work. True, maybe some small portion of luck is part of it too like with everything, but you worked your ass off. You got this job opportunity because DeeDee thought you would be great. And you aced the interview, because you are just that good. DeeDee didn't hand you the job; you just took the chance, proved yourself, and made it work. And I didn't free you from your debt magically. I am not above the law. It was possible because you were completely innocent in this."

"It shows how much it helps to have someone in your corner," I say quietly. "Maybe all of what you just said is true, but without you, and without Ster and Mateo, I don't think I would have found the strength. It shows how far even a little kindness can go."

"That's true," he says. "It's depressing to know how many people suffer without anyone reaching out a hand to them."

"Right," I exclaim, relieved he sees it the same way. "That's why I want to be thankful for my opportunities, and make the best out of it."

Aden chuckles. "And that's exactly what makes you so strong."

"Don't tease me!"

"I am not teasing you. Don't forget it took you coming to my family, for me to finally have some peaceful interaction with my brothers. Let alone when we bumped into each other years ago."

His words pique my interest. "You never told me why you were in such a bleak spot back then."

"I will," he promises. "But not today. You need some sleep. Besides, Lynn is coming over at any time."

"Right, for decluttering the attic!"

"Yes, but I promise I will tell you. Let's make sure to grab a glass of wine tomorrow and relax on our free day. I will answer all your questions."

I stir awake to the sound of voices coming from the entrance door. For a moment, I feel completely disoriented. I am at Aden's place, as much is obvious, but what even happened? When did I fall asleep?

There is a cup of tea in front of me, but the plates from breakfast are gone, and I am wrapped in a warm blanket.

Struggling free from the blanket and forcing my mind back into a waking state, I finally stumble off the couch. I have never coped well with taking a nap during the day. It just always pulls me down into some sort of dark pit, where my limbs get heavy and my mind drowsy. It's hard to wake up from it, even when I put on an alarm.

"Aden?" I trot through the living room, still fighting the drowsiness, when I bump into my boyfriend.

"You are awake?" He sneaks an arm around me and pulls me closer. "Lynn just arrived. I didn't want to wake you, I am sorry."

"Nah, it's fine! How long have I been gone for?"

"Two hours. It's noon," he says.

I furrow my brows. Wow, I wasted a lot of time. Talking to Aden helps wake me up fully, though, and I finally see Lynn in front of me. "Hi Lynn! Sorry, I am still not quite all here."

"Don't worry," she grins. "I figured."

She is dressed in jeans and a comfy sweater. It's the first time I have seen her like that, so casual and relaxed. I guess I have become a full part of Aden's life by now.

"Are you sure Mateo doesn't want to come in?" Aden asks.

"Mateo is here too?" I ask.

Lynn chuckles, first facing Aden. "Yes," she says, before turning towards me. "Was. He brought me but has some work to do with Sterling."

"When he picks you up again, we'll make sure to invite him in," Aden says.

I can't believe Mateo brought her to Aden's place. It means things have to be going really well! I don't comment on it so as not to embarrass Lynn or Mateo, but I am unbelievably happy for him. He only had on-off relationships for a while, and I don't know why. It seems like he always wanted more than his exes. He is the type of guy who wants to commit, but apparently, many thought he just wanted to fool around.

Seems like he and Lynn share the same values, though.

"So, what's the plan?" Lynn asks. "You mentioned the attic."

"Yes, I want to declutter it," Aden says.

"Are you really ready to do it?"

"Yes," he says. "Time to move on. I want to turn it back into my atelier."

"What exactly is in the attic?" I ask curiously.

Lynn stays quiet at my question, just glancing at Aden briefly. "Well," Aden starts. "I have put all my paintings there, and all my painting utensils. The plan is to go through everything and turn the attic into a small atelier again."

"You are going to paint again?" I ask carefully, finally realizing why Lynn sounded so enthusiastic.

"In private," Aden says. "I don't think I am ready to return to the public with my art. But I want to return to creating something again. I have only picked up drawing again recently."

"Ever since he met a certain someone," Lynn comments and winks at me.

I feel my cheeks heat up in both embarrassment and joy. "Why did you stop in the first place?"

At that, silence surrounds us long enough to feel uncomfortable. Eventually, Lynn clears her throat, tossing Aden a gaze I can't quite read, before walking towards the kitchen. "I will prepare us some coffee," she says.

She closes the door behind her, leaving us enwrapped in silence. "You don't need to talk about it when you aren't ready," I say.

"My boyfriend back then," Aden suddenly says. "His name was Emil. He died. And it was all so horrible it sucked all my creativity out of me."

"My god," I mutter. "Aden, I am so sorry."

"There is more to this story, Noel," he says. "A lot more than just his death. I was caught in a very toxic relationship with Emil. I will tell you the whole story when we are on our own. I promise."

I determine to be understanding, and not the pushy boyfriend who needs to get what he wants immediately. If Aden promised to tell me everything when we are on our own, then I will take him at face value.

"Alright!" I stretch slightly. "So, what's the plan for now? Should we go right to the attic?"

Aden smiles. "Yes, take Lynn with you, will you? Meanwhile, I will clean out the work desk in the living room."

I gaze at said desk, wiggling my eyebrows at Aden. "So, what do you usually do with that desk when you don't use me to have fun with it?"

Aden raises an eyebrow, a smirk curling his lips. "If only we'd be alone." He pauses. "When I don't fuck you over it, I usually use it for research."

Yeah, should have known my teasing would backfire, like it always does. That guy is just never embarrassed by anything! I sigh dramatically. "You won, okay?"

"No, really. I like its new purpose."

I glare, covering his mouth with my hand. Aden chuckles softly, taking my hand and placing a kiss against it.

"You started it."

"I know."

Aden reaches out his hand, brushing over my neck. "Like I said, I used it for research, for my art."

"You researched when you were painting?"

"Sometimes," he says. "I tried to learn a lot about different styles. Whenever I tried a new method or new material, I'd research beforehand. I also love everything concerning the history of art and would use it for personal research too."

"That's great," I point out. "Why not keep the desk here?"

"I don't think it fits anymore. I want to have my research place in the attic as well."

"And what do you want to put here instead?" I ask. "There'd be an empty space."

"How about a small bar?" he asks.

It takes a minute or more for me to grasp what he just said. "No way," I exclaim. "You... for me? I can't possibly accept that."

"Why just for you?" he says dryly. "My boyfriend is a professional bartender. Why not create a place where he can mix cocktails for me?"

For a moment, I see it in front of me: Aden sitting at a bar stool, while I mix a cocktail or try a new recipe to have him test it for me. "That would actually be nice," I admit.

"See." Aden squeezes my arm. "Don't always say no immediately when I suggest something."

I know he is right. I have a tendency of shooting him down when he offers something that looks like it benefits me more than him. It was the same when he offered to hire a lawyer for me. It's hard for me to accept help, even from those I love, but I am starting to understand that it doesn't mean I am weak when I accept help. I don't need to do everything on my own, and sometimes people want to do things for me because they love me.

Ster and Mateo always tried to help, as well. They both wanted me to move in with them instead of staying at my crappy apartment, but I was too stubborn and too prideful to accept their help. Good thing they never grew tired of me because damn, I sound exhausting as fuck.

TWENTY-EIGHT

NOEL

"Aden forgot to mention that he used this place to dump everything he doesn't need anymore," Lynn grumbles. "When he mentioned decluttering the attic, I thought it would just be the old drawings, painting utensils, and his former work that he had here."

I chuckle. "Well, it was unused space, so I can see why he wanted to use it to store stuff."

"Yeah, yeah, go and defend your husband," she mutters.

"Husband?" I squeal. "Lynn, we are not that far advanced!"

"I wouldn't be surprised if you two go on a vacation tomorrow and come back married," she points out. "Pretty much aligns with what you both would do. Don't you think so?"

I tap my nose thoughtfully. "Maybe. I could see it happen under certain circumstances," I groan. "Aden needs to put a stop to my impulsiveness, not support it even more."

Lynn laughs. "Aden is a romantic at heart," she says. "I think all artists have that side."

"I don't know. I don't think Ster does."

"Sterling?" she smiles. "I think if Sterling sets his mind to something, he would absolutely see it through, even if others would deem it as too fast, too illogical, or not thought through well enough. Don't you think so? He seems like a guy who goes with his intuition."

I frown. "I hate that you have a point, but we still can't make it an artist's thing. It's too much of a cliché."

"Well, Aden and Sterling share that sentiment," she says. "So, that's enough for me to know what I need to know."

She takes the bottle of wine she brought along and pours us both a glass. "Look," she says, revealing some canvas. "That was when Aden was experimenting with landscapes."

I gape at the paintings. "My god, he is good!"

She chuckles at my surprise. "How do you think he made a name for himself? Aden is a genius, a very rare talent. I am glad he picked up drawing again."

"I wish I'd have known him when he was still experimenting with art," I admit.

"I believe you met him exactly at the time that was right for you both," she points out. "He was ready to give love a second chance, and you..."

"I guess I was ready to give love a chance, in general. It was the first time for me to allow myself to fall in love."

"See? What use would it have been to meet Aden before that point in time? You might not have hit it off, but now the two of you work much better than anyone else I know."

"Do you really think so?"

"I know that Aden has never been with someone like he is with you," she says.

"Not even with Emil?"

"Oh, so you know about him?" Lynn asks, before she nods. "Not even with Emil." She pauses. "Being with Emil changed him, for the worse."

Her words surprise me. "What do you mean?"

"Well, you know his history with his family, don't you?" She rummages through some stuff and shows me more of Aden's early drawings. The date he signed it shows that he was in his late teens when he drew this. It's obvious how talented he already was back then. "I met him when I was Oliver's girlfriend. Instantly got weird vibes from the family dynamics, and at the same time clicked with Aden."

"Aden told me you were turned off immediately when you saw how the brothers treated him."

"Yeah, you can imagine, can't you? I was so pissed off."

I laugh. "I can absolutely imagine it." She looks to be the type of person who would immediately call someone out for their bullshit.

"Seriously," she grimaces. "Oliver was a nice guy, genuinely nice, you know? But it was a turnoff for me to see how he didn't stand up for his youngest brother. Maybe I am unfair, but back then, I thought, if he can't even stand up against the bullying of his youngest brother, will he ever stand up for me? Or for our future kids? I gave him a couple of chances, but realized he just wasn't the guy for me." She smiles. "Mateo, on the other hand, would totally stand up for someone in need."

"He would!" I agree enthusiastically. "And he always did!"

"See, I just knew."

"You said you and Aden immediately clicked?"

"We did." She takes a sip from her glass of wine while I continue going through the canvases. Now that we have freed them of all the surrounding mess, we can finally sort through them. "I am from a very conservative family. I know the struggle to grow up, not being able to be yourself, and holding back. Aden's struggles really spoke to me. Even back then, he was very strong. After I broke up with Oliver, I didn't see him for a while, but when we met again, we hit it off immediately."

"And Emil?" I ask.

"Emil just pulled him down again," she frowns. "Man, Noel. I know I shouldn't talk badly about the deceased, but Aden was a wreck thanks to that guy."

Maybe it's because I met Aden at a different time in his life, but it's hard to imagine him being truly broken. However, he did mention that meeting me in that small grocery store was a crucial moment for him also.

Lynn rummages through the paintings before pulling out two separate ones. One is dark and full of sorrow, the other much lighter. It still has its signature touch of melancholy. It seems that's definitely his style. Even his painting of a beautiful landscape has that touch of heaviness. However, it's also what makes his work so intriguing. She points at the dark painting. "Aden, when he was with Emil. Don't get me wrong, great painting, but obviously the artist struggled mentally." Then she points at the lighter one. "Still his style, but in a much more healthy way. Aden, when he met you."

"Wait a moment!" I exclaim, inspecting the painting with a frown and checking the date. "You are right, he already was with me when he drew this one."

"Like I said, he has never been with someone the way he is with you," she repeats. "I am very happy for him."

Her words make me insanely happy, but there is also a dull feeling in my stomach, something I can't quite put a finger on yet. What if I disappoint him? I am almost certain I will. I always do and end up disappointing those I love. Why should it be any different this time?

No, Noel, not the right time to panic.

There is no reason for it!

Lynn, fortunately, hasn't noticed my anxiety spiking and has turned towards a different painting. On it, I can see a young man with soft features, his eyes are red-rimmed, his face pale, the whole vibe around him is dark and depressed. It's not a particularly flattering image, but it strikes something in me. It's sad, and heavy, and almost desperate. It must be a painting from Aden's more depressive phase. Lynn shakes her head. "Emil," she mutters. "I wonder if things would have been different if you had let Aden help you."

"How did he die?" I hear myself ask.

"He overdosed," Lynn says quietly, still looking at the image sadly. "He broke Aden's heart every time he fell back into taking drugs. But when he died, it truly broke Aden."

He overdosed?!

That's what Aden meant when he said it wasn't a healthy relationship. He was an addict. That's why the picture just struck something so dark in me. He looks like Mom looked when she was younger and lived off her drugs.

And it looks like I did when the addiction started to chip away at all of my remaining personality, and all of the love I could feel, because I was too weak to stay away from what killed my father and ruined my mother.

"I need to go to the restroom," I say, barely able to keep myself upright, while stumbling downstairs. My heart beats so fast, it makes my head dizzy and my chest tight. It's hard to breathe, so hard to breathe. Everything around me seems to look dimmed all of a sudden, while spinning around me all the same time. It's getting so fucking hard to breathe.

I need some fresh air!

ADEN

There is much more stuff to go through in my desk's drawers than I thought. I am just glad Lynn and Noel took over in the attic. On my own, this would have taken me days. While I am sorting through some papers, my phone vibrates. It's a message from Oliver, which reminds me it has been a while since he wrote to me.

Hi Aden, just wanted to check in with you, to see how you are doing. Everything well? Hope Noel is well too.

Wow! Who would have thought, Noel telling him off, would be the one thing finally making Oliver rebuild some bridges. It's the first time in ages that he isn't trying to pressure me into meeting him or Kayden or one of the others.

And now?

Do I want to remain distant?

I sigh. If I wanted to completely cut them off, I would have done that already. I have never blocked them.

I am fine, thank you for asking.

I wonder if I should ask something in return, but I don't truly feel like it. To me, it's already quite a big step to reply at all. Putting my phone aside, I dive right back into my paperwork. The amount of stuff I have collected in the drawers is insane. For someone who is so nitpicky and organized at his work, I do have quite a chaotic, personal research table. I guess I have always worked differently as an artist than I did as a gallerist.

"Aden?"

I look up to see Lynn, her eyes are clouded in worry. "Did something happen?" I gaze outside, noticing the sun is setting. "Matao said he'd come around, didn't he?" Hopefully, he didn't cancel. I know she has high hopes for this relationship, and I do too. Mateo seems to be a good guy and a much better fit for Lynn than any of the other guys she dated during the last couple of years.

Also, Mateo is a better fit than Oliver was, and to be fair, he wasn't too bad as her boyfriend. It means that Mateo might actually be the right guy for her.

"Mateo is on his way. He sent me a message a couple of minutes ago." Lynn pauses. "It might be nothing, Aden, but... I... fuck, I don't know."

Now she certainly has my attention. "Where is Noel?" I ask.

"How did you know that's what this is about?" she exclaims.

"A feeling. Where is he?"

"I don't know. He went to the restroom an hour ago," she explains. "I am sorry, I was so deep into the work that I didn't notice how much time passed. Then I thought he might be with you, but—"

"He isn't," I say. A weird sense of deep calm fills me. It's not a good feeling, though, it's the type of calm that I usually forced forward when something in my life was going awry and I needed to cover it. "Tell me what happened, please."

"We were going through your paintings and chatting. Maybe I talked too much, Aden. I if I did, fuck, I am sorry. I had no idea."

"Why, what did you tell him?"

"About Oliver and me, and how much better you are today in comparison to back then, and especially in comparison to your time with Emil."

"You talked about Emil with him?" I ask.

"Shouldn't I have?" she asks, sudden panic on her face. "He knew his name, so I thought... Oh fuck! He had no clue, did he? I swear, I didn't say anything bad about you, and we just talked about Emil briefly."

"Lynn," I put the papers in my hand away and grab her hands. "Don't panic. I can't have you lose your nerve now. You did nothing wrong. You couldn't have known. Just tell me exactly what you said about him, okay?"

Lynn does, telling me step by step what they talked about. She was right when she said it wasn't an awful lot. Just my best friend being happy that I am so much better in this relationship and have picked up drawing again. She probably thought Noel knew more than he did. It's my fucking fault that he was unaware about everything, I probably should have been open with him much sooner.

"I am not even the gossiping type usually," she exclaims. "I just wanted to show Noel how well the two of you fit together. I am so sorry, Aden. I didn't mean to gossip about you or anything."

"Don't be ridiculous," I mutter. "You just chatted with my boyfriend. What you said isn't even anything big, just the basics."

Something triggered Noel, I just know it.

I try to dial his number once more, but it goes straight to voicemail. Like the last time when he ran from me. I remember he had an altercation with his mother back then, too, and panicked. Maybe it's similar today? Was it the aftermath of having a major fallout with his mother?

Or maybe it was what made him vulnerable and more prone to panicking?

"Here is Mateo," Lynn exclaims.

"Good," I say. "He knows Noel well. I am sure he can help."

TWENTY-NINE

ADEN

Mateo has a deep frown on his face when Lynn wraps up the whole story once more. Meanwhile, I try to remain calm and composed, while my thoughts are derailing again. Noel is smart, he is efficient, he is a survivor. I know him well enough by now to understand that he doesn't just run to be away from me, but that his anxiety pushes him into a fight-or-flight response, and his usual response is to flee. If he'd fight with me instead, I could catch him much better in the moment.

"You are pale, Aden," Lynn says all of a sudden. Contrary to me, she has calmed down now and is her usual practical self, while I am slowly losing my grip on everything. She takes my hands now. "I know where your thoughts are going."

"He could be dead," I press out.

"He is not dead," she emphasizes.

"You don't know that." My heart hammers against my chest, making my mind spin even more. "He could have run into a car, or someone could have assaulted him or..." My mind goes to the several times I picked up Emil somewhere, from a shelter, from the street, from one of his drug addict friends, from the police. It was never good when he disappeared. "What if he is somewhere hurt and alone, and no one is there to help him? Fuck, I can't even reach him."

"Noel isn't Emil," she says. "He is a stable young man; he just has some mental health issues like you do. But he is the type of guy to work for his future, to work on his problems, and to tackle them. That's what actually made you fall for him, isn't it?"

Her words are surprisingly sobering. "You are right," I mutter. "I was intrigued by Noel because he is my type, but fell for him because of the person he is."

"See? This time, my big mouth just triggered something in him, and he needed to get out." She glances at Mateo. "Did I get that correct?"

"Yeah," he says. "But your mouth isn't big, it's very pretty. Besides, it's not for me to say, but I don't think you said too much. Noel can usually handle something like that. And if not, he has to learn how to do it in a constructive way."

I am a little surprised by his words. Mateo and Sterling are Noel's closest friends. They know him in ways I have never gotten to know him. But it's also very relieving to know that despite them having his back, they don't enable him.

It's healthy for all of them.

It's like Lynn has always been with me. Even during the phases of my darkest depression, she was there to get me out of the dark hole I was in, with all the understanding and all the gentleness she had, but she also dragged me to a therapist and called me out when I fucked up.

"Did his mom contact him again?" Mateo asks all of a sudden.

My eyes snap up. "I can't believe I haven't told you yet," I say.

"Oh shit, something did happen?"

"She basically stalked him and followed him to my place. Then she assaulted him. I heard the commotion and went outside to make her leave."

"You actually managed to do that?" Mateo asks.

"Yes, I threatened her with my lawyer and the police," I say. "She looked terrified enough to back off."

"Aden can be scary if he wants to," Lynn explains to her boyfriend. "You wouldn't believe it."

"I am glad you did," Mateo says. "And even gladder Noel saw you defend him and successfully make her fuck off. Seriously, Sterlone tried and got assaulted by her. I tried once, too, and she broke a bottle over my head."

"What?" Lynn exclaims. "She did what? Wait, till I get my hands on that vile—"

"It was ages ago," Mateo reassures her, but he looks happy when he looks at Lynn. Despite my own dire situation, I can only smile. I get it. Having the person you love defend you and have your back means more than anything else could. Noel had my back against my family. He always has my back.

It's these final thoughts that sober me up completely. "I need to find him," I say. "I love Noel, I really do, and I won't leave him hanging in such a moment of weakness. I won't leave because he fucks up once. But we do need to move past this issue of him running when he is anxious, to be able to proceed with a healthy relationship."

Mateo nods. "I get that, Aden."

He looks thoughtful, almost distant. There is something he isn't telling me. "Do you think he was jealous of Emil?" I push.

"No, I don't think he is," Mateo mutters.

"What is it... tell me, please."

"Make him tell you about his past," Mateo says.

"I know about his past."

"I know you do, but maybe not of that part, and what it did to him and his confidence."

I nod tentatively. He is right, I need to get to the bottom of this to understand his triggers and to know how to avoid them. "Do you know where he could hide?"

"I tried the usual places," Mateo says. "But he isn't there."

"The usual places?"

"He has a set of places that feel emotionally safe to him," Mateo explains.

Well, that's not the worst situation then, and dims my internal image of him lying in a dark alley, hurt and assaulted, a little. However, Mateo just said he was nowhere to be found, making my heart sink once more. "Was he at none of these places?"

"I didn't say that," Mateo hurries to reassure me. "I was just able to check the places I know. Sterlone knows more. I will call him immediately."

"No, let me do that," I say. "He has me on emergency dial, so I can reach him when he is working. Besides, I want to hear from him directly where to look."

"I think that's for the best." Mateo takes Lynn's hand, and they move away a little to give me some privacy.

I don't waste any time and immediately call Sterling. True to his promise to pick up whenever I call him, he does answer the phone. "It's something with the next exhibit, isn't it?" he asks before even greeting me. "I had a feeling it would be. They probably don't want to show my work."

His words surprise me, but as his mentor and supporter, they also fill me with relief. He *is* nervous, and showing nerves before an exhibition is a sign that it is important to him. I made a good choice with him. "Everything is alright with the exhibition," I reassure him. "I am calling because of something else."

Sterling is quiet for a moment, and then. "What did he do? What happened?"

"How did you know?"

"The only time you call me when it's not for work is about Noel," he says.

"Perceptive as usual." I don't waste any time and summarize what happened, including the incident last night.

"My God," Sterling sighs. "I am sorry, Aden. I... Noel is such a good guy, I know you know that. But I also know how difficult it is to grasp him in moments of his anxiety, and this comes from his best friend. I don't even know what I'd do if he were my boyfriend. How are you holding up?"

With all our worry concerning Noel, no one–not even I–has asked this question. "I am scared," I admit.

"And?"

"I might be a tad angry," I admit.

"That's good, and healthy," Sterling reassures me. "Noel needs to be able to handle you being mad at him if he fucks up. Don't be afraid of showing him how you feel."

"I will." I used to hold back all the time when I was with Emil, and it ate me up. Not all of this is Emil's fault. I could have had more of a backbone, too, especially regarding myself and my own feelings. "But I know he runs when he is in panic. We'll need to work around that somehow. Do you have an idea where he could be?"

"Mateo said he checked all the usual spots?"

"Yes."

"There is one more," Sterling muses. "He hardly goes there because it's not the closest, but depending on what he needed when he left, he might have gone there."

"Depending on what he needed?"

"Usually, he runs to a safe place. It could be mine, for example, or Mateo's," Sterling explains. "But if he needs absolute silence around him, there is just one place he could have gone to. Do you have a pen? I am going to tell you the address."

I rummage in my pocket, taking out the pen and small notebook I always carry around. "Yes, go ahead."

After Sterling gave me the address, his previous words make so much more sense. "That's in the middle of nowhere," I mutter. "Don't tell me, he went there on foot?"

"He probably did run parts of it, but might have taken a cab for the remainder of the way," Sterling says. "He is on autopilot usually when he has an anxiety attack. He dissociates."

I remember last night, after his mother assaulted him. There was a moment when Noel seemed to be completely gone, far away in his mind.

"The place is safe, though," Sterling continues. "I promise. It's a small cottage next to a lake, on private property."

"How do you know that?"

"Because it belongs to me," Sterling says, a tremor in his voice. "Or rather, it belonged to my late grandfather, who abandoned us for years until he was at the end of his life, and wanted to make amends. Roxana and I both hate the place. I want to sell it, but it's hard to do so because it's run-down and in the middle of nowhere."

His words linger with me for a while, while I keep staring at the address. "You have it up for sale?"

“Yeah, been trying to sell it for two years now, but those who are interested either don’t have the money, or they want to tear the place down and put a hotel there or a golf course, and I am not ready to have the place ruined. It’s a beautiful spot, you know?”

“I’d need to look at it to make a decision,” I mutter.

“Excuse me?”

“I will go there immediately,” I tell him. “Once I have found him and scolded him, I will make sure you know he is okay. Well, maybe not exactly in that order. But I will send you and Mateo a message. For everything else, I will call you tomorrow.”

THIRTY

ADEN

It's night when I reach Sterling's cottage. He didn't exaggerate when he said it needs to have quite a lot of work done, but he didn't convey how beautiful the surroundings truly are. I am not surprised he doesn't want this to become a tourist spot. The lake has a sandy beach, a private area and is suitable for swimming. There is a bridge, and plenty of space to sit or lie comfortably. I was expecting a forest surrounding this place, but it's all free, just bushes, some grass and a sandy beach. Almost as if I am at the ocean, on a wild, deserted island.

Funny how such a place exists so close to the buzzing city, and I had no idea it was here. A true hidden gem.

"Aden..."

I turn around to see Noel. He must have heard the sound of my car and stepped outside the cottage. He looks pale and exhausted, and as though he has been crying. My eyes wander down to his hand, where he is holding his phone.

"I ran out of battery when I arrived here earlier today," he blurts out.

"Is that the reason no one was able to reach you?"

"Yes, though... I guess right at the beginning I wouldn't have been able to pick up either way."

Well, at least he is honest.

"I am so sorry," he says, sounding miserable. "I didn't mean to disappear like that. I just... ran. And when I came to my mind again, I was here. My phone wasn't working, and it was too late for me to walk back on foot."

"Are you telling me you dissociated the whole way from my place to this?" I ask, instantly alarmed.

Noel looks anxious at my words, as if he is scared that I might reprimand him in case he does. "It doesn't happen a lot," he hurries to explain. "Actually, it barely happens. It used to happen when my parents would"—he stops before breathing a sigh—"when they would beat me while they were drunk."

I look at him once more, noting how tired he looks. The run-in with his mother had a long-lasting effect on him, like the last time. It's worse this time because she sought him out in person. "I won't let her bother you ever again," I tell him. "Let's go inside and talk there."

The inside of the little house is spacious and surprisingly well-built, but everything is dusty, the furniture obviously ancient and run down, and it looks like there is some water damage from the last couple of thunderstorms. The worst is the kitchen. Now *that* could do with a face-lift.

But all in all, this place has a charm to it, much more than I expected it to have, and a lot of potential.

"How majorly did I fuck up?" Noel asks.

I turn to look at him. "You promised me you wouldn't run again," I say instead of an answer.

He looks crestfallen, but nods. "You are right."

"Why did you run this time?"

For a while, Noel stays quiet, then he sits down on the dusty sofa. "I used to take drugs," he tells me. "When I was a teen. I... my parents kept sending me to do their dirty business and had me buy their drugs for them. They said a kid would be less suspicious, and they were right." He pauses. "I made friends." He laughs bitterly, before repeating the last words and using his fingers to put them under quotation marks. "Obviously, not real friends, just people who wanted to sell stuff to me. I never did the hard drugs, but still, I was pretty deep in, and I guess any longer and I would have been sucked into the life and become my parents."

My heart sinks for him. I don't think I can truly imagine how horrible his upbringing and his life really were. He was a child, and instead of being protected, he was abused and taken advantage of. I finally close the distance between us and sit down next to him. "You did what you did to survive," I tell him while trying to figure out what had triggered him in his talk with Lynn. The puzzle pieces are slowly coming together.

"You lost your last boyfriend to drugs," he blurts out, his eyes filling with tears.

So, that's what it was. "Noel—"

"I know what you see when you look at me—"

"Noel," I interrupt him, this time sharply. "Would you let me get a word in, please?"

He shuts up, but his lips are still quivering.

"I did lose Emil to drugs. I was devastated, but I already told you that losing him was not all that ruined me; it was the toxicity of our relationship altogether. Because no matter what I did, how much I tried, how often I begged, and how much I wished my love would be the reason for him to at least try, he wouldn't let me help him. He would pretend to get better, just to take advantage of me and my money, and then fall even deeper. I completely stopped dating after he died, and instead went for guys who weren't my type at all because I knew they wouldn't get me hurt."

"I am your type," he mutters.

"Yes, and I took the leap for you, because you are honest and very straightforward. You want to know what I see when I look at you? I see a man who had it rough in his childhood, who was parentified and forced to be responsible for an alcoholic mother and an addicted father. He saw his parents rot, and had drugs thrown at him at a young age. He couldn't help but get into drugs himself. He was forced to steal food for his deadbeat parents. But he got free, and he got clean, and turned his life around completely."

"It's just..." he mutters. "I must remind you so much of Emil."

His words give me a stitch in my chest. This is my fault. I should have told him everything much sooner. Now he found out on his own, spiraled into an anxiety attack, and now, is struggling with his self-doubt. "You do, but not in the way you think you do. You showed me what could have been if Emil had allowed me to help him. If Emil were honest and genuine." I pause. "Noel, in case it isn't obvious, you are ***it*** for me. I have never acted around a partner like I have with you."

"I love you, too," he says before he lets out a frustrated groan. "And I ran again. I am so sorry. I disappointed you. I promised you I wouldn't."

"You didn't disappoint me, you hurt me, that's vastly different."

Noel pales at my words. "How is that any better? I don't want to hurt you, ever!"

"Because it will happen in any relationship. There will be times you will hurt me, and vice versa. We are just human, and we make mistakes. It doesn't mean I am disappointed. We only need to learn how to handle the issues we have and how we navigate them to have a healthy relationship."

Noel pinches his nose. "I need to do better in these situations."

I put an arm around his shoulder and nod. "We can agree on that. I know you act on instinct when your anxiety kicks in. But it *does* trigger me," I admit. "There were days when Emil disappeared, and I had to search for him until I'd find him half-dead somewhere. I know you are just retreating to calm down from your anxiety, but in my mind, I already see you being hurt, or worse..."

"I wasn't aware," he admits. "I... when my anxiety attacks, I just feel the need to run. Not necessarily away from you, just to run."

"Okay, I think I understand. But can we at least find a strategy? Something that doesn't make you run away and hide, and helps me know where you are."

"You are not going to leave me?!" He looks so scared that it hurts my chest. Maybe this is also part of why he runs in such a situation. He is anxious and lacks trust.

"No, why would I? I don't like having to chase you like that, because it worries me, but I am not going to leave you for having anxiety attacks."

"So, what can I do?" he asks.

"Let me hire a therapist for you, *without* arguing with me about money," I say, noting how he furrows his brows.

"Not fair," he mutters.

"But this is benefiting both of us," I point out. "If you want, I can occasionally join you."

"You would do that?"

"Sure, I have enough baggage to talk about."

This finally draws a smile from him. "Alright, then I accept the offer, *without* arguing... much."

"You could also send me a message; one word would be enough."

He nods, much to my relief, looking quite eager. "Yes, I... I will try doing that. But what if I forget my phone? Or like today, when my phone is dead?"

"Then go to a place I will find you at."

"Why the fuck did I not think about that?" he exclaims. "I can absolutely do that. But where to?"

"How about here?"

"Here." He blinks. "It's Sterling's old place. He got it from his grandpa."

"He told me he doesn't like it much because his grandpa pretty much disowned him and never helped him or his sister, until the very last," I say.

"That's true."

"He also said it's up for sale," I say.

"You... you want to buy it?" he asks, stunned.

"Why not? It's the type of place we both dreamed of as a retreat, didn't we?" I look around. "It needs some work, but it definitely can become a safe space."

Noel's eyes widen. "Under one condition."

"And what's that?"

"I want to contribute. I am going to be free of my debt soon, and your lawyer told me I probably will get some compensation, too, for the last couple of years. I know I can't add much to the deposit, but I want to put a little bit on it."

I want to tell him to save his money for his studies or just enjoy life a bit, but looking at him now, I know it's important to him. "I will tell Cedric to contact my lawyer," I say. "He will draft a contract for you. In case something happens to me, you will own the place. And in case we separate, you will own it too."

"But that's not fair."

"It is fair. You are contributing as much as you can, and it's just fair, you get something in case things turn wrong between us." I take his hand. "I know deep down you are a romantic, Noel, even if you try to be rational, and I love that about you. Actually, I think I am the same. But remember how you told me you can't quit your job, because you need to stay independent in case things go wrong between us?"

He nods.

"This is exactly the same situation. There are times you need to be selfish too, and think about your own safety and future."

Noel rubs over his face with the palm of his hand. "I am working on being more reasonable."

"For what it's worth, I don't think you are unreasonable."

"Then, I will try to be more trusting," he says. "Also, in myself." He looks around. "The place is romantic, isn't it? Wild and romantic."

"I thought the same."

"We'll plan this together, won't we?" he asks. "That alcove there, wouldn't that look nice for a place you could paint at?"

I nod. "And here,"—I point at the middle of the room—"is the perfect place for a carpet, where you could lie naked, and I could draw you."

Noel grins. "No one would ever believe me if I told them how silly you can be."

"That's why I save it for you," I say.

Noel tilts his head, a thoughtful expression on his face. "I like the sound of that," he admits. "Shall we go home? I don't think we can stay the night."

"We probably could," I mutter. "But I doubt we'd want to. Let's go."

Before we can leave, Noel halts, forcing me to stop. "I'd like to take you up on your offer," he finally says.

"Which one?"

"I want to move in with you."

My heart stutters for a moment. I thought it would take him a bit longer to agree to moving into my place.

He grins. "You look shocked."

"I didn't expect you to agree so soon," I admit.

"Does that mean you changed your mind?"

"Not at all. I told you, I am all in."

Noel smiles warmly. "I am all in, too."

THIRTY-ONE

NOEL

Mateo and Lynn carry my cupboard inside, both of them laughing because Mateo is so tall, he constantly hits his head somewhere. He has always been insecure about his height, but Lynn is pretty tall too, and it seems that together with her, he sees everything much lighter.

"This one goes in the corridor upstairs?" Lynn asks me.

"Yes. Are you two okay?"

"We are coping," Mateo grins. They put the cupboard down for a moment to catch their breath.

"This is nice," Lynn muses, brushing over the wooden surface with her hand. "Good quality."

"The only quality piece I own," I admit. "It was my dad's. He sold everything else, but somehow forgot he had that one in the garage. I always liked it. As a kid, it gave me fairytale vibes."

I don't own much, so moving isn't exactly a big deal for me. Aden wanted to hire someone to do it for us, but after I showed him what we needed to move, he saw reason and just rented a bigger car to be able to transport my stuff in one go.

Plus, all of our friends offered to help out. I am happy that Lynn and Mateo are here, in particular. After the drama I caused a week ago when I ran to the lake house, I am glad I can show Lynn that I am not that unstable.

I am lucky to have such amazing friends. No one called me out on what happened, not even Lynn, and she certainly had the most reason to do so. For one, she is Aden's friend and probably worried about him; and second, she was there and saw everything first-hand.

I talked to her briefly about what happened to make sure she knows I would never betray Aden, but she assured me that she knew what happened and why, and that I don't need to apologize to her.

As for Mateo and Sterling, they were just relieved to hear that Aden and I talked it out and found a constructive way around our issue.

"Did you and Aden truly buy that old house from Sterling?" Lynn asks, successfully pulling me out of my thoughts.

"Yes, we did. Aden had the contract set up yesterday," I say.

"He was over the moon," Mateo says. "I mean Sterling. I think that despite how much he despised his grandfather, he is glad that his old family property fell into your hands now, and he knows you are going to renovate it and not bulldoze the whole area. Plus, he can pay Roxanna's student loan now."

"So, that's how he will use the money," I muse. "I figured."

"He is going to pay for her education fully now," Mateo says. "And guess what, he paid some of my student debt too, plus put down the deposit for a new apartment. He wants to own a bigger place, so he can do his art there peacefully."

"That is amazing!" I exclaim.

Mateo smiles and nods. He doesn't mention it, but I know that ever since Sterling came under Aden's mentorship, Mateo's salary has increased a lot. He gets a certain percentage of the sales and also a salary from Sterling himself. At the beginning, he did most of it for free, but now it's a full-time job, and Ster is the last one who would rip off a friend. He couldn't have done it without Mateo, and he knows it.

I have also heard that there are other artists reaching out to Mateo now, to have him as their manager.

I am just so happy to see both my friends flourishing.

"Do you need help with the cupboard?" I ask.

"No, you were busy in the kitchen, weren't you?" Lynn asks.

"Yes, Aden and I ordered a bunch of utensils for me," I explain. "I am going to a few barkeeping courses soon and want to practice at home."

"Aden is lucky," Lynn sighs.

"All the more reason for you to visit us often," I point out.

Lynn grins. "Don't need to tell me again, because I will *definitely* come over plenty." She looks at me with a smile. "I told you once, Noel, and I stick to it: This is good. You and Aden are really good together."

Instead of rebuffing her by telling her how I think he is too good for me and that he brings more to the table than a nutcase like I do, I decide to have confidence in my relationship and show it. "I love being with Aden," I tell her. "He is amazing."

"He says the same about you," Mateo says. He stretches his muscles. "Well then, Lynn, love, are we ready to get this upstairs?"

"We are," Lynn turns to me with a soft smile. "He calls me 'babe'," she whispers. "And 'love'. No guy ever did that."

I give her the thumbs up and nod. It's very Mateo to shower his significant other with love and respect. I am glad she reciprocates.

While the two of them continue their way upstairs, another person comes through the front door. "Where do you want these two boxes?" Sterling asks, without putting them down.

"They should have a label," I say. "Wait, let me check." I study them before nodding. "Bedroom, please."

As Sterling walks past me, he smiles. "I am very happy for you," he says. Nothing more, but between him and Mateo, he is less forthcoming with words, so it makes me happy he comments on my decision. Knowing I have his and Mateo's approval means something special to me, actually more than I can imagine.

While Sterling stumbles upstairs, Cedric seeks me out. "I am going to organize some lunch for us. Mr. Randall usually eats around that time in the office."

"Thank you, try to keep it simple."

"I was thinking about wraps," he says. "Won't make much waste and are easy to eat."

I nod my approval, grinning when Cedric dashes off full of motivation. Despite his chipper attitude and his lack of experience, the guy is a born assistant. Strangely, he always knows what Aden wants. Thinking about Aden makes me want to look for him immediately.

He is in the living room, talking to the carpenter about the small bar we had designed for me. I wait for him to be done talking before hugging him from behind. Aden turns around, brushing through my hair. "Is everything okay?"

He is still worried about me. Well, after the way I had a full-fledged panic attack and ran to hide at Sterling's—our—house at the lake not even a week ago, I get why he is nervous. "I am fine," I reassure him. "I promise, if anything even remotely triggers me, I will tell you. But really, Mom hasn't reached out to me, and she is usually my biggest trigger."

"I am not trying to be patronizing," he says. "I am just a little worried."

It reminds me of how he said that my disappearing triggers him, too. I guess we'll both need some time to adapt to our new realities, and I probably need to be more aware of the things I do that might hurt him.

"I have reached out to the therapist Cedric recommended," I tell him.

"Oh, really?"

"Yes, I did so yesterday. I was early at work and did some paperwork for the boss, then figured I could use the thirty minutes I had before opening to make that call." I pause. "Cedric is really good."

"I know," Aden chuckles. "He has a passion for the job, which is why I hired him. Plus, I don't get on his nerves."

"You could never get on anyone's nerves!" I exclaim.

"You say that because you have rose-tinted glasses on and are obviously head over heels in love with me," he says in that usual dry humor, he only shows me and, sometimes, Lynn.

"I am confident you could never get on my nerves," I add.

"That's what I am hoping for, too," he says. "But at work, I guess, I can be a perfectionist. My other assistants hated my guts. Cedric, however, doesn't mind."

"You click with him," I agree. It's so funny, though, since Aden and Cedric are nothing alike. How in the world these two can work together so well is beyond my understanding, and I know it's also beyond Lynn's. She is just happy he finally has someone who can keep up with him, and I am happy that Cedric is nice, honest, and genuinely wants to do his job well.

Aden puts an arm around my shoulder. "So, you gave the therapist a call?"

"Yes, his first open spot is next month, but I'll definitely be seeing him then." I pause. "If... and I am not even sure it will happen–but if he wants to see you too, would you really come?"

"Yes," he says promptly, then hesitates for a moment. I am almost scared he will go back on his promise, but then Aden shrugs. "I think I should probably see someone myself. Wouldn't do any harm, would it?"

"I think it would be good," I admit. "You have a lot of baggage from your upbringing to boot, and... then there was Emil."

"I thought I moved past it all," he admits. "But I feel like I do carry some baggage in my relationship with you, and with Lynn and Mom."

I nod, making sure to put on a serious expression. "Wherever you go, go with all your heart."

"God, Noel," Aden snorts. "In which cheesy calendar did you read that one?"

I grin, happy that my little joke hit. "No calendar. A fortune cookie!"

Aden looks at me, amused. "It's amazing how you manage to surprise me daily."

"Is that good or bad?"

"Good," he says, winking at me. "Keep the surprises coming."

THIRTY-TWO

Epilogue

ADEN

Cedric dashes around us, as if he is being chased by something or someone. It would be annoying if he weren't totally focused on his task and eager to get the job done. As usual, he is brimming with motivation. "Make sure not to knock something over," I call after him, just to make sure.

He turns and nods. "Of course, sir, I will be careful!" With that, he skillfully runs past some sculptures as if he is in a video game, dodging like an expert.

I decided to let him handle things on his own. He has proven himself plenty by now, and I know he can handle the organization part, as well as the influencers in the art scene.

TV coverage is still on me, though, and this time it's going to be particularly important because Sterling will be covered also. Besides that, it's the first time I'll openly be attending such a huge event, not as a single man.

"I trust you to talk to the media as usual," Lynn says.

I nod. "Don't worry, I have it covered. Is Sterling ready?"

"As ready as he can be," Lynn chuckles. I turn my head to see how Sterling is standing in front of his most prominent new painting, looking like he wishes he could do some touch-ups. Mateo is next to him with a frown on his face.

"Mateo looks like he wants to drag him away from there."

"That's pretty close, actually." Lynn chuckles. "Sterling claims he isn't happy with the painting and wishes he could redo it."

"That's normal. I thought like that all the time," I reassure her. "Tell Mateo there is no need to worry."

"But I like him hot and bothered," Lynn grins.

Talking about hot... Noel has our stylist help with his suit and touch up his makeup, looking more nervous than Sterling. It's an official exhibition opening, and he will be there as my official plus one. I didn't want him to feel obliged, but he agreed to it on his own terms, claiming he wants to go fully official with me, for everyone to know.

Everyone we care for already knows anyway.

"Mr. Randall," Cedric pops up next to me. "Your mother and brother are already here. Should I let them enter?"

"Yes, definitely let my mother come in, so she can look around in peace. As for Oliver, he can come in early, as long as he doesn't get on my nerves," I say. "Keep an eye on him, please."

"Will do!" With that, Cedric dashes away, happily disappearing through a side exit, probably to pick up Oliver.

"First time you let one of them come," Lynn muses. "Are you sure you are okay with it?"

"No," I say honestly. "But he is really putting an effort into respecting my boundaries. I don't know, maybe it's an olive branch I am extending to him. Just him for now, though."

"Knowing him, that probably makes him happy," Lynn says.

"If you say it like that, it might make me change my mind."

Lynn elbows me and grins. "Instead of your brother, better worry about your boyfriend."

She isn't wrong. Noel looks more nervous than usual. He has had a couple of busy weeks, both with work and an extra class his boss sent him to. Then, we were also busy with renovating our lake house. It's all been a bit much, and I have promised to steal him away for a couple of days once the holidays approach.

"How come you look so confident when you are behind the bar, but now look like you are about to sneak away?" I tease.

"I am fine," he mutters. "This is just not my usual playing field. This is more your territory."

"Don't worry too much," I reassure him. "You look perfect, and you are still here as a guest. You don't need to be anything but yourself."

"You keep saying that," he sighs. "And I am trying to believe you, but it's not easy." He pauses. "We are going to spend the weekend in the house by the lake, aren't we?"

"Definitely. I want to have some peaceful, quality time with you," I say.

"When you say that, it sounds dirty."

"As if I'd ever think something dirty."

Noel furrows his brows. "Right. You are such an innocent soul."

I chuckle and take his hand. "Come, let's say hello to my mom."

His eyes instantly light up. Over the last couple of months, he has befriended my mother. It seems like she is giving him a bit of security and motherly love, something he missed from his own mom. The latter has tried to harass him once more, but this time, I made sure my lawyer was prepared. Here and there, she reaches out to him, and there is nothing we can do to stop her from doing it.

And every time she does, Noel hurts. Fortunately, he has his own place of retreat, now, that I can reach. If he genuinely needs to run, he goes to our house at the lake. We keep an extra phone there and a charger, in case his phone dies and he can't contact me any other way. I have noticed, though, that his anxiety doesn't kick in regularly anymore. Before, it was every time he talked to his mom or when she contacted him, but now he has better tools to deal with his panic attacks.

"So, I am only accompanying you. I don't need to talk to the media?"

"Don't worry," I reassure him for the nth time. "If anyone bothers you, just leave or give Lynn, Cedric, or me a sign."

"And I really don't have to do anything tonight?" he asks.

"Well, later tonight you can do—"

"Oh, my God, don't finish that sentence!" Noel elbows me before grabbing my arm. He is grinning now. "If only the media knew how dirty you can be."

I nudge him softly. "Good thing you are the only one who knows."

"Your secret is safe with me." He leans forward a little. "Actually, I love that side of you."

"My secret one?"

"The one that will make you drag me out of the car tonight and fuck me against the wall."

"So, that's what you want to do later," I muse. "I think I can oblige."

When Noel smiles and leans into my embrace, I feel my heart and chest swell with warmth and love. It's been so long since I felt so complete. To be honest, it might even be the first time in my life that I feel so whole and complete. Even with the smaller bumps in the road, even knowing that we still have issues ahead of us we'll need to tackle, I am confident we are going to be alright. Noel is willing to work on his anxiety, and I am willing to work on the baggage I still carry around.

Knowing that I have someone I love at my side, someone who loves me the same way I love them, is truly humbling. I was lucky to have met Noel, and lucky that Lynn was the friend she is, pushing me to step out of my comfort zone.

Now that I have found this luck, I will never let go of it again.

Acknowledgements

Allow me to start with the most important: Thank you to all of you who gave this book a chance! I honestly appreciate every single one of you who picked this book up and decided it's worth it to check out, and I sincerely hope that you enjoyed the read!

I had a lot of fun writing both Noel and Aden, and their journey from two hurt individuals to a strong couple which learned to communicate with each other. Admittedly I am having a bit of a hard time letting go. But "Hold Me" is the first book of the Men in Suits series, so we will get to meet this couple again, albeit not as the main protagonists. Each book of this series will feature a new couple.

On top of that I have plans for the holidays, meaning I am working on a cozy holiday-related novel which will be released in November.

Lastly, I want to thank my patrons and Inkitt subscribers, who once again showed their wonderful support to my work. Another thank you goes to my ARC readers, who didn't hesitate to point out errors to me when they spotted them, giving me the chance to do a last quality check on my final manuscript. And, another big thank you goes to my proof-reader who not only proof-read the manuscript but also pointed out potential inconsistencies and plotholes. I am constantly working on the quality of my books to provide my readers with a good experience. It takes some time and effort to build a good team, so, a sincere thank you to all of you who helped me with finalizing this book!

About the author

Isla Rayn is an MxM romance author. She studied linguistics and later technical writing. When she isn't creating fictional worlds, she is working as a Technical Writer. She started her journey as a writer with creating short stories first, before writing her first full-length novel in 2020.

From then on, she never stopped.

Isla specializes in contemporary romance novels with a focus on LGBTQIA+ related topics. She likes to write stories with healthy relationships and strong yet relateable characters, with a bit of steam and humour to them too.

You can find her on social media:

Instagram: isla.rayn

Printed in France by Amazon
Brétigny-sur-Orge, FR

33025617R10152